Also by Carolyn Mackler

❻  ❻  ❻  ❻

*The Earth, My Butt, and Other Big Round Things*

5/8

and So
Am I

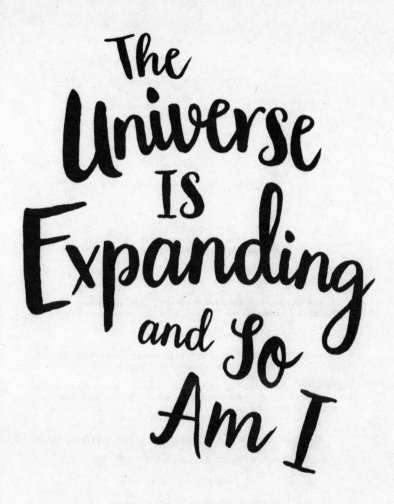

# The Universe IS Expanding and So Am I

## CAROLYN MACKLER

BLOOMSBURY

LONDON   OXFORD   NEW YORK   NEW DELHI   SYDNEY

BLOOMSBURY YA
Bloomsbury Publishing Plc
50 Bedford Square, London, WC1B 3DP, UK

BLOOMSBURY, BLOOMSBURY YA and the Diana logo
are trademarks of Bloomsbury Publishing Plc

First published in the United States of America in 2018 by Bloomsbury YA
This edition published in Great Britain in 2018 by Bloomsbury Publishing Plc

A catalogue record for this book is available from the British Library

ISBN: PB: 978-1-4088-9704-1; eBook: 978-1-4088-9706-5

2 4 6 8 10 9 7 5 3 1

Typeset by Westchester Publishing Services

Printed and bound in Great Britain by CPI Group (UK) Ltd, Croydon CR0 4YY

To find out more about our authors and books visit www.bloomsbury.com
and sign up for our newsletters

To the memory of my friend Jhoanna Robledo Wade,
who always appreciated a New York story

# 1

Froggy Welsh the Fourth is trying to get inside my jeans.

That should be fine because he's my boyfriend and we've been publicly and officially together for five months and we were privately together for two months last fall and we've already made out and he's gone up my shirt and right now we're locked in my bedroom on a sunny Wednesday afternoon in early June while my parents are at work and my brother is at the gym and my sister is thousands of miles from New York City, finishing her two-year stint in Africa.

But there's a big problem.

The problem is that I've fallen out of like with Froggy. It was never love, but Froggy is my first boyfriend, and the fact that he wanted to be with me, publicly and officially, seemed like a miracle. So I was okay with like. I could deal with like.

To be clear, I'm not saying that *Froggy* is the miracle. He's a dorky-in-a-good-way sixteen-year-old guy. He's medium height and skinny with fluffy hair, pinkish skin, and a stubby nose. He's talented at trombone and graphic design, and not altogether unpopular in our tenth-grade class. That's where the miracle comes in. While I'm not altogether unpopular either and I have some attributes of my own, I'm definitely not skinny. On good days, I consider myself curvy. On regular days, more like chunky. On bad days, I'm plain old fat. In my prestigious private school on the Upper East Side of Manhattan, there aren't a lot of fat girls. And the few plus-size girls who amble apologetically around the hallways never score boyfriends.

So, yeah, I've been super grateful to have Froggy, and I've also liked the making-out and up-my-shirt aspects, especially kissing until our lips are numb and various quadrants of our bodies are wriggling with desire. But then yesterday, as we were making out on a bench in Central Park, a few blocks from school, I had this weird feeling that I was kissing a golden retriever. This was new. Not the kissing part, because we've done a lot of that. But the new sensation was that his tongue felt slobbery and long, like it was trying to retrieve a dog treat from behind my molars. After a few minutes, I wiped my face with my hand and made an excuse about how I forgot a final exam review sheet and had to run back to Brewster before our Global Studies teacher left for the day.

All last night I was stressed. I kept wondering why kissing Froggy had grossed me out. Was I not into him anymore? But how can that happen when nothing between us changed from Monday when we had a perfectly fine good-bye kiss in the

2

empty stairwell near the computer cluster to Tuesday's slobber-fest on the bench? Also, if I truly wasn't into Froggy anymore, what was I supposed to do about that? Is canine-kissing grounds for a breakup?

As I was tossing in bed I decided that the slobbery kiss had to be a fluke. And the fluke had to be because Froggy was stressed about the end of school and therefore not exercising proper tongue control. Mom is an adolescent psychologist, and she frequently says that academic stress hits everyone in different ways. In our case, there are six days left of sophomore year and teachers are slamming us with homework. I decided I needed to forget yesterday and give Froggy and his tongue another shot.

That's why I invited him to my apartment today, and that's how we ended up making out in my room. But as soon as we closed my door, we sat on my bed and pressed our lips together and . . . nope. No chemistry. Not even a spark of physics or just plain human biology. And that's when I knew that—gasp, gulp, crap—I'm not into Froggy anymore.

This is a bad thing to realize as we're on my bed and he's sliding his hand across my stomach to the waistband of my jeans.

"Virginia." Froggy sighs, pushing up my shirt.

I used to cringe at the thought of him seeing my belly region. That was back when we were secretly hooking up. Once we publicly and officially got together, fooling around felt so good that I didn't stop him. But now that I've fallen out of like, I don't want to be doing this anymore. I glance longingly at my

3

bedside table, at the cover of *Fates and Furies*. I wish I could be reading right now. Not only are the main characters, Lotto and Mathilde, the cutest couple ever, but they met at Vassar, which is where I want to go to college.

Froggy sweeps his hand south and starts fiddling with the button on my jeans.

"Uhhhh," I mumble. I clasp my hand over his and drag him back up north. Froggy and I have never been inside each other's jeans before, and I'm definitely not ready to start now.

"Hmmm?" he asks.

I cough and, for lack of a more imaginative word, repeat my brilliant earlier statement. "Uhhhh."

Despite the fact that Froggy and I have been together, on and off, since the beginning of sophomore year, we still suck at talking to each other about what our hands are doing.

"Is everything . . . ?" Froggy pushes his hair out of his eyes.

I know he's asking if I'm okay, if *we're* okay. I don't know what to say because even though I've fallen out of like with Froggy, I can't break up with him. That exact item is at the top of my current list. I often create lists in my head about important things in my life, and sometimes I even write them down. Here's rule number one of a list that I've been thinking about this spring:

### HOW TO MAKE SURE SKINNY GIRLS AREN'T THE ONLY ONES WHO HAVE BOYFRIENDS, RULE #1:

It's no secret that the skinny girls score the bulk of the guys. It's not that I have anything against skinny girls as long as they're not bitchy and they don't make fat girls feel like slovenly slobs. But it's still not fair that skinny girls get first, second, third, fourth, and hundredth dibs on the pool of available guys. So if you're a chunky chick and you managed to get a nice boyfriend, don't ever let him go.

I know my lists tend toward the harsh, but whatever. There are very few places that girls, especially teen girls, especially fat teen girls, can be brutally honest. And my imagination is one of them.

Also, maybe it seems harsh when I call myself fat. The truth is that sometimes I *feel* harsh about it and I wish I were born into a skinny body with a kickass metabolism. The list I made up when Froggy and I first got together was called The Fat Girl Code of Conduct, and it smacked of low self-esteem. I've come a long way since then. In general I don't hate my body as much as I used to. I'll never be a twig, but I've learned to embrace my curves. Most days. Okay, some days.

"I have to pee," I say to Froggy.

That will buy me five minutes to figure out what to do. Maybe I can come back with a cold shower and push his horndog self into it.

But then, just as I'm standing up, I hear the front door unlock.

"Anyone home?" my brother shouts.

Froggy yanks down his shirt, rolls off my bed, and stands up so quickly he knocks into my lamp, which topples onto the floor. My door is locked, but I'm freaking out so much I can't

5

hook my bra. And it's not like my boobs are cooperating. By the time I rein them in, my hands are sticky with sweat.

It's not that Byron doesn't know about Froggy. My family is aware I have a boyfriend. Froggy comes over to watch movies, though usually we go to his apartment.

"I didn't think . . . your brother . . ." Froggy picks up the lamp and adjusts the shade.

"Me neither," I say. "He's always at the gym until dinner."

My chest is tight, making it hard to take a good breath. The last thing I want is to be caught midhookup by my *brother*. It's bad enough that Byron smirks when I mention Froggy, like the fact that I have a boyfriend is a joke to him.

I consider suggesting we hide in my room until Froggy has to leave for jazz ensemble. Usually I walk him uptown and then I grab dumplings or scallion pancakes at Pearls on the way home. Not that Upper West Side dumplings compare to the ones in Chinatown. On the weekends that I'm not forced to go to our country house in Connecticut, my friend Alyssa Wu, whose grandparents live in Chinatown, takes me to insider dim sum places.

"What should we do?" Froggy asks. He peers out my window like he's contemplating alternate exit routes. Not an option. My family lives on the top floor of a fifteen-story building on the Upper West Side of New York City. We face west, which means we can see the sunset and the Hudson River and New Jersey stretching out to the horizon.

I shouldn't be blindsided that my brother is here. Now that Columbia has let out for the semester he's living at home, but he's mostly at the gym or hanging out in Brooklyn with old high school friends. In a few weeks he's flying to Paris for an international relations program at the Sorbonne where he'll make up credits that he lost when he got suspended from college last semester. Byron's suspension, in our family, is referred to as "the ordeal."

Translation: It happened, it's over, and now we're not supposed to talk about it.

My summer plans do not involve eating baguettes and strolling along the Seine. My parents wanted me to go on Outward Bound. That's a mountain-climbing, character-building, pooping-in-the-woods expedition. Both my older sister, Anaïs, and then Byron did Outward Bound after their sophomore year of high school. I flat out refused. Even if it didn't involve pooping into a hole and wiping with a leaf, it didn't sound like my idea of a good time. My parents finally agreed to let me stay Inward Bound as long as I agreed to two terms.

1. I get a college-application-enhancing internship.
2. I get my driver's license.

Term one is going to be awesome. Dad is lining up an internship at the company where he's the chief operating officer. Not just for me, but for my best friend, Shannon, who's been on the West Coast since last August but is coming home soon. Dad works in the music industry, creating streaming software. His company is called Ciel Media. *Ciel* means sky in French, my least favorite language, but I try not to hold that

7

fact against the company. There's a pool table in the lounge area and a stocked fridge, and they sometimes receive free concert tickets and get to meet celebrities.

Fantasy: A hot celebrity guy, like a seventeen-year-old shaggy-haired drummer, notices me in the Ciel office and we fall madly in love and I drop out of Brewster and travel the country with him, the envy of drooling groupies.

Reality: I get a selfie with a hot celebrity guy's shaggy hair in the background.

The driver's license term is all sucky reality. I got my learner's permit when I turned sixteen in March, and every weekend since then my parents have forced me to take a driver's ed class at a driving school near our country house in Connecticut. Even with all that driver's ed, I still panic and forget what side of the road I'm supposed to drive on. Dad is determined to help me get my required forty hours behind the wheel, and he's already signed me up for my road test on July tenth.

So, yeah, that's the less-than-ideal part of my summer plan.

While Froggy is lacing his sneakers, I grab my phone and send a group text to Shannon and Alyssa. They don't know each other because Alyssa and I became friends while Shannon was in Washington State this year. But this is an emergency, and I need both of their advice as quickly as possible.

**My brother just walked in on Froggy and me, I tell them. Well, not IN-in. We're hiding in my bedroom, and he's in the living room. Help! What should we do?**

Nothing from Shannon, but Alyssa writes almost immediately.

**Too much info,** she texts. **Spare me.**

"Let's get out of here," I say to Froggy as I slide my phone in my bag. "We'll wave and make a quick exit. No time for questions."

"What if your brother asks what I'm doing here?"

"We won't engage," I tell him, borrowing some of Mom's TherapistSpeak. Mom is always peppering her language with phrases from the world of psychology like "don't engage" and "comfort zone."

"Uh, okay. Okay." Froggy tweaks his nose and grabs his trombone case. He's nervous about seeing my brother. I wish I could tell him about "the ordeal," about how Byron isn't actually that cool after all. I told Shannon about it. She was already away in Washington State so I texted the drama to her as it unfolded. But with my New York City people, like Froggy and Alyssa, I didn't say a word about the trouble my brother was in. For one, I didn't want either of them to dump me as a girlfriend/ friend if they found out the horrible thing he did. But also my family is private about anything that doesn't make us look perfect. I'm already on the low end of the Shreves Family Totem Pole, and blabbering our business would plummet me to subterranean levels.

I open the door, hoping Byron has decided to shower or lift weights in his room, but nope. He's strolling out of the kitchen with a bottle of Vitaminwater in his hand. And not Vitaminwater Zero. The full 120 calories.

My brother is twenty and tall with a lean athletic build, and he doesn't even have to work for it. He can consume a box of Nutter Butters, three cheeseburgers, and a gallon of Vita-minwater and not gain a pound. He has tousled brown hair, maple-syrup eyes, and a confident jaw. He plays rugby and wants to be an international lawyer someday. He's fluent in French, and even though he graduated from Brewster two years ago, his smile is still on the cover of their promotional brochures.

I didn't get his gene pool, but I'm okay with that. Most days.

"What's up, Gin?" Byron takes a sip of his Vitaminwater. Then he notices Froggy slinking out of my room behind me and says, "Okay . . . uh . . . *wow.*"

I head quickly toward the front door, hoping Froggy is behind me.

Byron leans against the foyer wall. "Do you know when Mom and Dad are getting home?"

"I don't know," I say.

My fingers are trembling as I twist the lock. When I finally open the door, Byron reaches over to fist-bump Froggy. In my brother's cool-people world, people fist-bump with ease. But Froggy thinks a high five is coming, so he presents an open palm.

"It's a fist bump," I offer.

Froggy lowers his hand and mumbles, "Sorry."

Byron laughs. "It's not like you need to apologize."

Froggy starts blinking fast. I catch his eye and motion him through the door, letting it slam behind us. In the elevator he rubs at his nose and I stare at the descending numbers. On the ninth floor, ancient Mrs. Myers hobbles on. She's about ninety and always thinks I'm my sister, then seems shocked that I'm no longer gorgeous and skinny like Anaïs. Yes, Mrs. Myers, with her thinning hair and raisin face, feels entitled to critique my appearance.

Sure enough, Mrs. Myers fastens her milky eyes on me, shifts her gaze over to Froggy, and then veers back to me.

"Be careful not to let yourself go, Anaïs," she warbles. "Men like their bank accounts big, not their women."

I stare at the ground, hoping we can pretend that comment never happened. But then Mrs. Myers clutches Froggy's arm and says, "Don't you agree with me, son, about the bank accounts?"

Froggy shrugs. No one says another word for the rest of the ride down.

On the street, the air is warm and green leaves are unfurling on the trees.

"Want to get dumplings?" Froggy says, clearing his throat. "There's this place called Pearls . . . my parents and I went last weekend. It's good."

"Pearls?" I ask innocently, like I have no clue what he's talking about, like it's not my favorite non-Chinatown place to indulge.

## HOW TO MAKE SURE SKINNY GIRLS AREN'T THE ONLY ONES WHO HAVE BOYFRIENDS, RULE #2:

Don't act like you're intimately acquainted with all the restaurants within a twenty-block radius of your apartment. That's between you and your slow-as-a-sloth metabolism.

"It's over on Amsterdam," Froggy says.

"I'm not hungry," I lie. "But I'll go with you."

## HOW TO MAKE SURE SKINNY GIRLS AREN'T THE ONLY ONES WHO HAVE BOYFRIENDS, RULE #2.5:

Duh. Of course you want dumplings. Fried pork dumplings! But he CAN'T see you chowing down and think, "So that's why she's big like a rich person's bank account." Even though you're not in like with him anymore, he's still your boyfriend and you still need him to think you live on kale and raw fruit.

"Are you sure?" Froggy asks. "You just had a plum at lunch."

"I'm fine," I say, smiling stiffly. "I'm great."

## HOW TO MAKE SURE SKINNY GIRLS AREN'T THE ONLY ONES WHO HAVE BOYFRIENDS, RULE #3:

You are always fine and great (and grateful he's with you). Moody and demanding? That's the domain of skinny girl-friends and nasty old ladies. Which you are neither.

# 2

I'm a girl who likes to itemize things, so here's what's going through my head as I'm walking home from not eating dumplings:

## BRAIN FARTS, COURTESY OF VIRGINIA SHREVES, AGE 16 ¼

1. I hate that Byron saw me with Froggy. Ever since "the ordeal," I've felt icky around my brother when it comes to anything having to do with sex or, in Froggy's and my case, all the stuff leading up to the act.
2. "The ordeal." One evening last October, Dad got a call from the dean of students at Columbia explaining that a woman, who I later found out was a Canadian college junior named Annie Mills, had accused Byron of date

rape. They'd gone to a party together. My brother got blackout drunk and says he doesn't remember anything. A committee assembled by the Office of Sexual Misconduct voted to suspend him for the semester. Yes, my brother who, for the first decade and a half of my life, I considered a god to be worshiped and idolized.

3. Byron's nosedive from the pedestal made me reassess everything—how I've always compared myself to the rest of my family and haven't measured up, how maybe that assessment was wrong, how I actually don't need my brother's approval, how maybe my family's negative comments about my body were their problem and not mine. Somewhere along the way I started having fun with my body instead of hating it. I even had the confidence to turn Froggy from a secret hookup to a public and official boyfriend.

4. Oh. Crap. Froggy.

I'm angsting over item number four when I step into the crosswalk.

"Cool hair," a hipster guy says as he's coming toward me.

I catch his eye and smile. As I do, I notice him checking me out. I have on a tank top that reveals some cleavage. Recently I ditched my tan grandma bras and bought hot pinks and multi-colored tie-dyes. Sometimes, like now, I even flaunt the bra straps through my tank top.

Last year, I NEVER would have shown off my bra straps. Last year, I hated girls who did that. Or maybe I hated myself because I didn't.

As I reach the west side of Broadway, I run my fingers through my shoulder-length hair. I dyed it purple back in December, mostly to piss Mom off. Since then, I tried pink for a while but eventually returned to purple. I added streaks of green bangs last week, a process that involved bleach and tinfoil and a plastic bag over my head.

"Hello, Virginia," the doorman says when I come into my lobby. His name is Alberto, and he works most afternoons. "You have a package."

"From Walla Walla?"

He nods and hands it to me. As I step into the elevator I sniff the parcel. It would be *so* like Shannon to send onions. She's random that way. Shannon and I have been best friends since we started Brewster in sixth grade. She has a stutter and I was the fat girl, so it was a match made in outcast heaven. For this whole school year, Shannon has been in Washington State while her dad researches the Walla Walla onion for his latest oddball coffee-table book.

As the elevator lifts, I think about how when Shannon left last August we both bawled. I doubted I would survive the first week. But I made it through the year and I even made new friends. In early July Shannon will be back and we're going to rock our summer internship together.

I tear open the package and pull out a homemade rainbow

pot holder and an index card on which she's written in green marker:

*V— Text as soon as you get this! I have big crazy news. xxS*

I pull out my phone and text Shannon, **Big crazy news? And what's up with the pot holder??**

Shannon doesn't write back, so I walk down the hall and unlock the front door to the apartment. Mom and Byron are in the kitchen drinking iced tea and laughing. Panic creeps over me. What if Byron told her about Froggy and me, and now they're having a hearty chuckle at my expense? I stuff Shannon's pot holder in my pocket and slip my phone into my bag. I'm about to reverse back out the door when I hear my sister's voice.

Anaïs has been in the Peace Corps for the past two years, doing health-care work in a rural village in a country in western Africa called Burkina Faso. No cell phones, no Wi-Fi, just letters that take a month to arrive and rare crackly phone calls.

"Virginia!" Mom says, gesturing me into the kitchen. "You've got to see Anaïs!"

"Is Virginia home?" I hear my sister saying.

I freeze in the doorway. I was fourteen the last time I saw Anaïs in person *or* on a screen. I hadn't started high school yet. I hadn't been kissed. I still worshiped Byron.

"Come quick." Mom points to the laptop on the counter. "She's in a hotel lobby and only has a few minutes."

I tentatively approach the screen. There's my sister, her eyes dark, her long brown hair hanging around her shoulders. Anaïs is brilliant and willowy and so beautiful that back when she was in New York City, people would come up to her on the street and ask if she was a model. She's eight years older than me, which is a good thing because I've never felt competitive with her. Which is a good thing because I'd lose whatever competition we were in.

"Oh my God . . . you're so old!" Anaïs says to me. "And look at your hair. I love it!"

I smile shyly. I'm not great at accepting compliments, especially when my family is four inches away. I glance behind my sister, at her hotel lobby, at the wall painted in bright blue and yellow.

"What about that eyebrow ring you told me about?" Anaïs asks. "Is it still in?"

I lean closer to the screen and show my sister. Mom clears her throat, no doubt remembering how last Thanksgiving I flew to Seattle to visit Shannon and we both got illegal underage piercings. Shannon pierced her tongue and I did my eyebrow. Mom flipped out and called it barbaric. Eventually, like with my hair, she got used to the eyebrow ring. She recently finished a book proposal about embracing your teenagers' rebellions, and she's calling it "Purple Hair and Piercings." I've read the proposal. It explains how her book would be about teenage behavior in general, but she's including stories about how she resisted her daughter's purple hair and eyebrow piercing, but now she's come to accept them. My secret hope is that her

17

agent will sell the proposal and she will write the book and it will become a bestseller and Mom will go on a book tour and I'll tag along and they'll hire a stylist to color my hair instead of my mediocre home jobs.

"Where are you, anyway?" I ask my sister.

"I'm in Ouagadougou," she says. "The capital. I finished the Peace Corps a few days ago."

"Then you're flying home through London?" Mom asks.

"I'm staying in London for a little bit." Anaïs pauses and glances to one side, out of the frame of the screen. It looks like there's something else she wants to say, but then she shrugs. "I land in New York City on June twenty-third."

"We'll be there to pick you up," Mom says. "I've already registered you for an MCAT course that starts in July. It's time to start preparing for medical school."

My sister was premed at Brown, and someday she's going to become a big-time doctor, like a heart surgeon or the surgeon general.

"I'd better go," Anaïs says after a second. "I love you guys."

When Byron says good-bye, I watch Anaïs's face to see if her expression changes. I wonder how she feels about our brother. When "the ordeal" first happened, I couldn't be in the same room as him without feeling nauseated. Nine months later, it's still confusing. Being blackout drunk is no excuse, ever. I remain mad at him for what he did to Annie Mills. But every so often Byron mentions an inside joke or does something unexpectedly kind, like charge my phone when it's dying. Then I forget to be mad. Then I feel guilty for not being mad.

I'm frowning about this when my brother touches my arm and gestures me across the kitchen.

"We're cool about this afternoon," he whispers. "You and Froggy. Let's just say I didn't see a thing. No one needs to know."

I give him a grateful smile. "Thanks."

As I said: totally confusing.

"Hey, Gin," Mom says when Byron goes into the living room and turns on the TV. "Wasn't that great to see Anaïs? How was your day?"

Before I can answer, Mom flips her honey-colored hair over her shoulder and scrolls through restaurant menu options on her phone. While Dad and my siblings are tall with brown hair and brown eyes, Mom and I are shorter with light hair and grayish-blue eyes. Supposedly when Mom was younger she used to struggle with her weight, but for as long as I've been around she's slim, she lives on leafy greens, and she works out seven days a week.

"Did you eat yet?" Mom asks me. "Dad's getting home in a half hour, so I'm about to order delivery."

My parents stopped cooking when my sister went to college six years ago. In our house, dinner is delivery or a restaurant.

"No," I say.

"I'll order us salads," Mom says. "After dinner, Dad and Byron are watching the baseball game and I'm going to the gym. Want to join? Get some exercise?"

"I've got a lot of homework. I have a final on Monday, two on Tuesday, one on Wednesday, and a big Humanities essay to finish by Thursday. Can you proofread my essay before I turn it in?"

I'll admit that was a pivot. But I'd do anything to avoid her gym. Mom and Dad belong to a private gym around the corner called Whole Fitness. In my head I call it Whole Fakeness. I hate trudging along the treadmill while Mom attacks the machines like she's doing battle with her bony thighs. When it comes to exercise, I used to believe the concept should be abolished. But then I discovered kickboxing. Or, more specifically, my kickboxing class with Tisha. My pediatrician gave me Tisha's name over the winter when I was hating my body and doing too many things to hurt it. Even though I was skeptical about joining an exercise class, it's turned out to be awesome. For an hour and a half every Friday afternoon, Tisha leads a bunch of girls as we kick and punch and groove to music. The other girls in the class are from different schools around the city so it's a break from Brewster bitchiness. Also, unlike Whole Fakeness, the walls of the studio aren't lined with mirrors, which makes the class more about feeling good than scowling at your cellulite.

I lug my backpack into my room. We don't have school tomorrow because the teachers have a clerical day, but we're overloaded with review sheets due Friday. I come out for a quick dinner and then dive back into studying. I'm deep in my chemistry review when there's a knock at my door.

"Come in!" I shout.

It's Dad, which is weird. He rarely drops by my room for a chat. With Dad, it's more like we have Things We Do Together: he brings me to see the Knicks or the Yankees, we eat Chinese food and watch games on TV, he takes me to driver's ed. But as far as cozying up in my bedroom and having spontaneous chats, that never happens. When I was younger I thought it was because he was too busy being a chief operating officer and competing in golf tournaments. But as I got older I realized that Dad doesn't have much to say to me. He can't show me off to his friends like he did with gorgeous Anaïs, and he can't male bond like he does with Byron. At least he's not as critical of my body as he used to be. He finally chilled on that when I worked up the nerve to tell him that my body wasn't his to discuss. But that doesn't mean we're going to win any father-daughter-relationship prizes.

"Aren't you watching the game?" I ask.

"Commercial break. Yankees are up two."

I blink a few times. Did he really come here to tell me the Yankee score?

"Mom mentioned there's no school tomorrow," Dad says. "I'm taking the afternoon off to head to Connecticut and meet with a tree guy at the house. You can come along, and we'll get in some driving practice."

My heart drops into that place in my stomach that dreads and fears driving. I completed driver's ed last weekend and even had to suffer through the required two-hour parent-teen safety class. Dad was so pumped about it he took notes and raised his hand in class and later had us both sign a contract about safe practices for once I have my license. I didn't tell him that it's optimistic to imagine I'll actually get a license out of all this.

"I have to study," I say. "I have a bunch of things due Friday."

"Your road test is a month away, Gin. You can study in the morning, and even while I'm walking the property with the tree guy. Plus, as we talked about in the safety class, you need forty hours of practice before you're allowed to take your road test. I would guess we're only at thirty-one hours. And that's being generous."

When Dad uses his chief-operating-officer voice, there's no use arguing with him. I'm a lowly employee in his executive universe.

"Meet me at the garage at noon," Dad says. "Tomorrow will be our day of three-point turns."

In three-point-three seconds he's going to remind me that no Shreves has ever failed their road test.

"You know," Dad says, clearing his throat. "No Shreves has ever failed their road test."

Boom.

# 3

I set my alarm for seven, a crime on clerical day. The teachers have to work, but we're supposed to get the day off. It's not like I was going to slack, not with finals coming up, but Dad's driving lesson has thwarted my plan to half-ass it. The apartment is quiet all morning. I get a lot of studying done and even manage to take a shower and change my eyebrow ring from the gold one to a silver hoop. At eleven, a text from Dad comes in.

**I'm leaving the office in 15 minutes and taking the subway uptown. I'm craving bagels. Can you run up to Absolute and get us a few? Don't tell Mom! #carbpolice**

Dad thinks his hashtags are funny, but they make me cringe. Especially this one. Like, is he saying that Mom is HIS carb police? Because Dad is thin and fit and has no reason to avoid carbs. Or is he saying that Mom shouldn't know about the bagels because I need policing? Mom would love nothing more than to be the prison warden guarding me from tempting carbs. Whatever it is, I *do* see Dad's point. If Mom discovers I bought him a bagel, then she'll ask if I got myself a bagel, and then she'll wonder if I scooped out the bready center like she's suggested and she'll inquire whether I ordered a thin layer of butter or cream cheese. And neither Dad nor I want to invite that line of inquisition.

I'm also cringing about going all the way up to Absolute Bagels. It's hot and humid today. Our air-conditioners are wheezing in their attempt to cool the apartment. Absolute makes the best bagels in the city, which I would never ruin by scooping out the bready center, but they're nearly thirty blocks uptown, practically at Columbia. I suppose I could take a subway, but it will be stinky and crowded in this heat. I'd rather walk.

I throw on shorts and a red-checkered tank top, stuff my notebooks and *Fates and Furies* into my backpack, and trek for a half hour until I get to the bagel store. As usual, there's a line spilling onto the sidewalk. It smells incredible inside, which sucks because I've decided I'm not going to indulge in a bagel and risk getting busted by the #carbpolice. Also eating with Dad is weird. He'll take me out to gorge on Shake Shack or General Tso's Chicken, and then if a skinny woman walks by, he'll praise her body like he doesn't realize that, oops, this kind of caloric consumption will never earn me a praiseworthy body. Not that I want him to praise my body because that's gross, but it still messes with my head. Better to enjoy bagels on my own time.

I wipe the sweat off my forehead and get in line behind

a woman standing with her son. She's holding a rust-colored puppy on a purple leash. I fish my novel out of my bag. Maybe it's dorky to read on the sidewalk, but whatever. It's not like I know anyone who lives up here.

"So these really are the best bagels in New York City?" someone behind me says.

I turn around, and I'm face-to-face with the most beautiful eyes I've ever seen. They're blue-green like sea glass and garnished with long lashes. The eyes belong to a guy around my age, maybe a little older. He's super tall with shoulder-length blond hair and a scar on his right jaw. He's holding a battered white skateboard in one hand and a sketch pad in the other.

"Yeah," I say. "I love them."

*More like I love you, you sea-glass-eyed, long-haired artist/ skater boy.*

"Which kind would you recommend?"

I have to crack up. A New Yorker wouldn't ask someone for a bagel recommendation. I'm guessing he's not from here, like maybe he time-traveled from my imagination to appear behind me on the bagel line.

"Are you laughing at me?" he asks, grinning.

I smile back at him. "Sort of."

"I guess it's obvious I'm not from New York."

"Really?" I say. He has an accent I can't place. "I never would have guessed."

"Snob," he teases.

"Tourist," I say.

The woman in front of me hands the dog's leash to her son, tells him to stay put, and then follows the line into Absolute. I tuck my book into my backpack, and we step in after her.

"So . . . which one's the best?" he asks.

I survey the vats heaped with poppy, sesame, everything, cinnamon-raisin, onion.

"Everything," I say after a second.

*That's what I would give you*, I say to him in my mind. Of course once we properly fell in love, like Lotto and Mathilde in *Fates and Furies*.

"An everything bagel," he says, nodding.

"Toasted with butter," I add. Then I point to his skateboard. "Where do you skate around here?"

He shakes his head. "Oh no! This isn't mine. If I wanted to die I'd get on a skateboard. I'm way too uncoordinated." He spins the wheel a few times. "It's my sister's. We were on our way over here, but she said the queue at this place drives her crazy. She ran to the bank machine and asked me to bring the skateboard home for her."

"Queue." "Bank machine." This guy might be the most adorable alien I've ever encountered. Also, I love that he has a sister he hangs out with. Byron and I used to be close when we were younger. We'd spend whole weekends in the apartment when our parents went to Connecticut, baking sugary concoctions and having movie marathons. All that changed the summer after his freshman year at Brewster when he got gorgeous and had girlfriends and parties to go to. And I was the chunky little sister who tarnished his image.

"I've never attempted to skateboard," I say, swallowing back my thoughts about Byron. "I put it in the category of Horrible Things like snowboarding and skiing. Capital 'H,' capital 'T.' When my family skis I hang out in the lodge and drink hot chocolate and read."

I have no idea how I'm able to babble right now. Even though I'm with Froggy and therefore off the boyfriend market, I always freeze around cute guys. For instance, there's a lusty boy in my grade named Cole Nevins. Whenever I'm seated near Cole in class, I stare at his brawny arms and forget I have a brain and vocal cords.

"Don't even talk to me about snowboarding," this guy says, groaning. "I've broken my wrist twice and cut up my face, and I'll never try it again." He touches the scar on his cheek and flashes me a smile that is in competition with his eyes for Most Beautiful Ever. "What else is in your Horrible Things category?"

Just then, Dad texts me. I glance at my phone. **Get me an onion bagel with extra scallion cream cheese. #yum**

**Okay,** I write. **I'm almost at the front of the line.**

**And I'm just walking from the subway to the parking garage. I'll pick you up outside Absolute Bagels in a few. Did you bring your learner's permit?**

I wish I could text him that I dropped my learner's permit in a volcano full of hot lava. Instead I write back that yes, I have it.

The person at the front asks to take my order.

"One onion bagel with extra scallion cream cheese," I call out. I glance quickly at the guy behind me and then add, "And one everything bagel toasted with butter."

27

Screw the #carbpolice. Screw Dad's obsession with skinny women. I'll eat my everything bagel and I'll love it.

As I'm paying I hear the cute guy ordering an everything bagel toasted with butter, too.

"See you around," he says to me. "I like your hair, by the way. Purple and green."

"Thanks," I say. Then I add, "New York City has almost nine million people. The likelihood that I'll see you again is nonexistent."

"That would be a Horrible Thing."

"So is Greek yogurt," I say. "So is when people say 'any-hoo' or 'coinkydink,' I hate that."

He starts laughing. I wave to him, grab a few extra napkins, and walk out, swinging my bagel bag in my hand.

ⓖ ⓖ ⓖ ⓖ

As soon as I get to the sidewalk, the hot air engulfs me. My underarms are slick. Or maybe I'm sweating from my conversation with that guy. On top of being incredibly cute, he was funny, and he had this way of laughing at what I said like I was the most hilarious person ever.

I'm standing at the curb, simultaneously sweating and smiling, looking for Dad's silver car zipping up Broadway, when a text comes in.

An important call just got scheduled, Dad has written. I'm in the car but had to double-park outside the garage because I need to take notes. It's going to be a while.

I bite down on the inside of my cheeks. I could be home studying. Or sleeping. Or not being stranded on Broadway and 108th Street in ninety-degree mugginess.

**How long?** I write.

**Not sure. Grab an iced tea. I'll text.**

That's it. No mention of whether "a while" is a half hour or an hour or six hours. No "sorry" for making me trek to Absolute Bagels and then ditching me for an important call. In Dad's world, calls are always important calls. It could be an investor, a client, or an old friend from Dartmouth, and they will always get priority over me.

That thought makes me sad, and, all of a sudden, I'm swallowing back tears.

"Hey."

It's him. He's standing next to me, and his eyes are wide with concern. "You okay?"

I shrug and gesture to my phone. "Family stuff," I say vaguely. It's not like I want to tell this beautiful guy that I have Dad Issues—no, actually, Entire Family Issues.

"Yeah," he says, nodding. "Family sucks sometimes."

I glance curiously at him.

He shrugs. "I'm dealing with some family stuff now. Pretty intense."

"Want to talk about it?" I ask. The second it's out of my mouth, I can't believe I said that. I've never been one of those confident girls who has cute guys confiding in her and crying on her shoulder.

He shakes his head. "I would actually love *not* to talk about it. I would love to spend time with someone who has no idea about any of it or what's been going on. That sounds like a dream."

I exhale. I know exactly what he's saying.

"I was supposed to be getting picked up by a family member right now," I say. It's tumbling out of my mouth before I can tell myself, *Virginia, you don't do this kind of thing either.* "But I actually have some time, so do you want to hang out and take a walk?"

He grins. "That would be the opposite of a Horrible Thing."

I smile back at him. "Agreed. And we won't talk about family."

"Or drama. Or any details of our lives."

"Unless, of course, the drama is that you're an ax murderer," I say. "In that case, you should inform me now."

He shifts the skateboard to his arm with the sketch pad, holds up his free hand like *scout's honor*, and says, "No axes. Promise. No murder for that matter."

As my insides churn with excitement and, I'll admit it, lust, I remind myself I have a boyfriend. Even though I've fallen out of like with Froggy, I probably shouldn't be doing this. But then I argue with my brain that *this* isn't anything. *This* is a walk and maybe eating a bagel.

"There's a cathedral I've been wanting to check out," he says. "Saint John the Divine. I think it's near here?"

*This* is walking to a cathedral. Innocent. G-rated.

"Yeah," I say. "My best friend and I used to go there and look for peacock feathers."

"Peacock feathers?"

"There are some peacocks wandering the grounds. I think two of them."

"New York City is so cool," he says, taking out his phone. As we begin walking, he starts typing, but then he stumbles into a trash can on the corner.

"Shit!" he says, leaning over and pressing his palm against his shin. I try not to notice that his calves are muscular and coated in toasted-almond hair. "That's what I get for walking and looking up directions. I'm totally not a New Yorker."

I have to crack up. "You were looking up directions to Saint John the Divine? It's like four blocks from here."

"There you go being a snob again," he says.

"And I won't even comment on the tourist thing," I mutter back.

He laughs as he slides his phone in his pocket, and I steer him toward Amsterdam. Saint John the Divine is a neo-Gothic cathedral around 111th Street with acres of lawns and stone buildings and a little garden with a fountain. Shannon and I came here a lot in middle school because she wanted to find turquoise peacock feathers and whittle them into supersized quills.

"You know the book *A Wrinkle in Time*?" he says as we hit Amsterdam and start walking north. "I heard that the author, Madeleine L'Engle, used to have an office at the cathedral.

That's why I want to see it. Isn't that crazy? I've probably read that book ten times."

"Charles Wallace was the genius kid, right?"

He nods enthusiastically. "And there was Meg, the main character. And IT. And—" He pauses at the steps and gapes at the massive stone cathedral. "Wow."

I look upward with him. I forget how amazing the cathedral is, tall and imposing with ornate windows and arches over the entryways. I've seen it so many times over the years that it seems like a regular part of the landscape of Amsterdam. Along with the peacock phase, Shannon had a medieval birthday party in the basement of the cathedral. When I was a lot younger I had a nanny who would bring Byron and me here to have picnics on the grounds.

"Wow," he says again, exhaling loudly. "It's wild to think about Madeleine L'Engle walking up those exact steps with ideas for a new book in her head."

"There's a garden in the back," I say. "Want to check it out? My brother and I used to play tag there when we were little."

"Do you have an older or younger brother?" he asks, but then quickly shakes his head. "Hang on. No family details. A garden? Hang on. Before I agree to walk to a remote garden with you I should ask if *you* have an ax. I don't want to be sexist and assume that only men are ax murderers."

I have to laugh. I love the way he talks, all fast and funny and semiscattered. I hold out my hands to show him I have nothing except the bag of bagels looped over one wrist, and my backpack is too obviously stuffed with books to conceal any weapons. "No ax. No machete. No ice pick."

"Glad that's settled," he says as we amble through the gate and follow the driveway around the side of the cathedral. I glance up to the stone landing where the peacocks sometimes hang out, but none are there now. Just a mom following a toddler up the stairs, holding her arms out to catch her if she tumbles.

Even though I haven't been to the garden in a few years, it's exactly how I remembered. We navigate along the little stone paths, around the neatly trimmed hedges, and over the floral mosaic in the center until we get to a tall bench shaded by a wooden canopy. The weird thing is, it's not like we discuss sitting down, but in one easy motion we both lower ourselves onto the bench. I set my backpack next to me and he drops the skateboard and sketch pad on the ground, and we unwrap our bagels.

"It's perfect," he says after a few silent bites. "Chewy and crunchy and garlicky and the perfect butter-to-dough ratio."

My mouth is full of bagel, so I just nod yes, agreed. A perfect butter-to-dough ratio is something Mom would never admit exists. She'd be too busy scooping out the dough and going light on the butter.

After a few more bites, I ask him, "Since you love *A Wrinkle in Time*, I was wondering if you've read *When You Reach Me*?"

He shakes his head. "Never heard of it."

"Oh!" I say, clapping my hands together. Yes, dorky. But

*When You Reach Me* was one of my favorite books in middle school, and I get hyper about things like that. "First of all, it's amazing. You won't be able to put it down. Also, it takes place in this neighborhood, but in the 1970s. It's an homage to *A Wrinkle in Time*. That's why I think you'd like it."

He's grinning so hard there are crinkly lines around his eyes. "That is so cute"—he pauses to wipe his lips with a small paper napkin—"that you just word-dropped 'homage.' I've never met a girl who uses the word homage."

"So your guy friends are into homages?" I shoot back.

"Come to think of it . . . nope."

"For years I'd only read the word and I thought it was 'ho-mage.' Hard 'h.'"

He laughs. "Oh, like 'cha-ohs' instead of 'chaos.' That was mine."

My phone vibrates in my back pocket. I slide it out.

My call wrapped up, Dad has texted. I'm almost at the bagel store.

I swallow hard. What happened to *It's going to be a while*? The thing is, I'm not ready to say good-bye to this guy. I wish I could blow Dad off, but that is obviously not an option.

Before I have a chance to write back, another text comes in.

I'm at the light at 103rd and Broadway. Are you out front?

Shit. I guess I have to do this.

I'm in the garden behind Saint John the Divine, I write quickly.

I'll turn on 106th, Dad texts. Be there in two minutes. Come to the sidewalk on the east side of Amsterdam.

34

I sigh heavily. I can feel the guy watching me. As I slide my phone back in my pocket, he says, "Do you have to go?"

"Yeah." I sigh.

"Family stuff again?"

"Pretty much."

I stand up and sling my backpack over my shoulder. Twenty minutes ago, I was biting back tears because Dad wasn't coming and now I want to cry because he's almost here.

The guy stands up next to me. I notice all over again that he's really tall. He also happens to have broad shoulders and arms that look like they could pull me into a serious hug.

"Are you—?" I start to ask, but he's talking at the exact same time.

"Do you think we should—?"

As soon as he hears me, he halts and shakes his head. "What were you going to say?"

I shrug. "I was just going to ask if you're leaving now, too."

He stares at me for a second and bites his bottom lip. It suddenly hits me that he was going to ask something entirely different, that maybe the *Do you think we should* was the beginning of *Do you think we should*:

1. Exchange names?
2. Exchange numbers?
3. Have sex?
4. Get married and live happily ever after?

35

"I think I'll stay and finish my bagel," he says. "Then I'm going to go inside and sketch and try to channel the spirit of Madeleine L'Engle."

My phone vibrates in my pocket. I don't have to take it out to know it's Dad telling me he's out front.

"Well . . . 'bye," I say. As I do, my heart lurches a little.

"Yeah . . . 'bye."

I turn and walk out of the garden. I don't let myself look back until I get to the sidewalk. By that point, it's too late. There's nothing left to see.

# 4

Because of the delay from Dad's call, he has to haul ass on the highway. We get to our Connecticut house at the same moment as the Tree Man is arriving in her blue pickup truck. Yes, the Tree Man turns out to be a Tree Babe. I swear, I can hear Dad mentally whistling as she walks with us up our front path and into the house.

She's about twenty-five and skinny with huge boobs, a body-type combo I will never understand because breasts are fat cells and boy hips are lack thereof. Also, she's totally working the landscaper-meets-porn-star angle, with her minuscule green shorts and thin white T-shirt, her mane of blond hair barely contained by a green baseball cap.

Dad is loving it. They're in the kitchen, and he's supposed to be telling her about the trees on our property that need pruning so they don't cause damage in a storm, but he's offered her seltzer three times and now he's in brag mode. He's leaning against the marble counter describing how they bought this country house at the right time in the market, like she cares, and how his older daughter is planning to go to medical school and his son will head to law school after Columbia. Not like I want to be on the brag bingo card, but I'm feeling a tad invisible right about now.

I cross the room and flop onto the sectional couch. If we had a TV, I would blast the volume and send Dad the message to take his middle-aged married self outside. But my parents have always been insistent that we don't have television or Wi-Fi in the country. We don't even get a cell phone signal out here. Based on my morning texting, I know that Froggy and his friend Hudson are visiting his grandparents on Fire Island, and Alyssa is baking cookies and working on her Humanities essay. Shannon still hasn't texted me back about her big crazy news.

"Let's take a stroll," Dad says to Tree Babe as he slides open the glass door to our porch.

Barf. Like he's inviting her to walk with him along a moonlit beach and not to inspect a bunch of maples and oaks.

I allow myself to read *Fates and Furies* for fifteen minutes. Then I pull a chemistry sheet out of my backpack and attempt to focus on chemical equilibrium and rates of reactions, but my mind keeps wandering back to the nonskater artist boy who bumped into garbage cans and gazed up at cathedrals and made my stomach flip with a yearning I didn't even know existed.

Fates: I met him.

Furies: We will probably never see each other again.

6  6  6  6

"Well, she was lovely," Dad says to me. "I can see why Green Arbor sent her over."

"Uh," I say. What else is there to say? It's not like I'm going to bond with Dad about how lucky he is that he got the hot tree pruner.

We're in the driveway. I'm at the wheel of his car, and Dad is in the passenger seat. I've turned the ignition, and I'm waiting for him to start Dadsplaining. That's the endless lecture he gives before every lesson—mirrors, signals, blind spots—but today he seems to be thinking more about trees and the people who service them.

I shift into drive and press my toes on the gas. It turns out to be more like a lurch, jerking my seat belt into lock mode. I refuse to look at Dad. I hate this so much. Most New York City kids don't even get their license until the summer before college because there's a plethora of ways to get around—subway, bus, cab, bike, walk—that don't involve the insane act of maneuvering a four-thousand-pound machine and putting your life and others in danger. But Dad doesn't get that. Teaching his kids to drive at sixteen is another bragging point for him. Also, he's obsessed with the practical aspects of having a license, like what if I'm stranded in the middle of nowhere and the person driving becomes deathly ill? The thing is, most places I go have public transportation, and most people I hang out with aren't dying.

"She had a great figure," Dad says. "Really top notch."

I hit the brake hard, but suddenly the car is careening into the road and I realize, crap, I pushed the gas instead.

"Dammit, Virginia!" Dad shouts, grabbing the wheel and turning us quickly so we don't ram into the mailbox across the street.

"Sorry." I slide my foot over to the brake. I'm biting down on the inside of my cheeks, already raw from when I was gnawing them this morning, and my hands are trembling.

"Don't apologize," Dad says, exhaling slowly. "Just don't do that again. You should know your gas from your brake by now. If a car was coming from either direction we could have been hit. This is real life. This isn't one of your video games."

I'm not sure how Dad doesn't know that I don't like video games and never play them.

"Now, let's get going," Dad says. "What are you waiting for?"

I'm waiting to stop shaking. I'm waiting for you to realize I hate driving. I'm waiting to remember what side of the road I drive on. I'm waiting for you to understand that it's not appropriate to drool over hot young tree pruners to your sixteen-year-old daughter.

I ease my foot onto the gas and position my hands at ten and two and try not to hit the curb or drift over the yellow line on the trip to the parking lot where we practice turns.

One horrible hour later, it's obvious that I suck at

three-point turns. Despite Dad's stream of commands, I can't seem to accomplish a turn in less than seven points.

"I don't get it," Dad says once we've traded seats. "You took thirty hours of driver's ed, and we've gotten in thirty-two hours of practice. What's not clicking? Byron and Anaïs picked up driving so quickly."

*Ah, yes*, I want to say. *That's because I was switched at birth. Don't you realize that one of these offspring is not like the others?*

Dad adjusts the mirrors, takes a left on the main road, and merges onto the highway toward the city. It's a ninety-minute drive. He puts on NPR, and I slide on my headphones. A few minutes before the Cross County Parkway, Dad takes a conference call on speakerphone. I turn off my music and listen to him talking about licensing and rights management. Since I'll be interning at Ciel Media this summer, it'll be good to get some of the terminology down.

Once Dad hangs up, I say, "Should I come by next week to do the internship paperwork or wait until Shannon gets back?"

Shannon is flying home next Saturday, and we're starting as interns the week after.

Dad shakes his head. "I'll call Holly in HR and see what I can figure out. She says she's on it, but these things take a while. You and Shannon aren't traditional college interns."

We head down the West Side Highway. I can see kids in Riverside Park taking soccer classes in their matching white shirts and blue shorts. Mom forced me to do those soccer classes all through elementary school. I didn't tell this to the cute boy from the bagel store, but soccer is another bullet point on the list of Horrible Things. So was dressing the same as fifteen other girls. Their soccer outfits draped loosely over their skinny bodies while mine stretched tight across my stomach and thighs.

Dad pulls up in front of our building before dropping off the car at the parking garage. "We'll get more practice on Saturday," he says as I'm climbing out. "You might not have the instincts, but plenty of hard work should get you there."

I nod at his C-minus pep talk and close the door.

Just as I'm walking into the apartment, Shannon finally texts.

Sorry for the delay! I was on an awesome end-of-year class camping trip and didn't have my phone. I'm assuming you figured out how to sneak Froggy past Byron yesterday? AWKWARD!!!

I quickly respond. Did you really put "awesome" and "camping trip" in the same sentence? Shannon is an indoor artsy type. Or at least she used to be.

Ha! Shannon writes. Do you like the pot holder I sent? I bought a loom at a yard sale. I may sew a bunch of pot holders into a quilt. Oh, and I want to tell you the news, but promise you won't be mad.

Mad??? I write, hopping onto my bed. It's weird to think how yesterday Froggy and I were fooling around here, that he was trying to undo my jeans. It's been a relief not to deal with him today, but I'm dreading seeing him back at school tomorrow. It's confusing. I just can't figure out how I could have been into Froggy for so many months and then suddenly not. And does "suddenly not" last forever, or will I fall back in like with him if I stick with it? Of course I have to stick with it! It's rule number one.

Then again, I can't chase away this niggling little thought that Froggy was a fine starter boyfriend, but maybe I could hope for true love someday. And maybe true love could come in the form of a tall guy with blue-green sea-glass eyes who likes books and bagels and who makes me laugh. I'm not saying the guy from this morning was my true love, because I don't know his name and he's not from here and for all I know he's leaving the city tomorrow. But something about meeting him and hanging out this morning made me feel something I've never felt before—that getting a boyfriend isn't about settling for who will take me, that maybe I could hope for more than that.

A text comes in. I lunge for my phone thinking it's Shannon with her news, but it's just Mom, writing from her office.

**Be sure to pack for the weekend in CT,** she's written. **Dad and I are coming home from work early tomorrow and we'll leave right after you get back from kickboxing. How did driving go?**

I guess she hasn't talked to Dad yet.

**It went,** I write back.

I open my drawers and toss shirts and shorts and magazines into a tote for the weekend. Just as I'm zipping up the bag, Shannon texts me back, **You know how we're supposed to come home from Washington in nine days?**

**I've only been counting down since last August,** I write to her.

**And you know how we have a pact to always be honest with each other?**

Yeah, I write.

I'm worried you're going to be upset about some news I have to tell you.

I won't, I write. Promise.

Since we're already on the West Coast, my parents and I have decided to hike the PCT. Well, 600 miles of it. Through Central and Northern California.

Googling PCT, I text her.

A moment later, I write, Oh.

It turns out the PCT is the Pacific Crest Trail, a hiking trail that runs along the entire West Coast from the Canadian border to the Mexican border. I'm guessing she can't hike six hundred miles and return home in time for our summer internship.

While I'm waiting for Shannon to respond, I stare out my window at the Hudson River. My hands are clenched into fists when her text finally comes in.

I'm sorry I can't work at Ciel with you. Please tell your dad sorry/thanks. I'll be back for school at the end of August.

When I don't write back immediately, Shannon adds, You promised you wouldn't be mad.

Maadd? I write. I'm fine. Have fun out there.

I consider saying, Maybe you can weave your pot holders into a thermal sleeping bag, but instead I power off my phone and stuff it deep in my tote bag.

# 5

As I walk across Central Park on my way to school on Friday, I keep reaching into my dress pocket and touching my phone. I still haven't turned it on since yesterday. I know it's not fair to blow off Shannon and I should be happy she's hiking six hundred miles, but the truth is that I *am* mad she's not coming home and doing the internship with me. That was our plan. We've been excited about it for months.

Also, when my parents were pushing me to do Outward Bound, Shannon was my number one supporter in my quest to stay Inward Bound. We spent an entire night texting about the atrocities of pooping in the woods. Shannon was the one who pointed out that you could get your period in the wilderness and a bear could smell the fresh blood and track you and eat you. So what's up with Shannon suddenly wanting to spend her summer trekking through the wild?

I have to turn on my phone soon, though. Otherwise Froggy and Alyssa will think I'm dead. Actually, Froggy thinking I'm dead could be a solution to my out-of-like situation. Clerical day was a break, but unless I can decide what do about him, like whether I should acknowledge that starter boyfriends must have ends, I'll have to keep suffering through slobbery make-out sessions every day until he goes to band camp in late June. Part of my brain is insisting, *Break up with Froggy.* But what if I hurt his feelings? Also, what if he's the best guy I'll ever get and if I dump him then I'll never be half of a couple again?

Central Park is quiet, just dogs loping around and owners clustered in groups chatting. I used to take the crosstown bus to school, but ever since "the ordeal," I've needed my walk across the park to clear my head before I can deal with people. "The ordeal" has definitely taken its toll in many different ways. Right after I found out what Byron did, during the phase when I could barely look at him, I snuck up to Columbia and located Annie Mills, the student who accused him of date rape. I found her through the college directory and apologized on my brother's behalf. I've never told a soul about that. When I knocked on Annie's dorm-room door and announced who I was, she was like, *What are you doing here?* But after a while, she realized I wasn't a psychopath and we drank herbal tea and talked about not being victims. In the end, she even gave me a hug. It didn't magically make everything better, or make what Byron did go away, but it felt like the tiniest twig of an olive branch.

That was back in December. I saw Annie another time, a

few months ago. I was uptown at Columbia writing poetry for a Humanities assignment, and I popped into the Hungarian Pastry Shop to indulge in a chocolate éclair. There she was, waiting tables. As soon as I saw her, I hurried out before she could spot me. I've never told anyone that either.

It's a warm morning, already in the high seventies, and I'm wearing a black tank dress and strappy sandals. I glance over at Turtle Pond. I used to love passing this pond, with Belvedere Castle hovering on a rocky outcrop above it. That's the first place Froggy and I kissed in public, on January twentieth at 1:21 p.m.

Back then it felt really important. Back then I couldn't imagine not wanting to be with him.

As I hit the East Side, I see Brewster down the block. It's a small private school in a redbrick building draped in ivy. I climb the front steps, wave at the guard, and walk down the corridor toward my locker. School doesn't start for fifteen more minutes. I'll probably kill time at the library. I round the corner at the sophomore wing and—

Froggy is standing next to my locker.

He waves when he sees me. I used to think he was cute. Now he looks needy, like a rescue dog begging for a kibble. Okay, this is getting bad. Kissing like a golden retriever. Pleading rescue-dog expression. Remember, Virginia: *Froggy is your boyfriend. He is a fine boyfriend. He will most likely be your boyfriend forever. So stop thinking canine thoughts about him.*

"Hey," he says.

"Hey." I sling my backpack onto the floor and cross my arms over my chest.

"I texted you a bunch of times."

"Oh . . . uh . . . thanks . . . sorry. My phone's off."

"How was the driving lesson?"

"Yeah, it sucked. I suck." His nose is sunburned from the beach yesterday. I should ask if he and Hudson had fun at Fire Island.

"I'm sure you're not that bad," he says. He moves in to kiss me. My instinct is to duck, but Froggy is my boyfriend and kissing is what couples do. I angle forward and give him a dry peck. I allow myself a fleeting second to imagine what it would be like to kiss the boy from the bagel store. I definitely wouldn't dodge his mouth. But then I remind myself that I don't know his name and I'll never see him again and I'm not living in reality by thinking about kissing him.

"Yeah . . . so . . . Hudson and I are leaving right after school," Froggy says. "You know that Minecraft Marathon I told you about? At the Brooklyn Public Library?"

"Oh, right," I say. "Are you really staying up all night?"

"We're going to, you know, try. Twenty-four hours of Minecraft."

I don't get the obsession with Minecraft. I have no interest in building pretend castles and slaughtering pretend animals to pretend survive. Whenever Froggy and Hudson and Alyssa geek out over Minecraft, which is every day at lunch, I pull out a book or check my phone.

"Are you going back to Connecticut tomorrow?" Froggy asks.

"Yep."

Froggy comes in for another kiss. This time I sidestep him and lean over to scoop up my bag.

"Is . . . uuuuhhhh . . . ?" Froggy asks, rubbing his nose.

I clutch my hands to my neck. "I have a sore throat."

I can't use that excuse every day, but it'll get me through this moment.

⑤ ⑤ ⑤ ⑤

Alyssa and I spend lunch hidden in the computer cluster. This is where we used to work on our blog. It was called Earthquack. We're taking a break from the blog because end-of-year school-work got too intense, but I convinced her to stow away here for lunch today. I white-lied and said I was stressed about finals and needed her to be my study partner. If I told Alyssa the real reason, that we came here to hide from Froggy, she'd be crushed. Alyssa thinks Froggy and I are the perfect couple and it's amazing we're together because no one has real relationships in high school anymore.

It's Brunch for Lunch. We make a quick cafeteria run to grab waffles, sausages, and orange juice. Once we're done eating, we read over the Global Studies documents and quiz each other for the final.

"Why's your phone off again?" Alyssa asks.

"The answer is no. Scotland did not vote to leave the European Union during Brexit." I pause. "And I want an unplugged day. That's why I'm keeping my phone off."

Lie. But I don't want to go into the Shannon stuff. It's not that I don't love Alyssa, because I do. She saved me from a friendless oblivion this year, and I'm bummed that she'll be staying with family in New Jersey all summer. But Alyssa and I don't do deep confessions. Our friendship is more about the day-to-day.

"Who's the Prime Minister who stepped down after Brexit?" I ask her.

"David Cameron," she says. "I love your dress."

"Thanks," I say. "Total credit to Torrid. I love their stuff."

"It's cute how you and Froggy are both wearing black."

I nod vaguely. It will definitely crush Alyssa if Froggy and I break up.

As the bell rings, we toss our paper plates into the recycling bin. Ms. Crowley, my favorite teacher from ninth grade, walks by and says, "Hi, girls!"

We both smile and say hello back. But as soon as she passes, Alyssa leans close to me. "Are you sure you're okay? You seem quiet."

"No, I'm great," I say. "I mean, I'm stressed about finals, but otherwise everything is fine."

"Want to go to Chinatown tomorrow?" Alyssa asks. "My grandma told me about a new restaurant with a cheap lunch special. We could study for finals at my place and then drown our academic woes in dim sum."

"I wish. My parents are making me go back to Connecticut."

Alyssa shrugs sympathetically. Her parents are from New York City and so are her grandparents. Three generations who don't know how to drive, a dream family to me.

We clomp up three flights. Alyssa veers into the bathroom

and says she'll see me in a minute. When I get to Madame Kiefer's classroom, Froggy is standing outside the door, holding up a bag of honey-lemon cough drops.

"For your sore throat," he says. "When I didn't see you at lunch, I got permission to go out and buy them."

"Thanks." I force a smile as I take the cough drops.

I'm the worst girlfriend ever.

⑥ ⑥ ⑥ ⑥

As the final bell rings, I hand in my Global Studies review questions and hurry down the stairs, taking caution to sidestep Froggy's locker. Ideally, I'd like to avoid him before he leaves for the Minecraft Marathon in Brooklyn. Even back when things were good and kissing didn't involve Canine Tongue, we rarely smooched at his locker. Brie Newhart, Queen Bee of the Tenth Grade, is two lockers down from Froggy. Kissing my boyfriend in front of her is offering myself up as a punch line.

At the beginning of sophomore year, I overheard Brie making fun of my body. That was the same conversation where Brie told them that she flirted with my brother on the subway and he's so hot and how on earth could we be related? Soon after that, Brie developed an eating disorder and was absent from school to get treatment. While she was gone, a different clique formed with Brinna Livingston at the helm. When Brie returned, she was subdued for a while and actually a little nice. She even helped me with French homework. But after a few months, Brie reclaimed her Queen Bee position, ushering in a new reign of mean and bitchy.

Big freaking sigh of relief that the summer vacation means a three-month vacation from Brie Newhart and her friends.

I slam my locker and head outside. Kickboxing doesn't start until four. If someone asked me a year ago whether I would voluntarily go to an exercise class on a Friday afternoon when every cell in my body wants to curl up with Netflix and a bag of honey-wheat pretzels, I would have asked that crazy person what hallucinogenic drug they were on. But kickboxing is different. Tisha creates an upbeat vibe in her studio where we laugh and punch and kick and we're so into what we're doing that we don't even realize we're getting exercise.

On Fridays, I usually walk across Central Park, with a pit stop at Sephora to try on lipstick and eye shadow. It's warm but overcast today, with a hint of rain in the air. In an ideal world, it will rain so hard this weekend that the roads will flood and Dad won't take me driving and I'll get to read and study for finals and remain in denial that my road test is coming in four weeks.

Anaïs and Mom used to fight about denial. My sister would say that Mom was Cleopatra, Queen of Denial, and Mom would get mad and deny that she lives in a world of denial. As I'm crossing the park I decide that when it comes to things like road tests that I'll fail and boyfriends that I can't bring myself to break up with, a little denial might not be so bad.

# 6

Forty-five minutes later, Brie Newhart walks into my kick-boxing class.

When I see her, I gasp so loudly I have to pretend I'm having a coughing fit. I wish I could run back to Sephora and see if they sell foundation that will not only cover my flushed cheeks but make my entire self disappear.

By the time I see Brie, I've already changed into my workout clothes and I'm chatting with the girl next to me. It's a small class, usually around ten girls of all different body types. We worship our teacher, Tisha. She has cornrowed hair, a full figure, and she's both a jujitsu black belt and a former Alvin Ailey dancer. For an hour and a half every Friday, Tisha gets us to sweat bullets combining dance and cardio and martial arts.

But Brie.

Here.

This is the opposite of awesome on so many levels.

"Hey!" Tisha says as she ushers Brie into the gym, a studio on West 105th with hardwood floors, no mirrors, and plenty of bags to kick and punch.

"You must be Brie," Tisha says. "Did you bring hand wraps?"

"No, Tisha," Brie says brightly. "I'm so sorry."

Teachers love Brie because she does the eye-contact thing and makes plentiful use of their names. They never seem to see through to her evil, fat-shaming core. Except it's not even a core. It's all of who she is, even in the DNA of her pigtails and charcoal workout shorts and skimpy jog bra.

"No worries." Tisha hands Brie some spare gloves. Then she turns to us. "Girls, this is Brie. She's joining our class."

There's a chorus of "heys" and "what's ups." I press my lips tight. Of all the millions of exercise classes in Manhattan, how is it possible that Brie wound up here? I don't even think she lives on the Upper West Side.

Brie positions herself next to me but doesn't say a word. I pretend to be adjusting my hand wraps, but really I'm just unwinding the gauze and winding it up again. I pick up my jump rope. I *so* don't want to jump in front of Brie, my boobs bouncing all over the place.

When Tisha signals us to start, I squeeze my arms hard into my chest, attempting to contain the boob jiggle. I glance over at Brie. She's doing perfect jiggle-free jumping jacks.

Partway through class, as Tisha is switching the music, Brie whispers to me, "Thanks, Virginia. But I mean that sarcastically, so instead of 'you're welcome' you should say 'sorry.'"

I stare at her, confused. My bangs are sticky against my forehead, and my underarms are leaking through my shirt.

"Your mom told my mom about this class," Brie says, "and now my mom is forcing me to take it."

"My mom told her?" I manage.

"They ran into each other at Saks," Brie says. "Supposedly your mom couldn't stop talking about kickboxing and how physically and emotionally therapeutic this class has been for you. So . . . yeah . . . thanks."

No. Way. Brie wound up here because of Mom? Mom, who is supposed to understand what teenagers need, totally betrayed me.

"I liked your purple hair," Brie adds, "but don't you think the green bangs are a little much? Like, you're not a clown. You're not getting paid to entertain young children at birthday parties."

I stare at her, my mouth open in shock.

At that moment, Tisha pumps the music and tells everyone to punch the heavy bags. I spend the next several minutes attacking my bag. I don't hear Tisha when she says it's time to start the cooldown. She has to come over and tap my shoulder and tell me to stop punching.

ⓖ ⓖ ⓖ ⓖ

After class, I don't even change out of my shorts and sweat-soaked Columbia T-shirt. I used to wear this shirt obsessively when Byron started college. Back then I was so proud of my brother. Now I just wear it to kickboxing or to dye my hair. I hurry down the stairs and storm angrily toward home. I'm going to text Mom that we need to talk as soon as possible. I reach in my bag and turn on my phone.

The last day's worth of texts appears on my screen. There are texts from Froggy, Alyssa, a bunch from Mom, one from Dad. I pause in the middle of the sidewalk and scroll up and down the messages, trying to see if I've missed a text from Shannon.

Nope. Doesn't look like it.

Shannon hasn't texted since I snapped at her last night. I've been so busy being mad that she's ditching me for a six-hundred-mile hike that I never realized she might be upset back.

I put away my phone without texting Mom.

"Where have you been?" Mom asks when I walk into the apartment ten minutes later. She's carrying her tote bag into the foyer. "I've been texting you all afternoon."

"Whatever," I mutter. "My phone was off."

"We have an agreement," she says. "We let you travel around the city, and we expect we can reach you anytime. What if there was an emergency?" Mom scrutinizes my T-shirt and shorts. "Did you wear that to school? Please tell me you didn't wear that to school. There are purple stains all around the neck."

I don't answer. I don't owe her any explanations. "Why were you texting me all afternoon, anyway?"

"Dad got home from work early, and I ordered Thai food,"

she says. "We're going to eat dinner first and then leave for Connecticut. Let the traffic thin out a little. You can do homework. I know you wanted me to proofread your final Humanities essay, but I don't think I'll have time until—"

"*That* was the emergency?" I snap.

Mom pauses to take a TherapistBreath, inhaling through her nose and exhaling through her mouth. It's the Dr. Shreves that she is around her patients, all calm and composed.

I set down my backpack and cross my arms over my chest. "How could you tell Brie Newhart's mom about kickboxing?"

Mom presses her lips together. She's busted and she knows it. "I ran into Simone Newhart at—"

"Saks," I say. "I know. But why did you tell her about my class?"

Mom walks into the kitchen. I follow her in and watch her take the seltzer out of the fridge.

"First," she says calmly, "you don't need to use that tone. Let's make this into a constructive conversation, not a battle."

Before I've had a chance to respond to that garble of TherapistSpeak, Byron walks in from the gym.

"Hey, Gin, what's up?" he asks. Then to Mom, he says, "I got your text that you were ordering Thai food. Did you order for me, too?"

"Yeah," she says, "Dad got you shrimp Pad Thai and spring rolls." Mom opens the fridge, gets out the lemon juice, and squeezes a few drops into her seltzer. "You're not coming to Connecticut, right?"

"Nah," my brother says as he leans over and unlaces his

sneakers. "The golfing is going to be crap because of the rain. I'll just chill here. I've got a lot to do to get ready for Paris. I'm supposed to write this doctrine about international relations after World War Two. In French."

"I can look it over when you're done," Mom offers. "That would be a fun challenge for me."

I often feel like barfing about how my whole family speaks French. Even though I've taken years of the language, I still struggle to conjugate verbs in the present tense. Once I finish my sophomore language requirement at Brewster, I'm going to switch over to Mandarin.

"What day do you leave for Paris?" Mom asks.

"The twenty-sixth." Byron shoots her a charming grin, all teeth and deep dimples. "And yes, I'll still be here to see Anaïs. She arrives three days before I leave. So you can wave that impending anxiety attack good-bye."

Mom swats his arm like she's annoyed, but it's obvious she thinks he's adorable.

I clear my throat loudly and tap my foot on the ground. "I'm waiting," I say. "I'd appreciate an explanation this decade."

Byron whistles under his breath, opens the fridge, and pulls out a Vitaminwater. Even though Mom has never said it out loud, those bottles are clearly not for me. Whenever they arrive from Fresh Direct, she scribbles *Byron* in Sharpie on each case. She says it's because he works out and needs to replenish his electrolytes.

Mom looks up from her phone and fixes her eyes on me. "I

told Simone Newhart about kickboxing because it's been wonderful for you. Brie has been going through a hard time, and I thought she could use something positive, something out of her comfort zone."

"The class has been good for me because people like Brie aren't in it. Brie is a bitch. At class today she said my hair looks like a clown's." I decide not to go into how Brie has called me fat. The last thing I want is for Mom to nod and say, *Well, she has a point, Gin*.

"Language, Virginia," Mom says, sitting on a stool and writing on her phone.

"Brie who?" Byron asks.

"Brie Newhart," I tell him. "She's in my grade. You know her."

Byron guzzles his Vitaminwater and alley-oops the bottle into the recycling bin. It lands with a thud. "Never heard of her. That was a bitchy thing to say about your hair, though."

"Yes, you have heard of her!" I say to him. "You flirted with her on the subway last fall."

I can't believe I'm upset for Brie. No, I'm actually not. It's about girls in general. If my brother flirted with someone on the subway, wouldn't he remember it? Or do so many girls fawn over him that there are too many to keep straight?

"Virginia," Mom says, looking up. "Let it go, okay?"

"Let it go" is Mom's code-phrase for sweeping it under the rug. That's where she likes to put things that are less than perfect.

Byron starts down the hall toward the shower but then turns, smiles at me, and says, "Mom, you shouldn't have told that Brie girl about Gin's class. That's her sanctuary."

As the bathroom door closes, I'm plummeted onto the I-love-him-I-hate-him roller coaster I've been on since last fall. "Sanctuary" is the perfect word for how I feel about kickboxing. I can't believe Byron knows that.

The buzzer rings from our lobby, a short buzz followed by a longer one.

"That's the Thai food," Mom says to me. "Can you get it? And, Gin, you're right. We'll talk about the Brie thing later. I'm handling a situation with a patient right now. She didn't get accepted to ballet camp, and she's falling apart."

"No ballet camp . . . that's devastating."

Mom ignores the sarcasm in my voice.

The buzzer rings again.

Mom shouts in the direction of the bathroom, "Byron, the food's here! You can shower later. And get Dad, too! He's in our room."

I go to the intercom and say, "Hello?"

No answer. Usually Alberto is there to announce who's coming, but he takes a break every few hours. I push the button to unlock our lobby door and send the delivery guy up. Then I open our front door and lean against the frame. A moment later, the elevator opens and two police officers step onto our floor.

I look down the hall, waiting to see the delivery guy come out of the elevator after them.

No delivery guy.

The police officers are walking toward me. One of the guys is tall and bald, and the other is short with a stubby nose. They both have guns on their belts.

My heart starts pounding as the bald one clears his throat. "Is this the home of Byron Shreves?"

I stare at him.

"Remember to add on a tip!" Mom calls from the kitchen.

"Is it?" the policeman asks.

I nod slowly.

"Is he around?"

I have forgotten how to talk.

"Excuse me," the short guy says. His voice is harsher, more demanding. "We need to know if Byron Shreves is home."

Mom appears behind me. "What is this regarding?" she asks, her voice tight and high.

"I'm Officer Culkin," the bald guy says, "and this is Officer Hernandez. We are detectives in the Sex Crimes Unit."

"Get Dad," Mom barks at me, "and tell him to call Mark Levy. Tell him it's urgent."

Mark Levy is the lawyer that my parents hired when Byron got suspended from college. For a while, they were talking to him every day. The big fear was that Annie Mills would report the sexual assault to the police, but once it seemed like it was going to be handled within Columbia, like Byron got suspended and had to drop out of the rugby team, they stopped huddling with the lawyer all the time.

I'm trying to get Dad, but my feet aren't moving. Five

seconds pass where no one says anything. But then I hear various doors opening and Byron and Dad are coming down the hall. They're laughing, and Dad's arm is slung around Byron's shoulder. When they see the police, Dad's hand slips to his side.

"Are you Byron Shreves?" Officer Hernandez asks, stepping through our doorway.

Byron glances nervously at Mom. The color has drained from her face.

"Yes," Byron finally says. "Why?"

"We need to bring you to the precinct and ask you some questions about the night of September thirtieth."

"Are you arresting him?" Dad asks.

"Call Mark Levy," Mom hisses to Dad.

Dad takes his phone out of his pocket but then drops it. It skids loudly across the hardwood floor.

The officers don't even look at my parents. They just focus on Byron. The bald one says, "Get your shoes on. We're going to the precinct."

"But—" Mom starts, but Officer Hernandez cuts her off.

"Mrs. Shreves," he says, touching his hand to his gun, "we can cuff your son and bring him down, or he can walk out willingly with us. We have the car out front."

Usually when someone calls her Mrs. Shreves, Mom corrects them and says "Dr. Shreves." This time she doesn't say a word.

I dig my fingernails into my palms. It's my fault for buzzing the police up. I should have asked through the intercom who it was, given us some warning. Or if I'd gotten Dad as soon as

Mom told me to, then maybe he could have called the lawyer and stopped these guys from taking Byron.

Byron slides his feet into his sneakers. He's wearing the same shorts and gray T-shirt that he worked out in. I wonder if I should grab him a fresh shirt, but I still can't move.

"We'll follow you in a cab," Dad says quietly. "We'll see you there."

With that, Byron and the detectives walk to the elevator. The bald guy pushes the down button. Dad grabs his wallet, and Mom slings her purse onto her shoulder. The elevator door opens and they all step in.

I'm standing in the empty hallway, completely in shock, when the buzzer rings again.

This time I ask who it is.

This time it's the Thai food.

⚅ ⚅ ⚅ ⚅

I can't stop shivering, so I go into the bathroom, yank off my clothes, and step into the shower. The instant the hot water hits my shoulders, I start crying. I stay in the shower bawling until my back is stinging and my throat is raw, and when I finally get out, I'm feeling dizzy. I wrap myself in a towel, sit on the toilet seat lid, and lower my head between my knees. I have no idea what happened at the door just now. Did Byron get arrested for what he did last fall? But why now, almost nine months later? And if he did get arrested, does that mean he's going to jail?

The home phone is ringing in the distance. I pull the towel around my chest and hurry into the living room to grab it.

"Hello?"

"It's Mark Levy," the guy on the other end says. "Is Mike there? Or Phyllis?"

Mark Levy is the lawyer. Mike is my dad. Phyllis is my mom. I'm having a hard time forming any clear thoughts around these facts.

Also, I'm not sure what to tell him. It's not like I can say that the police hauled my brother off. Then again, he's a lawyer, so I'm guessing that's key information. "My parents . . . sort of . . . went with Byron . . . to the police station."

"Isn't this Mike's cell phone?" he says quickly. "I thought that's what my assistant gave me."

I'm explaining to him that no, this is our home phone, when he hangs up without saying good-bye.

I clutch the towel tighter and survey our living room. There's the bag of Thai food and the plates and silverware set on the table and the totes packed for the weekend. I grab my phone out of my bag and head into my room. I pull on shorts, a bra, and a tank top, and text my parents to ask if everything's okay even though it's obviously not. While I'm waiting for them to write back, I allow myself to think about Annie Mills for a second. I feel horrible for what Byron did to her, but I also thought she said she wasn't going to let herself be a victim. So what made her go to the police now, all these months later?

We are still figuring things out, Mom finally texts.

I pace around the apartment. I consider eating a few spring rolls from the bag of Thai food. Maybe it will ease the gnawing in my gut. But what if my parents and brother walk in while

I'm chowing down and they're like, "We've been at the *police station* and you're enjoying Thai food like it's any other evening???"

Instead I pour a bowl of Life, douse it with milk, and go into my room. As I spoon up the cereal, I stare at my phone.

Should I call Alyssa? No. We don't go below the surface. Not about stuff like this. Froggy? No way. We can barely even talk about us, much less major life events like my brother getting arrested. Anaïs is somewhere between Burkina Faso and London, and I have no idea how to reach her.

**Hey,** I text to Shannon.

She's the one person who knows everything about me and still loves me. I can see three dots like she's writing back and then . . . nothing. Maybe I should say she *used* to love me until I was a bitch to her yesterday about the hiking thing.

**I'm sorry for yesterday,** I add. **Can you talk?**

This time Shannon responds immediately. **You SAID you wouldn't get MAADD and then you got MAADD and now I'M MAADD. Did you ever THINK about the fact that hiking the PCT is cool and you should be happy for me?**

I set my half-eaten bowl of cereal on my bedside table.

**I'm sorry,** I write. My eyes are prickling with tears, and the mush in my bowl is making me queasy. **You're right. The PCT is going to be amazing.**

**LIAR,** Shannon writes. **You would never in a million years think amazing thoughts about the Pacific Crest Trail. Camping & pooping outdoors = your idea of hell. You're forgiven by the way. Will you send me care packages?**

Of course, I write. I'll smuggle you contraband toilet paper. Ha!

It feels good to text with Shannon like it's any other day. Or night. But it's not.

I have something to tell you, I write. I swallow hard, glance into the hallway to make sure my parents aren't walking in, and then add, Byron just got arrested. At least I think he did.

The instant after I send it, my phone rings.

"What happened?" Shannon asks.

I tell her about the buzzer and the police and how they took Byron away.

"Is it another rape?" she asks.

My breath catches in my throat. There's something about thinking "rape" in my head, and another entirely hearing it out loud.

"No," I say. "The police said it was about September thirtieth. So it's from last year."

"Virginia," Shannon says quietly. "This isn't about you."

"What do you mean?"

"I know you well enough to know that you've been beating yourself up ever since they left the apartment. This is Byron's problem, and Byron will have to deal with it. You have to keep living your life."

"I wish you were here," I whisper.

"I'm always here for you," Shannon says.

I almost say *Not this summer*, but I press my lips together and remind myself to be a good friend.

By ten, they're still not home. I grab the bag of Thai food and throw it down the garbage chute. Then I turn off my ringer and get into bed.

At midnight, I'm lying awake when I hear voices in the apartment. My parents, for sure. I listen for Byron. Nope. Just Mom and Dad.

# 7

I wake up with a neck cramp. It's pouring rain outside my window, and the sky is steely gray, definitely not driving-practice weather. But it's not like I'm even happy about that anymore.

My parents are talking in the other room. Their phones keep ringing and chiming. I press my thumb into my neck to massage a knot. I want to find out what happened to Byron, but I'm not ready to deal with my parents yet. I reach for my phone on the bedside table. Several texts came in while I was sleeping.

A half hour ago, Alyssa wrote, **Hey to you in CT. I'm up at the crack of butt. Final review sheet for math is brutal. Text when you get home on Sunday so we can do it together. And remember, no hitting anything with your car!**

I don't write back. I'm not sure how to tell Alyssa that I'm still in the city. If I went for the truth, my parents would kill me. They're really private about not airing our dirty laundry. Mom frames it as a loyalty thing, but I think it's more about protecting the perfect Shreves image. They'd kill me if they found out I told Shannon that Byron got arrested last night, but Shannon knows everything about me so I'd take death over lying to her.

I can see that Shannon texted at three in the morning, midnight in Walla Walla: Thinking of you, Virginia. Hang in there.

At two in the morning, Froggy wrote, Hello from Minecraft Marathon hour 10.5. In survival mode. xoxo

I frown at the xoxo. Often he adds a heart, too. Good thing there's not an emoji for taking off someone's jeans. Okay, that's gross. I can't believe that a few days ago that was my biggest worry.

Just then, Mom turns the knob on my door. I quickly stash my phone under my covers.

"You need to get up," she says. Her hair is blown out and she's done her makeup. Weird. On Saturday mornings that we're not in Connecticut, Mom lives at the gym.

"What's going on?" I ask. "What happened to Byron last night? Is he home?"

Mom opens my closet door and pushes through my hangers. "I don't get it," she says, ignoring my questions. She's slamming my clothes from right to left. "I've gotten you so many nice things to wear. Where are they? All your new clothes look so cheap."

I roll over in bed and look out the window at the rain splattering onto the grayish Hudson River. There's a barge plodding toward the George Washington Bridge. If I were to answer Mom with a list, I would say:

## NICE THINGS IF "NICE" MEANT "HORRIBLE"

1. The Nice Things you got me were not nice. They were beige and shapeless.
2. You would never talk to your patients like this. Though I bet the girl who didn't get into ballet camp wears pleated skirts and sweater sets.
3. You bought me those Nice Things last fall and, hello, teenagers grow. Also, teenagers discover awesome stores like Torrid that acknowledge that style comes in shapes other than string bean.
4. As to the location of the Nice Things? Sorry, but I donated a heap of them to Housing Works back in March.

"This will do." Mom plucks out a beige blazer and a knee-length skirt. She got them for me to wear to a friend's daughter's bat mitzvah last summer.

I reach under the covers and squeeze my belly. I doubt the skirt still fits, and my boobs have definitely surpassed the girth of the blazer.

"Dad will rush it to the dry cleaner," she says. She takes a white blouse off my hanger. "At the very least they can steam these things. And your hair appointment is at eleven. Talia is doing me a favor by fitting you in. We leave at one."

Before I can ask where we're going at one, Mom walks out of my room with the blazer and skirt. I pull my covers over my head and close my eyes.

"Virginia!" Mom bursts back into my room. "Don't you get the gravity of this? Get up and let's have breakfast. The last thing I need is additional stress. Mark says we should be at the arraignment by two."

As Mom about-faces into the hallway, I glance at my phone. It's twenty minutes later. I must have fallen asleep. I wriggle up in bed and google "arraignment."

*A formal reading of a criminal-charging document in the presence of the defendant.*

A shiver runs up my spine. So it's true. My brother has been arrested.

ⓖ ⓖ ⓖ ⓖ

This, by the way, is only the beginning of Mark Says.

As I'm walking toward the dining area for breakfast, I stop short. Dad is on the phone with Mark Levy, the criminal-defense lawyer who called last night. Dad's shirt is rumpled and he's unshaven, with shadowy creases under his eyes. He's sipping coffee at the table and saying into the phone, "Yes, Mark. Yes . . . got it." Pause. "Yes . . . yes . . . okay, Mark." Pause. "Okay . . . yes."

Mom is staring intently at Dad, her nails clicking on the tabletop. She has a new manicure, pale peach with squared tops.

As soon as Dad hangs up, Mom says, "What did Mark say about SORA?"

Dad shakes his head. "I didn't ask."

"Come on, Mike—"

Dad cuts her off. "For now we're just talking about the arraignment. Mark says we should take this one step at a time."

Mom picks up her phone. "I'm calling him back about SORA. That's the one thing I told you to ask. SORA could negatively impact Byron for his entire life."

I take a step backward into the shadows, slide my phone out of my pocket, and quickly type in SORA. After a few clicks, I realize that SORA is the Sex Offender Registry Act.

"Phyllis," Dad says, his voice rising, "we're going to need Mark on our side. We don't want to alienate him now."

"I told you we should have sued Columbia after they suspended him," Mom says. "I said they were making an example out of Byron. You disregarded that, and now it looks like we conceded."

"Don't start second-guessing our decision," Dad says. "We always knew there was the possibility she could press criminal charges. We didn't want to make it worse by suing Columbia. Since Byron doesn't remember much about that night, we didn't have a case. It was her word against his."

"Don't tell me not to second-guess our decision. This is my son! Don't you care that he might end up in jail? Or have to register as a sex offender?"

"*Our* son," Dad says.

"Well, I don't feel like you're protecting him," Mom snaps.

"And I don't feel like you're being rational," Dad shoots back.

I'm frozen in the entryway, my eyes pinging between the two of them. They never fight in front of me, and I rarely hear them argue in private either. I slowly back down the hall, but then knock into a side table, causing them to whip their heads in my direction.

"Come on, Virginia!" Mom shouts. "It's not like we have time to spare."

"Why do I have an appointment with Talia?" I ask, reluctantly sitting down with them. I fork a few nectarine slices into my bowl alongside a dribble of Greek yogurt. Mom and Dad are obsessed with Greek yogurt, but I find it thick and disgustingly sour.

Talia is Mom's temperamental hairstylist. I usually go to Supercuts, but for my birthday Mom gave me a gift certificate for a cut and deep condition with Talia. That was the month that my hair was pink. Talia spent the entire time lecturing me for coloring my hair and said I was stripping it of its natural luster. There is no way I can deal with her today.

Mom shakes her head. "Do you have any idea how busy Talia is? She's coming in early to take care of you. I texted her this morning. Mark says we need to present the image of a wholesome family at the arraignment." Mom picks up a slice of nectarine and sets it down again.

"What wholesome thing has to happen to my hair?" I ask.

Mom presses her lips together and, in that pause, I know. She's making me get rid of my purple and green. Which is not happening.

"No," I say.

"You're going back to blond," Mom says. "Your natural color. If the judge looks at our family, we don't want him to think we let you guys run wild."

I push my bowl away. "What about your 'Purple Hair and Piercings' book proposal? It was all about how you like my hair. Also, I don't see how having a daughter with purple-and-green hair is in the same category as having a son who's been arrested for rape."

Mom looks away like she's been slapped. Dad clears his throat.

"If it's going to be a fight," he says to Mom, "let it go. Virginia's hair color is not going to make or break this."

"You're undermining me," Mom hisses to him. To me she says, "I can't believe you're challenging me at a time like this."

I wipe at my eyes. "Mom—"

"That's enough," she says sharply.

I stare into my lap, trying to think of a comeback that will show how irrational she is being.

"Phyllis," Dad says. "You need to conserve your energy for what's ahead. A world war over hair color won't help this morning."

This may be the first time in my sixteen and a quarter years that Dad has had my back.

Mom grabs her phone. "Fine. I'll text Talia and cancel. Don't you care that your brother could go to jail?"

A meteor-sized lump has lodged in my throat.

Mom pushes back her chair and storms into her office.

I cry quietly into my hands. Dad pretends not to notice.

When he leaves the table, I carry my bowl to the sink, filling it with water. Tiny blobs of Greek yogurt float to the surface. In my shorts pocket, my phone buzzes.

Alyssa has texted again: I came to Brooklyn to cheer on Froggy and Hudson. Total Minecraft geekdom. Froggy says, "Hi, babe." How's CT?

In town this weekend after all, I write back. I ignore the Froggy/babe part and head into the shower.

A few minutes later, I'm wrapped in a towel and walking to my bedroom when I nearly collide with Dad. He's coming out of Mom's office.

"Thanks for backing me up about my hair," I say quickly. I feel instantly awkward in a towel in front of Dad.

"You've really upset your mom."

"It's not like I did anything," I say, wishing I had a bigger towel or a bathrobe or, better yet, a floor-to-ceiling parka. "Byron is the one who—"

"Virginia," Dad says, and his voice is low and cold, "this is not all about you."

Then he brushes by me and closes his door.

6 6 6 6

At 1 p.m., Dad calls for a car. As we ride down in the elevator, I'm humming the Funeral March in my head because that's what this feels like, somber and depressing.

Random fact: The Funeral March was written by Chopin.

I know this because Alyssa and I are on the planning committee for Mr. Mooney's tribute. He was our prehistoric math teacher. He always used to sing to us in class. Last winter he had a heart attack and died over winter break. At Brewster Field Day on Thursday afternoon, which is also the last day of school, we're having a ceremony in Central Park in Mr. Mooney's honor and releasing balloons and playing his favorite songs. Our playlist skews more to old-timey folk than Chopin funeral sonatas, though.

"The driver's name is Rosalie," Dad says, looking up from his phone. "She's out front."

"What kind of woman drives a taxi?" Mom asks.

Dad shrugs. "Strange career choice."

I want to say that the kind of woman who drives a taxi is similar to the kind of woman who is a Tree Man, and Dad had no problem with that.

As we walk wordlessly through the lobby, Alberto leans out from behind the doorman desk.

"Looking good, Shreves family!" he says, reaching out to high-five me. "Where are you headed all dressed up like that?"

I stumble in Mom's one-size-too-small heels that she's forcing me to wear and twist my right ankle.

Mom says coolly to Alberto, "Family obligation."

I blow my bangs out of my face, high-five Alberto, and limp to the sidewalk.

A black SUV is waiting at the curb. Dad climbs into the first row of seats. He gestures for me to squeeze through the four-inch space to the way back. If I were a prepubescent gymnast, this would be a cinch. But I'm not. Not to mention that my linen skirt is too stiff for acrobatics. Not to mention that the blazer is pinching my armpits and the blouse is popping at my boobs, revealing a peep show between button two and button three.

"Let's go, Virginia." Mom has produced a massive umbrella, and she's standing behind me, sheltering her perfectly styled hair from the drizzle. "I'm not getting any drier."

I angle sideways and heave myself into the back. Nothing rips, but my ankle is throbbing from when I tripped in the lobby. Mom climbs into the row in front of me, buckles up, and the driver steers us to the West Side Highway.

As we're cruising downtown, I lean forward in my seat. "Is it true that Byron could go to jail today?"

"Consider where you are right now," Mom says quietly. "Is that really appropriate?"

Location: In a car going to see my brother get charged with a crime.

Mom gestures her chin toward the driver.

Oh, my bad. There's Rosalie the Taxi Driver who doesn't even know who Byron is and doesn't give a damn if our family is perfect or not.

Dad turns in his seat. "We're prepared to make bail. It should be fine. Now that's enough."

I swallow hard. No one says anything for twenty blocks. As we pass Chelsea Piers I think about how Shannon and I once came here to play laser tag.

"Shannon isn't coming home until August now," I tell my parents. "That means it'll just be me working at Ciel Media.

I'm pretty bummed about that. Not about Ciel, but that I have to wait two extra months to see Shannon."

"Uh-huh," Dad says but doesn't look up from his phone.

Mom doesn't say anything.

After a minute, she gets on her phone and, in a chirpy voice, cancels her private golf lesson for tomorrow. When she hangs up, I make one more attempt at conversation.

"The reason Shannon isn't coming home," I say, "is because she and her parents are hiking the PCT. Isn't that crazy?"

No response.

"That's the Pacific Crest Trail," I add.

Still nothing. I stare out the rain-splattered window for the rest of the drive downtown.

As we're nearing the city court buildings, Mom rotates to the back. "Mark will meet us outside and fill us in on the protocol," she says to me. "What I need you to keep in mind is no drama. Only speak when spoken to. Basically, be invisible."

The car comes to a stop at a massive concrete building. *Criminal Court* is etched into the stone on the front.

I suddenly can't breathe. My brother is inside that building.

"Do you understand?" Mom presses at her hip, unbuckling her seat belt.

*No drama. Only speak when spoken to. Be invisible.*

I nod. That should be easy because it's basically the story of my life. Or my life story if Mom wrote it.

# 8

No one seems to notice my purple-and-green hair as we go through the security clearance and enter the lobby of the criminal courthouse. In fact, no one seems to notice us at all. People are gathered in small groups, frowning and whispering into their phones. There's an ATM machine with a hand-scribbled sign taped to it that says *out of order* and industrial-sized fans blowing stale air around. Alyssa and I have walked past this court building a bunch of times on our way to Chinatown, but I never knew what it actually was until today.

"There's Mark Levy," Mom says, collapsing her umbrella and walking quickly toward a short guy wearing a pinstripe suit. He smiles stiffly, revealing a horselike gap between his front teeth, and shakes my parents' hands. As I nod at the lawyer—*only speak when spoken to, only speak when spoken to*—I realize he's *really* short, like five-one. Mom is five-three, and she's taller than him.

"I'll start with the bad news," Mark says. He rises onto his toes like he's trying to make himself appear taller. He's also pudgy, built like a cardboard box. "We have Judge Harrison today. She's tough on sex crimes and tends to set a high bail." When he says that, Mom jabs my arm. I'm not sure what she's trying to tell me so I shift my weight from one foot to the other. Bad idea because my right ankle is still hurting a lot.

Mark continues. "But Judge Harrison can also be fair if she's having a good day, and I've never known her *not* to set bail for a sex crime unless there are extenuating circumstances involved. I've talked to Byron and explained all this. He hasn't been brought out yet, but it's looking like they'll call his case within the hour."

Mom jabs me again. I look at her like *what?* but before she can say anything Dad clears his throat.

"How's he doing?" he asks.

"As can be expected—" Mark starts.

Just then, Mom holds up a finger and leans close to me, frowning hard. Her breath smells like cinnamon Altoids, which she chain-chews when she's stressed.

"I'm trying to tell you to go over there." She points to a bench on the other side of the lobby. "Wait until we call you."

I limp across the lobby in Mom's shoes. A lot of girls at school have been prancing around in heels since they were toddlers, but not me. For one, I look stupid in heels, like I'm faking the part of a girlie girl. And for two, I hate the double standard that men are allowed to walk around like regular humans in regular shoes while women are expected to wince and wobble on their tippy toes.

I sit on the bench and hug my arms around my middle. There's a tired-looking woman on the other end of the bench, her lips pressed tight, mascara stains under her eyes. She's wearing denim shorts, a T-shirt, and sneakers. Upon glancing around, I realize that everyone but us has on whatever they happen to be wearing on this Saturday morning. It's mostly shorts, tank tops, jeans, and sweatpants. I'm guessing most people don't have expensive lawyers to instruct them to present the image of a wholesome, linen-garbed family. I guess that's Mark Levy's goal, to set Byron apart from the real criminals. Then again, if Byron sexually assaulted Annie Mills, doesn't that make him a real criminal?

Stop! I shouldn't be thinking that. I should be hoping that Judge Harrison is having an awesome and spectacular day and goes easy on my brother.

"Okay," Dad says, beckoning to me. "Let's go."

I join them at the door leading to the courtroom. There's a steel-gray sign saying *No photography*. Damn. I was planning to get some family shots for our holiday card. Kidding.

"Where's Byron?" I ask.

Mom shoots me a glance. Oh yeah. Seen but not heard.

"He's in a cell behind the courtroom with the others who've been arrested. He's been held there since last night." Mark pauses at the door. "Now put your phones away and don't take them out. Judge Harrison hates when phones ring in here."

81

I silenced my phone in the car, but I check again just to be sure.

"People call it the Pen," Mark adds, "and that's putting it nicely."

Mom sucks in her breath. I shudder in my too-tight blazer and follow her into the courtroom.

⑤ ⑤ ⑥ ⑥

An hour later, we're still waiting. We're sitting in the third row—Dad, Mom, and me. Mark Levy is in front of us and on the aisle. Every now and then he walks up and confers with a police officer or a clerk. Then he returns to his row where he whispers something to Dad, who whispers something to Mom, who doesn't whisper anything to me.

The lack of information has resulted in me cobbling together random observations.

### RANDOM OBSERVATION #1:

I thought Judge Harrison would be old and severe, like a mean teacher who yells at you for being loud in the hall. But she's got long auburn hair and full pink cheeks. She looks like the library assistant at Brewster.

### RANDOM OBSERVATION #2:

Arraignment court is a traffic jam of police officers and people handing paper to each other. Every so often they bring a person from the Pen, usually a stony-faced guy who is subjected to a retina scan. Then that stony-faced guy has to wait on a bench until he's called up in front of the judge, who determines whether he will get out on bail or be locked up again.

**RANDOM OBSERVATION #3:**
It sucks, okay? Some of the people are even handcuffed.

All of a sudden, the door from the Pen opens, and, holy crap, it's my brother. As a guard guides him to the retina scan, Byron looks as stony-faced as everyone else. He's not handcuffed, but his arms are clasped behind his back. He's wearing the same shorts and gray T-shirt he had on yesterday, and his brown hair is matted and greasy.

After the scan, a police officer guides my brother to the bench, pushing him down with a shove.

Mom gasps. Dad's face has gone pale. Mark Levy stands up quickly and walks to the front to confer with a clerk. In that second, Byron makes eye contact with Dad. He raises his eyebrows as if to say *help*. I can tell he's two seconds from crying. Which makes me want to cry, seeing my successful, smart, sometimes asshole brother barely holding it together.

"Excuse me," I whisper to the woman to my left.

I squeeze past her on my way to the aisle. I don't look back at Mom or Dad. I'm getting out of here.

☙ ☙ ☙ ☙

The rain has stopped, but the steps of the courthouse are still wet. I lean against a metal railing and cry for my brother and for every stony-faced person getting arraigned in there.

Once I'm done crying, I breathe in the steamy, slightly putrid air. There's a loud drilling sound, some nearby street getting jackhammered. People are hurrying past, shaking out umbrellas and pushing babies in strollers like it's any other day, like they have no idea people's fates are being decided one cement wall away.

I wipe my nose with my blazer sleeve. I'm combusting with sweat, and the stiff sleeves are binding my arms to my sides. There's a trash can at the bottom of the stairs. I peel off the blazer and chuck it in

Good-bye, Horrible Thing.

I cross the street and wander into a park where old Chinese women are dancing to music from a battered boom box. Across the park I can see the yellow awning for Tasty Dumpling. Alyssa's grandmother usually makes her dumplings from scratch, but when she doesn't have time she buys them by the frozen bagful here. Not only are they delicious, they are also cheap, which is good because I only have five or six dollars in my wallet.

I curl my toes in Mom's too-small heels and limp toward Tasty Dumpling.

Ten minutes later, I'm consuming a plate of fried pork dumplings, dousing them with soy sauce. My phone is on the table next to me, and I'm texting with Shannon, filling her in on the Byron stuff. I'm also texting a little with Alyssa. Apparently she hung out with Froggy and Hudson at the Brooklyn

Public Library all day, and the three of them are walking to the subway now.

Hey you, Froggy writes. Are you feeling better?

I have no idea what he's talking about. It's not like I told him about what's happening with Byron.

Better? I ask.

Your sore throat, he writes.

Oh, right. That.

Yeah, I say. All better.

Froggy texts me a row of thumbs-ups and then adds, I need to go home and sleep, but want to hang out tomorrow?

Sure, I say. Maybe it'll be good to see Froggy, to do something normal to get my mind off Byron.

Central Park at noon? Froggy asks. The regular spot?

The regular spot is Belvedere Castle, where we first kissed in public. Froggy lives on the East Side and I'm on the West Side, so it's our midway point. Back when we were madly in like, meeting at the castle was cheesy in a cute way. Maybe it still could be.

Great, I write to him. Regular spot at noon.

ⓖ ⓖ ⓖ ⓖ

On the walk back to the courthouse, I watch the old Chinese dancers. The women have paired off, and they're ballroom dancing, spinning and stepping and clutching their partners' outstretched hands. The late-afternoon sun has come out, and I notice that my blazer has already been plucked from the trash. Right at this moment, someone could be excited about their

85

new beige blazer, oblivious as to why I was forced to wear it today.

I turn the corner onto Centre Street and spot Mom, Dad, Byron, and Mark Levy in front of the courthouse. Mom is nodding, and Dad's arm is touching Byron's back.

So Byron is free. The judge must have set bail, and my parents must have paid it.

Mom looks over at me. She doesn't comment on my courtroom escape or my missing blazer. I guess Mom's tendency to sweep things under the rug can work to my advantage sometimes.

An SUV pulls up to the curb. Mark waves good-bye and walks away. Dad opens the door and climbs in. Byron gets in after him. They both go into the way back. Mom slides in next. I walk over, step in after her, and the car takes off.

"I forgot my umbrella," Mom says after a minute.

"Want to go back?" Dad asks.

"Hell, no."

No one says anything else on the drive home. Byron's eyes are closed, and he reeks like sweat and pee and maybe even vomit. I press my fingers over my nose and focus on breathing through my mouth.

"Want an Altoids?" Mom says as the car pulls into our neighborhood. She offers the red-and-white tin over the back of the seat.

"Thanks," Dad says, pinching up a few.

I take an Altoids, too. Byron, who is staring flatly out the window, shakes his head.

"I hadn't remembered that Mark was so short," Mom says to Dad. "And doesn't it look like he's gained weight?"

Dad nods. "He should watch it or he's headed for a triple bypass."

"He was already doughy when we met him last fall," Mom says.

Dad laughs for the first time all day. "That's putting it nicely."

I feel like I've been punched in the gut. I know I come from a family of fat-shamers, but I would have thought at a time like this, when my brother could wind up in jail and Mark Levy is the guy who could save him, they would put their judgments on hold.

"He's good, though, right?" Byron asks, suddenly tuned in.

*Though.* As if body type has anything to do with ability.

"Of course," Dad says. "He's the best."

As the car pulls up in front of our building, Mom adds, "Anyway, most of this is over the phone. No one will even see him."

I push the door open, jump onto the curb, and storm into our lobby.

# 9

As soon as we walk into the apartment, Byron disappears into the bathroom and the shower starts up. Dad pours himself a glass of red wine and one for Mom, too. He downs the entire glass like it's water and fills another. Mom orders Thai food, which seems like a weird choice, as if they're re-creating last night just without the arrest. When Dad is on his third glass of wine and Mom is on her second, I decide that things are bad, maybe even worse than I thought.

I'm on my bed working on a draft of my Humanities essay. It's not due until Thursday, but it counts for 40 percent of our grade. I've told myself that if I can finish three pages of the essay I'll allot myself thirty minutes of *Fates and Furies*. Things are falling apart with Lotto. It's hard to see. But fictional hard is better than real-life hard. As I'm struggling to come up with a thesis sentence, I can hear Dad on the phone in his room.

When he drinks his voice gets louder than usual. I can hear him talking with his financial advisor, and I can even hear him saying the number they paid to make Byron's bail. It's a crazy high number, the cost of a year of college.

I gnaw at my thumbnail until it bleeds, push aside my laptop, and go to the bathroom for a Band-Aid. I haven't chewed my nails much since I was in sixth grade and Byron joked that chubby girls chew their nails because they have oral fixations.

On my way back from the bathroom, I can see Mom sitting at her desk. Mom uses my sister's old room as her office. On her laptop, there's an image of the Eiffel Tower. Mom's glass of wine, now empty, is positioned next to her.

"Why are you looking up Paris?" I ask.

Mom quickly closes that screen. Now I just see her wallpaper, which is a photo of the five of us, back when I was ten and we were on a family vacation in Nantucket. Mom had me on a gluten-free diet that summer, and I remember being frustrated that I couldn't eat lobster rolls with everyone else. That was the summer before Anaïs left for Brown, before Byron started high school. On Mom's desk, I notice a copy of her book proposal. The cover page says "Purple Hair and Piercings: Embracing Your Teen's Rebellions" by Dr. Phyllis Shreves. I touch my eyebrow ring. Since I switched rings a few days ago, it's feeling a little sore. On the cover of the proposal, Mom's agent has inserted a picture of a skinny teenage girl with purple hair and an eyebrow ring.

Mom sighs heavily. "I may as well tell you because you'll find out soon enough. Mark says that Byron can't go to Paris.

I was just contacting the study-abroad program to ask about a refund."

"Why can't he go to Paris?"

"It's complicated," she says quickly. That's when I notice that her new peach manicure is chipped off her thumbs. Mom never picks at her nail polish. She routinely swats my fingers when I scratch at mine.

"Did they take his passport away?" I ask, hugging my hands over my stomach. When I googled details about arrests earlier, it said that you can get your passport taken away.

"No." Mom pauses. "But Mark says that Byron needs to stick to intrastate travel while we figure this out. If he tries to leave the country it could appear like he's a flight risk, like he might not come back."

My knees feel watery. I clutch the door frame to support myself.

"What's going to happen to Byron?" I ask. "Like from here on out?"

Mom reaches for her wineglass even though there's nothing left. I know from what I've overheard so far that if the prosecuting lawyer can prove beyond a reasonable doubt that Byron is guilty, he could get jail time. He could get that sex offender registry that Mom was worried about. Those are some worst-case scenarios. But it also sounds like the lawyers could agree on a deal, like for Byron to plead guilty to a reduced charge, and then he wouldn't have to go to jail.

"There's no set outcome," Mom says after a moment. Then she closes her laptop, strides over to Anaïs's old bed, and starts stripping the sheets. She's yanking them hard with her fists and chucking them onto the floor.

Later, when the Thai food arrives, Dad answers the front door. Mom sets out plates and napkins and I carry in the seltzer glasses, but Byron doesn't come to the table. As Dad knocks on his door, Mom and I go quiet.

"I'm not hungry," Byron says through the closed door.

"At least come sit with us," Dad says. "We ordered your favorite. Shrimp Pad Thai and spring rolls."

No response. Dad stands there for a moment, his arms crossed over his chest, then sighs and comes to the table.

"He hasn't eaten all day," Dad says to Mom. "Mark says he brought him a nut bar this morning and he refused that, too."

Mom scratches a fleck of polish off her fingernail. I watch it flutter onto the floor.

Enter: Another glass of wine per parent.

They are getting soused. Dad is repeating a golf story that he told two days ago, and Mom's eyelids are drooping. They don't notice I'm sneaking miniservings of Pad Thai and texting with Shannon in my lap. She's sending me the address of various stops along the PCT where I can mail her packages, places called Tuolumne Meadows and Red Moose Inn.

Near the end of the meal, Mom leans toward me and says, "We've decided not to tell your sister about the arrest." She folds her napkin once, then twice, and runs her finger back and forth along the crease. "Just in case Anaïs calls, please don't say anything."

"But she already knows about Byron," I say. "About what he did."

Mom shakes her head. "We don't want to upset her. She'll find out when she gets home in two weeks. Let her have fun in London."

"Okay," I say. "Sure."

"That's my girl," Mom says, draining her glass of wine.

ⓖ ⓖ ⓖ ⓖ

I don't wake up until ten. I pull on a bra, a pink camisole, and loose cutoff overalls. I check out a blog with braid and pony-tail ideas and then fix my hair into pigtails. When I come out to the kitchen, I can see that my parents have stepped up their efforts to get Byron to eat. Instead of going to Whole Fitness aka Whole Fakeness like they usually do, they took a run in Riverside Park so they could veer over to Absolute and get Byron his favorite poppy seed bagels. Then they jogged down to Zabar's to buy him lox and scallion cream cheese and rasp-berry Danishes.

Absolute Bagels. That blond-haired artist boy who likes *A Wrinkle in Time* and girls who say "homage." Sigh.

"I'm not hungry," Byron says. He's hunched over the coun-ter sipping black coffee. "Besides, my head is killing."

"You have a headache because your body needs food." Mom reaches over to touch his hair, but he bristles. "At least have a few bites."

"Byron, you need to keep your energy up," Dad says.

"For what?" Byron sets down his coffee cup hard. "For

Paris? For Columbia next semester? For rugby team and law internships? Forget all that. My life is over."

And then—seriously, for real, holy crap—Byron starts to cry. He slumps his head down, and he's gasping and hiccuping. I haven't seen my brother cry in a decade. And then it was probably because Mom snatched his game player away so he'd finish his homework.

My parents swarm in and hug him and pat his back.

I'm leaning against the fridge, trying to stay as motionless as possible. I am not meant to be witnessing this. If they remember I'm here I will be exiled to the far reaches of the apartment.

"Honey," Mom says as Byron's crying winds down to a sputter. "We will figure this out. Remember what Dad said? Mark Levy is a fantastic defense lawyer, the best in the city. He's going to be in constant conversation with the district attorney, and they'll work out a plea bargain or maybe even throw it out."

"But we accepted my punishment at Columbia fall semester," Byron says. "The dean of students suspended me, and we didn't challenge it. Mark says that's going to work against me. It's going to make it look like we admitted guilt."

Even though I should be feeling sorry for Byron, I'm annoyed at how he's saying "we." It's not like my *parents* did anything wrong. Mom looks at Dad like *help me out here*, but he's crossing his arms over his chest, his cheeks flushed with anger. I wonder if Dad's going to tell Byron that this isn't a "we" situation. Yes, we are here for you, and, yes, we will do our best to make sure you don't go to jail, but you are the one who got drunk and forced a girl to have sex. You. Not us.

"And what about SORA?" Byron says. "Even if I avoid jail time, what if I have to register as a sex offender? Do you realize that, if that happens, I won't be able to go near schools or children? Columbia will expel me if I'm found guilty. And forget law school. You think I'll ever be accepted to a law school, even a shitty one, after this?"

Byron starts crying again. As Mom rests her hand on his shoulder, she says, "We will figure this out."

"Mom!" my brother says, lurching away. "Do you even understand what last semester was like for me? Do you know that people wrote my name in Sharpie on bathroom stalls all over campus next to the word 'rapist'! Don't you get it? You can't gloss this over like you do everything else in your life."

Mom drops her hand to her side and her mouth falls open.

"He's right, Phyllis," Dad says. "It is awful, and let's not pretend it isn't."

Mom stares wordlessly at Dad. Byron isn't saying anything either. I'm still pressed against the fridge, barely blinking and only taking oxygen when absolutely necessary.

"You know what makes me angry?" Dad says. "I know what Byron did was wrong, but it was a twenty-minute mistake. A drunken mistake that could quite possibly ruin his life."

A twenty-minute drunken *mistake*???!!!!!!

Okay, that's not cool.

Hearing Dad put it that way, as a mistake, is CRAZY. It

94

wasn't a mistake. It was a horrible, mean, entitled choice, and Dad shouldn't frame it as some kind of accident. I clench my hands into fists. I'm starting to feel anger building up in my ears and shooting down my arms.

"What I don't understand is this," Dad continues. "Byron was already punished last semester. Isn't that enough? Why did that girl have to take it to the police?"

Before I can stop myself, I'm saying, "Did any of you think she went to the police because what Byron did was wrong? And her name is Annie Mills. Not 'that girl.'"

Dead silence.

"Virginia Shreves," Mom finally says, "whose side are you on?"

"I'm not talking sides," I say. "I'm just saying—"

"Don't say," Dad says, raising his voice. "Go to your room. Now."

I haven't been sent to my room since I was little. I reach over, grab a raspberry Danish, and storm down the hall. I don't even bother closing my door. I hold the pastry between my front teeth while I toss things into my backpack—notebooks, novel, phone, money, gum. Then I wriggle my feet into my Converse and hurry out the front door.

I'm eating the raspberry Danish and riding the elevator down when it stops on nine. Mrs. Myers shuffles on. She takes one look at my overall cutoffs, leans into her cane, and says, "What kind of outfit is that? It looks like you're wearing a tent that's—"

"Please don't comment on what I'm wearing," I say sharply.

"Don't interrupt me, young lady." Mrs. Myers's face tightens into a scowl. "When I was your—"

The elevator arrives at the lobby. I step through the doors and hurry out onto the street.

# 10

I know exactly where I'm going even though I'm aware that I would get in massive trouble if anyone found out. But they're mad at me already, so what have I got to lose? I put on my music and walk up Broadway, past all the Starbucks and dollar stores and pizza shops rolling up their metal gates. When I approach 105th Street, I can see down the sidewalk to the gym where I take kickboxing. I wonder if Tisha is there. I consider stopping by to tell her how it's going to ruin the class if Brie is in it. But what's Tisha going to say, other than to call me a spineless wimp? She teaches kickboxing to earn money, so it's not like she's going to turn away a new client just because I'm scared of her.

I cross over to Amsterdam and walk until I get to Saint John the Divine. It's crazy to think that meeting that guy and sitting in the garden with him only happened three days ago. So much has gone down since then, I barely even remember what it felt like to be that version of me, laughing and chatting and not feeling like my world is collapsing.

But I'm not here for reminiscing about buttered bagels on benches with boys.

I'm here because across the street from the cathedral is the Hungarian Pastry Shop.

Yep.

The Hungarian Pastry Shop is where Annie Mills works, or at least where she was working when I came in to buy an éclair back in March. As soon as I saw her, I reversed out the door and sprinted all the way to the subway.

Maybe she's not even here now. Columbia is out, and most of the students have gone home. Then again, she's from western Canada, so there's a possibility she's staying in New York City for the summer.

I'm standing under the red-striped awning of the Hungarian Pastry Shop, twisting my pigtails around my fingers and trying to figure out whether or not to do this completely stupid thing for which I have no plan. There are tables outside the café with droplets of water splattered across the tabletops and metal chairs. It rained hard last night. I smudge a few raindrops with my finger, sliding the water until it forms a bigger puddle.

Should I? Shouldn't I?

I just want to ask Annie why she went to the police. That's all. When I talked to her in December she said she was doing okay.

Okay. That's my plan. Ask why. Then leave quickly.

I push open the door and step into the café. Heaps of cookies are jammed into display cases, and there's a messy arrangement of chairs and wobbly tables and random paintings on the walls. I glance around the room at the grad students on laptops, parents sipping lattes, and toddlers picking at pastries. The guy behind the counter has long dreadlocks, and he's tapping on his phone.

No waiters in sight, Annie or otherwise.

I weave through the café, finally settling onto a red-painted bench at the back. It's far enough from the crowd that it will give me a good vantage point. I set my backpack onto the bench next to me and pull out *Fates and Furies*. I doubt I'll be able to focus on Lotto and Mathilde, but I can pretend to read so I don't look like a stalker.

"Leela? I was hoping to see you again even though you said it was statistically impossible. Cute ponytails. You look like Pippi Longstocking if her hair were purple and green."

I look up fast. Even though this is the worst possible time for something as wonderful as this, my face breaks into a smile. Because right down the bench from me is the boy from the bagel store, the boy who wasn't an ax murderer, the boy who knew the importance of butter-to-dough ratios. There's a mug on his table and a phone, a sketch pad, and a scattering of crayons.

"Do you actually draw in that," I ask him, "or just carry it around like you did with the skateboard?"

"Real funny, Leela," he says, tucking his hair behind his ears. "I also carry around a hammer to look like I build houses."

"But still no ax?"

He cracks up. "This is actually awesome. I needed to see you again because I started a sketch from the other day but I couldn't remember the color of your eyes, so I left them blank. Yes, *them*. I gave you two eyes."

He flips a few pages back in his sketch pad and then rotates it so I can see.

Color me stunned.

Inside this beautiful boy's sketch pad, drawn by this beautiful boy, is *me*. I'm wearing the denim shorts I had on last Thursday and the checkered tank top and I've got my backpack over my shoulders and one fist pumped in the air. I can't be positive, but it looks like I'm clutching a bagel. My hair is swept into a high purple ponytail, and I'm grinning but my eyes are blank.

"Blue," I say, pointing to my eyes. "And what about my bangs? Don't you have a green crayon?"

"Leela has all purple hair, so I deleted your green bangs. Artistic license. And they're not crayons. They're oil pastels. Sennelier."

"Sennelier?" I ask. That sounds suspiciously French.

"He's the guy who created pastels for Picasso. And if they're good enough for Picasso . . ."

"Snob," I say, grinning.

He leans into me, so close I could touch his cheek. "Gray-blue, Leela. Very pretty eyes. I'll have to mix a few shades for that. And I hadn't realized you have an eyebrow ring."

I watch him selecting his pastels and testing out streaks on another page of the sketch pad.

"What's with the 'Leela'?" I ask.

His face is fixed on the drawing. "She's a superhero," he says after a moment. "Turanga Leela. From *Futurama*. An animated series? The guy who made *The Simpsons* made that for a while. She's a kickass Cyclops who's strong and awesome but gets insecure because of her one eye." He adds a thin swirl of gray to my right eye, then my left. "She's the main character's love interest. His name is Fry. Yes, I'm a dork."

A purple-haired superhero? I had no idea.

"But you gave me two eyes," I say, gesturing to his drawing.

He looks up for a second. "You're too pretty to have one."

That word again. *Pretty.*

"Can I take a picture of it?" I ask. Seriously, I want proof that on this day in my life a beautiful boy called me pretty and wanted to draw me.

He shakes his head. "Not yet. I didn't get your chin right." He smudges at the peachy-pink line of my chin. "If you put your number in my phone, I'll text it to you when I'm done."

He unlocks his phone and hands it to me, then gets back to work. It's a tarnished phone with a picture of a brown-and-white dog on the home page. Of course he has a dog. I bet it's a rescue dog. I bet they go hiking together and her name is Bailey or Mya.

"I know we're not doing details, but whatever. I'm Virginia." I add my number to his contacts. I can't believe he's asking for my number. "Not Leela."

"Virginia," he says. "Like the state."

"And Woolf." I set his phone back on his table. Mom named me after the author Virginia Woolf. My sister is named after Anaïs Nin, and my brother is named after Lord Byron. Mom wasn't fooling around with her aspirations for her offspring. I try not to take it personally that Anaïs Nin was a sex goddess and Virginia Woolf killed herself by filling her pockets with stones and walking into a river.

"She wrote *A Room of One's Own*," he says.

"You know that?" I ask. Most people, especially most guys, haven't heard of Virginia Woolf's book of feminist essays.

"I have a sister," he says, rolling his eyes. "I've also heard of Lena Dunham and *Are You There God? It's Me, Margaret*." He glances at the waitress approaching his table and says, "Speaking of my sister."

"Hey, Sebastian!" she says. "Sorry it took me so long. A big catering order just got picked up."

Oh no. *Oh no no no no no.*

The waitress is Annie Mills. She's smiling as she sets down a plate of cookies on his table. Then she notices me sitting on the bench and her face goes pale.

# 11

After a few nauseating seconds, Annie turns to him—to *Sebastian*—and hoarsely asks, "Do you two know each other?"

Sebastian, who hasn't clued into the tsunami of tension crashing in, grins and says, "Oh, sure. We go way back, Virginia and I."

I lift my backpack onto my lap and hug it tight.

Annie is looking between Sebastian and me like she's trying to puzzle it together. She seems different from the other time I met her, back in December, or even when I spotted her in March. She's got shadows under her eyes and her cheeks are splotchy with acne and her hair is cut short, the front portion wrapped in a charcoal headband.

"What's going on?" Sebastian asks, reaching for a rainbow-striped cookie. He downs it in one bite. "You're being kind of . . ." He shrugs his shoulders as if to say *Fill me in*.

Annie leans close to his ear. I don't have to be a mind reader to know that she's telling him who my brother is. Sure enough, as soon as she pulls back, he gapes at me and then shakes his head at his sister.

"No way." Sebastian closes his sketch pad and sets it on the table. I wonder if he's going to crumple the portrait of me or shred it into a million pieces. I shove my book in my backpack.

"Listen," Annie says. "You shouldn't be here."

My throat is tightening, and my phone starts going off in my pocket. I reach in and silence the ringer. "I just wanted to come and ask you about—"

Annie crosses her arms over her chest. "So you *knew* I'd be here?"

"No, that's not it. I knew . . . because I once saw you . . . I didn't know that he . . ." I glance toward Sebastian. *Sebastian*. Even his name. And his accent. Now I realize it's a Canadian accent. I learned last fall that Annie is from Saskatchewan, which is a province out west, above Montana.

"Stop," she says. Her eyes are also blue-green, but they're stormy, not tranquil like sea glass.

"Annie," Sebastian says. "I don't think you're being fair."

I glance gratefully at him. My phone is ringing in my pocket again. My parents are probably furious.

"Listen, I don't want to talk about this here." Annie looks around the café. There's a waiter in the front taking an order, but other than that it's pretty quiet. "You know what? Let's go outside for a second."

Annie grabs her purse from behind the counter, says some-thing to the guy working, and then pushes through the door. I don't even look at Sebastian as I strap on my backpack and hurry after her. I wish I could say good-bye, to explain that I never would have talked to him if I knew he was Annie Mills's brother. But I can't look at him because I don't want to see his expression, to see that he's disgusted by me and my family and what my brother did and even the fact that I came here today.

Even so, I hate walking through the café and knowing I'll never see him again.

⑥ ⑥ ⑥ ⑥

"What on earth are you doing here?" Annie says once we're on the sidewalk. Her face is tight and she looks mad. "You realize this is completely inappropriate. And you *knew* I worked here?"

She's close enough to me that I can smell her breath. It's sour, like coffee, and her bottom lip is cracked.

"I saw you working here once . . . ," I start to say, but my voice catches in my throat. My legs are jelly. And it doesn't help that my phone is vibrating with calls and texts. "I just wanted to—"

"No, don't say anything, actually. I need a second to think. I shouldn't even be talking to you. The DA would . . . this is so messed up."

I'm close to tears, but I can't cry, because I have to be strong. Annie was the one who inspired me to be strong back when I visited her dorm room last winter. Her long brown hair—now cut short—hung down her back, and she made me a mug of herbal tea. As the snow flurried outside the window, she said that she wasn't going to let Byron turn her into a victim. Even though he physically overpowered her, she wouldn't give him mental power over her. This Annie now seems so different, almost like another person entirely.

Annie closes her eyes for a long second. "Okay," she says, opening them again. "You can talk. I'm sorry . . . this is all just really hard."

I swallow back tears and quickly say, "I wanted to ask why you went to the police. I thought you were letting Columbia take care of the punishment. Did you know that Byron got arrested on Friday? He's out on bail, but this is only the beginning. I'm not saying he should be let off the hook, but I'm confused because I thought you were moving on with your life."

I suck in a shallow breath. Not the most eloquent of speeches. I didn't go into the stuff about how my brother could get kicked out of Columbia or have to register as a sex offender. But I said most of what I wanted to say and I avoided crying.

Annie shakes her head. The freckles on her nose are washed out, graying like dishwater. "I'm not sure I understand. Are you trying to say I shouldn't have gone to the police?"

"I just thought you said you were okay," I mumble, looking down at my feet. I notice my ankle is swollen from where I tripped in our lobby yesterday. The weird thing is, I'm not even feeling the pain, like my head is detached from the rest of my body. "Remember how you said you're not a victim and you're not going to let him make you into one?"

Annie reaches into her purse and pulls out a pack of

cigarettes, smacking it against her palm. I watch her, totally shocked. Sure, people at school smoke cigarettes, mostly the popular kids, and it's mostly for show. But Annie Mills made me herbal tea and had a yoga mat in her room! She didn't seem like the smoking type.

Annie lights the cigarette and takes a long draw. "It's horrible, I know. This is just sort of where I am right now. Not a great place."

I'm beginning to feel like it was a mistake to come here. I hope it hasn't made her feel even worse.

"I told everyone I was okay last fall," Annie finally says, "but I was actually a mess. Did you know that Byron and I were friends? And I trusted him? That's why I went to his room that night. Now it's completely messed with my head. I can't go out, not even to a small party. And forget about guys. Never again." Annie chokes up. "He took away a part of myself that I'll never get back. Sorry it's your brother I'm talking about, but you should know what you're dealing with."

Annie clears her throat and then raises her cigarette to her lips. That's when I notice that her hand is trembling.

"I'm sorry," I say quickly. "I'm sorry. I shouldn't have come. I'm just so confused about this."

Annie nods. "Did you know that people on campus yelled things at me, accusing me of crying rape and ruining Byron's life so I could get attention? But do you know what really got me? When your brother came to school this semester, I'd see him around with girls. Younger girls. Freshmen. And all I could think was, *Please don't let it happen to them.*"

Annie makes a gagging sound and turns away.

I lower my head. I'm done. I get it. I was wrong to come, and now I need to go somewhere and crawl in a hole and never come out.

"I didn't tell anyone I was coming," I whisper to her. "No one told me you work here. I just saw you up here once. I'm sorry."

Annie points her cigarette in the direction of the Hungarian Pastry Shop. "What's up with you and my brother?"

"I didn't know he was your brother," I say. Just thinking about Sebastian makes me feel quivery.

"Either way, it's not okay."

I shrug my shoulders and mumble, "Okay, well . . . I guess I should go."

"Yeah," Annie says. "Probably a good idea."

I start toward Broadway but then she calls out, "Hey!"

I quickly turn around.

Annie drops the cigarette onto the sidewalk and grinds it with her sneaker. "It's just . . ."

She trails off and I don't know what to say either, so we both head in opposite directions.

6 6 6 6

I don't stop when I get to Broadway or even Riverside. My sneakers are slapping against the sidewalk, and my temples are pounding in my skull. I can't stop thinking about how different Annie looked from six months ago. I'm also thinking about Sebastian and how when I met him at the bagel store he was carrying his sister's skateboard. He said his sister had gone to the bank. What if Annie had come back to the bagel store while we were there? Had she told the police about my brother yet? If she hadn't gone to the police yet, would it have changed her mind if she saw me? I guess it wouldn't, but it's still so confusing.

I turn left in Riverside Park and walk down the promenade. After a while I sit on a bench and lower my head between my knees. I'm a little dizzy, and my underarms are moist with sweat.

My phone vibrates in my pocket again. I wipe my hands on my cutoffs and pull it out.

I'm leaving, Froggy has just written. I notice it's the most recent of eight or nine texts from him over the past hour. He's also called twice. So it wasn't Mom. Huh.

I read Froggy's texts. I totally forgot that we were supposed to meet at Belvedere Castle at noon. It's currently 1:04.

I'm sorry, I write to Froggy. Something came up.

I watch the three dots come and go, come and go. Finally, he writes me back.

Yeah. Well. See you around.

I feel terrible that I blew him off. It's not like he's been a bad boyfriend. I'm just not into him, and now, with my brother getting arrested and possibly going to jail, I can't fake it anymore.

I consider writing back and apologizing or making an excuse, but since I can't decide what I want to say, I end up doing nothing.

I stay on the bench for an hour studying chemistry. The final is tomorrow, and I still haven't looked over the nomenclature stuff yet. I also review my French vocabulary for Tuesday's final and read an essay on the rise of nationalism that we have to analyze for the Global Studies final on Wednesday.

While I'm studying, I try not to think about Sebastian and how long he'll be in New York City. I try not to think about the fact that his sister is Annie Mills.

After a while, I head to Jerusalem deli, grab a falafel sandwich, and carry it back to the park. I walk all the way down to the Hudson River. There are bikers and joggers streaming by. The grass is damp, so I sit on a rock by the river, arrange paper napkins across my thighs, and unwrap my sandwich. The river is calm and sparkly with diamonds. I think about Virginia Woolf and wonder how things got so bad that she decided to kill herself. Or maybe it wasn't a choice. Maybe she had no choices left.

There are times that I've hated my body so much that I didn't think I deserved to take up room on this earth. But I've always found reasons to live, like books and Shannon and cute boys and kickboxing and movies and carbs and Vassar and just the fact that things always get better and I want to be there when it happens.

Before I get back to studying I allow myself a quick google search for Leela from *Futurama*. Sebastian was right. She's a curvy chick with a high purple ponytail. If I could be a super-hero, I would totally pick her.

Not that I can think about purple-haired superheroes or anything having to do with Sebastian. Not that it even *was* anything, just some guy who sketched me.

Hang on.

Some cute guy sketched *ME*? I'll give myself a millisecond to revel in that.

Sigh. Smile.

Then I think about what Annie said, about how people on campus harassed her for reporting Byron. And I suddenly hate the world all over again.

Around four, I pack up my stuff and walk toward home. My ankle is starting to hurt again. I stop at a Starbucks to pee and buy a decaf Mocha Frappuccino.

Decaf Mocha Frappuccino = another reason to live.

Not that Mom would ever understand this caloric indul-gence. I throw away the empty plastic cup before I turn onto our block and drag my ankle the final stretch home.

As I unlock the front door, the home phone is ringing.

"Anyone home?" I shout into the apartment. No answer. The phone is still ringing, so I scoop it up.

"Hello?"

"Hey, Ginny!" It's Anaïs. Other than last Wednesday, I've barely heard my sister's voice in two years.

"Hey, Anaïs. Where are you?"

"London. I got here Friday night."

"Wow." I reach into the freezer for an ice pack. "What's it like there?"

As Anaïs talks about London and riding the Tube and how she already misses Burkina Faso, I hold the ice against my ankle and stall for time. All I'm thinking is, how long can I talk to my sister and act normal? Byron's arrest is major family news, yet Mom made it crystal clear that I'm not supposed to say a word about it to Anaïs.

"Is everything okay?" she finally asks. "You're being so quiet. Is anyone else home?"

"I just walked in. I don't think anyone's home."

"Are you okay, sweetie?"

"Sweetie" does me in. I sink onto the couch and wipe back tears as I tell her about the Thai food and the police and the arraignment and the bail and the fact that Byron could go to jail and have to register as a sex offender. I also tell her that I'm not supposed to be telling her, that I would be in deep trouble for the rest of my life if Mom finds out.

"When were they planning to tell me?" Anaïs asks.

"I'm guessing when you get home."

When she doesn't respond, I reach for a tissue and blow my nose.

"What?" I ask. "Are you mad I told you?"

"No . . . that's not it. I'm just remembering why I left. All the secrets. I hate it."

"But you're coming back, right?" I've always seen my sister as my ally in the family. Sure, she's gorgeous and thin and speaks French and plays golf, but when push comes to shove

I think she has my back. I'm ready for her to return to this continent.

"What's that?" Anaïs says. She sounds distracted. "I mean, yeah. Not forever, though. Don't tell Mom and Dad. Just tell them I called."

After we hang up, I sit cross-legged on the couch, the ice pack stinging my ankle, and I think about how Anaïs has the choice to come and go as she pleases. I don't have that choice. I'm stuck here.

And just like that, I opt for no more pretending. At least in my own life. No more faking it. No more denial. Tomorrow, when I see Froggy at school, I'm ending it. I'm breaking up with him.

# 12

When I wake up Monday morning, I don't feel quite as bold. It doesn't help that I have my period and can't find any tampons, so I have to wear a big bulky diaper pad. If that's not bad enough, Mom and Dad stay home from their morning workout to lecture me about family loyalty and how I'm not to mention the name "Annie Mills" in our house ever again.

It's almost a relief when I get to school. But then, nine minutes before the chemistry final, I pass Froggy at his locker.

As soon as I see him, my teeth start chattering.

"So," he says, frowning. His cheeks are flushed with white splotches, like thumbs pressed into a sunburn.

"So," I respond.

*Say it*, I tell myself. *Say it's over. Be nice but don't chicken out.*

The thing is, I'm having a hard time breathing, much less

putting syllables together. It doesn't help that Brie Newhart is walking toward us, headed for her locker. She's wearing a tiny yellow dress and heels. Brie dresses for Paris Fashion Week more than for finals week at school. I think about how she made fun of me in kickboxing on Friday. The last thing I need is for her to see me breaking up with my boyfriend. Cool kids are allowed to fight in public and make out and make up. The rest of us have to conduct our business as invisibly as possible.

Froggy and I wait while she scoops folders out of her purse and checks her phone. He knows where he stands at school, too.

Once Brie walks away, he again says, "So."

"So," I again say back.

Froggy glances at the floor and then mumbles, "I think we should just be, you know, friends."

*Oh crap.* I was going to break up with him, but now he's breaking up with me.

"Okay." I touch my hand to my eyebrow ring.

Froggy closes his locker. "Okay."

"Okay," I say.

"Okay," Froggy says.

Nearly ninth months together, and it's over in three seconds and a handful of "sos" and "okays."

As Froggy turns and walks down the hall, I watch him go. I wonder if I should cry. Not because I didn't want it to happen, but because that's what you're supposed to do when you and your boyfriend break up. The truth is, I'm relieved. I don't want to stay with someone that I'm not in like with because I don't think I can get anyone else. I don't want to suffer through kisses that gross me out. I don't want to pretend I only eat kale and plums.

*So . . . okay*, I tell myself. *I will be okay.*

⑥ ⑥ ⑥ ⑥

Tuesday. Three days left of school. I still don't feel sad about Froggy, but I'll admit I'm a little adrift. Alyssa walks close to me in the halls and keeps asking if I'm okay, but she doesn't seem quite as heartbroken as I thought she'd be that Froggy and I are over. When I first told her about the breakup, she sighed and hugged me and said, "All good things must come to an end."

I don't tell Alyssa what happened with my brother, of course. Mostly we talk about Field Day on Thursday. We're putting together a playlist for the Mr. Mooney tribute and bringing bubble guns because it turns out a helium balloon release isn't green. We also talk about summer vacation. I tell her that Shannon is hiking the PCT, and she agrees that that sounds terrible.

Speaking of Shannon, I get a text from her when I go into the bathroom after my French final. She wrote an hour ago that she's leaving for the hike today and won't have her phone for the next two months. I tell her not to get eaten by a bear or fall off a mountain.

During the math final Cole Nevins is wearing a cologne that smells super sexy. At one point, it looks like he's smiling at me, but maybe he's just checking the clock.

116

⑥ ⑥ ⑥ ⑥

On Wednesday, I see Froggy in the hall near the computer cluster. Alyssa and I are walking back from lunch. He waves at Alyssa but frowns at me. I didn't expect it to sting, but it does.

After lunch, I go upstairs early to get settled in for the Global Studies final. On the way, I pass Cole Nevins. It's just the two of us in the hall, which is weird. I've never seen him *not* surrounded by his cool-guy posse.

"What's up, Virginia?" he says, grinning at me. "You finished the math final early yesterday, right?"

First: He knows my name?

Second: He saw me leave the math final early?

Third: We've got a problem. The problem is that whenever I'm around Cole my brain shuts down.

*Math, Virginia. He's asking if you finished the math final early.*

"Yeah," I say, nodding. I'm trying to smile, but my face feels twitchy and tight.

"Crazy finals stress, right?" Cole asks. "I've already decided I'm applying early to Brown, so all these grades count."

*Brown. Where my sister went. I could tell him that. That would be the obvious response.*

"Where are you applying?" he asks. "Or thinking about applying?"

"Vassar," I manage. "Maybe Wesleyan and Oberlin."

"Just send them a picture of your purple-and-green hair

117

and you'll get in right away," he says. "You've got a great look going on."

I have no idea why he's being so nice to me all of a sudden.

"See you around," Cole says.

I don't remember to wave until he's halfway down the hall.

⑥ ⑥ ⑥ ⑥

That afternoon, when I get home from school, Byron is on the couch watching a rugby match.

"Hey there," Byron says. "What's up?"

"Hey," I say, standing behind him.

I study my brother's tannish neck and his muscular shoulders. I think how Annie Mills said that she and Byron were friends and she trusted him. On the television, the rugby players are running and tackling each other. One team is wearing red jerseys and the other is in blue. Byron plays rugby at Columbia, and he used to play at Brewster, too. Whenever we went to his matches, Mom and Dad would marvel at how my brother takes no prisoners. When Byron was in possession of the ball, he would run and pivot and pass and receive and not stop until he made it to the goal line.

"Want to watch?" Byron asks. "It's France versus Wales. It's from last month. I'm just catching up."

Maybe it's because of what Annie said, but I totally don't want to sit next to Byron on the couch. The thought of it disgusts me. She trusted him. He raped her.

"What did you say?" he asks.

"Nothing." I pause. "I have to finish my Humanities essay."

I go into the bathroom and splash my face. The skin around my eyebrow pierce is pink, so I rub some Neosporin on it and then switch back to the gold ring.

Once I'm in my room, I make edits to my essay and print out the final copy. I wish I could share it with my teacher online and not have to go to school again until September, but we're required to hand in our essays in person. Also, I have to be at Field Day tomorrow even if I weren't co-chairing Mr. Mooney's tribute. In the student handbook it reads: "We strongly encourage everyone to attend all school functions and display the energy and enthusiasm we expect from Brewster students."

Barf.

I wish my parents would let me transfer to a public high school, but I know they believe a private school like Brewster will feed me into a good college, which will ensure a good future.

I tuck my essay in my backpack and pull out *Fates and Furies*. Flopping onto my pillow, I read fifty pages of Mathilde's section. Then I turn onto my side and read fifty more. I can't believe what I'm learning about Mathilde. I can't believe that the great love I thought existed between Lotto and Mathilde may not have been so great after all.

I'm propped on my elbows when I read the final page. Once I'm done, I let *Fates and Furies* drop onto the bed. I curl up on top of my comforter thinking about love and whether it really exists. Even though I didn't have it with Froggy, I want to believe it does. I want to believe Lotto and Mathilde loved each other. I want to believe that love can be messy and complicated but it's for real.

A text comes in. It's probably Mom, letting me know she's working late or meeting Dad for dinner. I dig into my bag, retrieve my phone, and—

Someone has sent me a sketch of a purple-haired girl with gray-blue eyes and an eyebrow ring waving a bagel in her raised fist.

Not someone.

Sebastian.

◎ ◎ ◎ ◎

I stare at the picture in shock. My eyes are resplendent swirls of gray and blue, and he's added a sun and clouds behind me. The sky is wavy, like Van Gogh's *Starry Night*.

Hi, I write, sitting up in bed. **Thanks for sending the drawing. Glad you gave me two eyes.**

Three dots. Three dots. Three dots.

Finally, his response comes in. He writes: **I'm calling it "In which Leela teaches Fry about the best bagels in NYC."**

I smile. I used to love the Winnie-the-Pooh books when I was younger and how the chapters started with "In which," all proper and British. I remember being fascinated by "In which Pooh goes visiting and gets into a tight place." When I think about it now, it's messed up that I liked a chapter about a bear who overeats and gets stuck in a hole and has to starve himself to get out.

**In which,** I write to Sebastian. **Like Winnie-the-Pooh?**

**Yes!** he writes. **A. A. Milne is my rock star. When I was little I wanted to be Christopher Robin.**

**Cute,** I write to him and add a bunch of smiling emojis.

I can hear Byron in the living room. I hear the fridge open and close, which I guess means Byron is finally eating. Or maybe he's surviving on fluid. It's after seven. Mom and Dad will be home soon. What would they say if they knew I was texting with Annie Mills's brother? Duh. They'd say I'm a traitor. I'm not even allowed to say her name in the house.

I tap at my phone. **Should we be texting?**

**No,** Sebastian writes.

I sigh. I'm not sure whether to be happy or sad that we're on the same page about this.

Another text from Sebastian comes in. **But I've been thinking about it, and I've decided that what they don't know won't hurt them. I'll change your name to Leela in my contacts. You put me in as Fry. We can live in Futurama land and text with reckless abandon.**

I think about his sea-glass eyes and his smile and how I felt when he was drawing me.

**Okay,** I say.

**Better go,** he writes. **My family is getting home.**

**Family?** I write.

**Yeah. We're all here.**

As I add "Fry" to my contacts, I think about how his family includes Annie Mills. Talk about messy and complicated. I save Sebastian's sketch to my phone and quickly delete everything else.

# 13

"Virginia, is it true?"

"Is what true?" I say to Alyssa.

It's finally Thursday. The last day of school. I just turned in my Humanities essay and carried twelve jumbo bubble guns over to Central Park, where I've been lining them up on a table and filling them with soapy liquid. Alyssa stayed at Brewster to get markers and paper from the art room. When I waved good-bye to her ten minutes ago, she was smiling.

Now, as she approaches me, her face is drawn and her eyes are filled with tears.

"Is it true about your brother?" Alyssa asks. "When I was leaving school just now I passed the principal talking to the public relations lady. You know that one with the helmet hair and fake eyelashes who's always taking pictures of us?"

I nod *yes* even though the public relations lady never takes pictures of me. Alyssa is Asian so Brewster loves to put her on their website as an example of the diversity at our school. Same goes for the three Muslim girls who wear hijabs and the boy with cerebral palsy who walks with leg braces. Brewster isn't as excited about posting photos of weight diversity, though.

"Anyway, I heard the principal telling the PR lady to find all the promotional brochures with Byron Shreves on the cover and destroy them," Alyssa says. "She said that now that the news is out, Brewster has to distance itself from Byron."

I hug my hands around my stomach, feeling way too exposed in my midthigh skirt and tank top. My fingers are sticky from the bubble liquid. I wish I could wash my hands. I wish I could disappear. I wish I could erase what Alyssa is about to tell me.

Alyssa kicks the toe of her sneaker into the grass. "I looked up your brother as I was walking over here and—" She pauses and hands me her phone. "Virginia, I'm so sorry."

I look around to make sure no one is watching us. The cafeteria workers are setting up drinks and cookie platters, and the gym teachers are prepping for a three-legged race. Gym teachers will jump at any chance to let the sporty kids flaunt their physical prowess and make the nonsporty kids look like losers. I shade my hand over Alyssa's screen. It's open to an article from the West Side Resident, a local news blog.

## UPPER WEST SIDE COLLEGE STUDENT
## ARRESTED FOR RAPE

Upper West Side resident Byron Shreves, 20, was arrested on Friday evening for allegedly raping 21-year-old Annabelle Mills on Columbia University's Morningside Heights campus last September 30. Even though the alleged incident occurred more than eight months ago, Mills only recently reported it. Shreves was picked up from his family's West 81st Street home on Friday and charged in the attack. He pleaded not guilty and posted bail. Shreves and Mills are both students at Columbia University, and Shreves is also a graduate of the prestigious Brimmer School on the Upper East Side. A spokesperson for the university had no comment.

I hand Alyssa's phone back to her. I wonder if my parents know about this article.

"I'm so sorry, Virginia," Alyssa says, wiping her eyes with the back of her hand. "I had no idea what you were going through this week. Why didn't you tell me?"

*Because I'm not allowed to talk about it*, I want to say. Instead, I just shrug.

Alyssa hugs me. I try to hug her back, but I feel stiff and robotic.

"Did you tell Froggy yet?" Alyssa asks.

I shake my head. "We're not talking."

"Want me to tell him? Maybe it would change his—"

"No," I say quickly. "It's okay."

"Is there anything I can do? I leave for New Jersey tomorrow morning, but I'll check in over the summer."

"Sure. But it's okay. Really."

Obviously it's not okay. Obviously it sucks and I'm horrified by what my brother did, but I'm also worried he's going to wind up in jail, and that thought is so sad and scary that I feel like there's a noose tightening around my neck.

I reach into my bag and touch my phone. Should I tell my parents that Byron's arrest has hit the news? I wonder what time this article came out. They didn't say anything about it when I saw them in the kitchen this morning.

I glance toward Fifth Avenue. Swarms of Brewster students are heading toward Central Park for Field Day. The public relations lady is following them with a camera. As one group nears, I can see it's the popular sophomores, Brie and her friends, Cole and his buddies. Bonus is that Cole is African American *and* popular, gold for Brewster PR. He'll probably replace my brother on the new brochures.

"We should finish setting up," I say to Alyssa. "We're doing the Mr. Mooney tribute first, right? You're going to connect your phone to the speakers?"

"Yep." She frowns at me. "Are you sure you're okay?"

"Not really . . ."

Alyssa leans over and squeezes me into another hug.

"Chick on chick!" Cole shouts, approaching our table and helping himself to a bubble gun. "What's up, Virginia? That was a sexy hug."

"Dude, are you serious?" asks his friend Josh. "You honestly thought that was sexy?"

I can't stand Josh. He lives for making fun of people. His mom is a multimillionaire, and he's always taking people with him on vacations, which is probably how he's achieved such elevated popularity status. But I don't ever get the sense that people actually like him.

Cole aims the gun to the sky and lets loose a burst of shimmery bubbles. He looks embarrassed. I'm remembering how we talked in the hall yesterday, how he asked where I'm applying to college and then told me he likes my look.

A moment later, Brie sidles over and loops elbows with Cole. She's got a mischievous grin on her face as she says to him, "You thought that was sexy? I didn't know you're such a chubby chaser."

She says it loudly. She says it so I can hear.

Cole laughs awkwardly and shakes his head. As they walk away, Josh and Brie and a few others are cracking up like it's the most hilarious comment in the world.

"Fuck off!" Alyssa shouts after them, but they don't even turn around. Then, to me, she says, "Can you believe—"

But I'm gone. I've grabbed my backpack and I'm walking toward Fifth Avenue. Fuck Brewster. Fuck Field Day. As I wipe back tears, all I can think is that I can't believe I ever imagined someone as beautiful as Sebastian might be interested in me. Unless he's a chubby chaser. Fuck chubby chasers.

I don't stop walking until I get to the 6 train. I take the

subway all the way to Canal Street. When I get out, I take a deep breath, push the tears down for good, and navigate the narrow sidewalks until I'm in the heart of Chinatown. I'm sweaty and my thighs are sticking together, but I'm feeling better. Being here is helping. I like being surrounded by the chaotic drivers, the plucked duck carcasses hanging in restaurant windows, the old Chinese women selling lumpy vegetables on street corners. It makes me feel like I've traveled to a different country. It makes me feel invisible, or at least anonymous.

Unlike at Brewster, where I stand out like a swollen thumb.

Fuck Cole and his sidekicks. Fuck Brie. Fuck sophomore year with Shannon in Walla Walla and my brother getting kicked out of college and then arrested.

I try not to think about the fact that I'm a few blocks from criminal court. I try not to think about how eventually I have to go home and deal with the fallout from Byron's arrest hitting the news. For now I just clip my damp bangs into a barrette, buy an order of scallion pancakes, and walk and walk and walk.

૯ ૯ ૭ ૯

I get home around four. Mom and Dad are sitting on the couch. They're never home on a Thursday afternoon. When I step into the apartment, Dad gestures to a chair and says, "Sit down."

"I saw the article," I say as I lower myself into the chair. I can see down the hall that Byron's door is closed.

"Which one?" Mom asks. Her eyes are bloodshot, and she doesn't have any makeup on. "No, never mind. It's everywhere."

I make an executive decision not to tell them that Alyssa is the one who clued me in. If my parents discover that Alyssa knows about Byron's arrest they'll never feel comfortable with her at our apartment again.

"When you were at Brewster today," Dad asks, "did anyone say anything to you about Byron?"

*Brewster.* The mention of school makes me think about those assholes in the park and that, in turn, makes me want to puke.

"No," I say, swallowing back a mouthful of saliva. I decide not to tell them how Brewster is shredding the brochures with Byron on the cover.

"They'll find out soon enough," Dad concludes. "Mom lost eleven patients today. People were calling and canceling all morning. Her book proposal is over, too. Her agent said it would be impossible to sell a parenting book now, even though her reputation as an adolescent psychologist is impeccable."

Mom is staring into her hands. I've never seen her look so sad.

"What about your job?" I ask Dad.

Dad pauses. "It'll be fine. Ciel is a different situation than Mom's."

"Have you talked about it with your friends?" Mom asks. "Or texted about it?"

I shake my head. As soon as I'm in my room, I'll delete all my texts with Shannon.

"Good," Dad says. "Don't."

"Virginia, Dad is serious." Mom leans forward on the couch so she's eye level with me. "Mark says we need to keep this under wraps. The less publicity, the better. Also, we don't want to say anything over text that could be used in court."

"I'm not texting anyone about it, okay?" It's actually worrisome seeing them like this. There's a certain comfort in their usual sweep-under-the-rug attitude.

"We're going to Connecticut today," Dad says.

"Not tomorrow?" I ask.

"We need to hunker down for a few days," Mom says. "Unplug and metabolize everything that's going on."

"Okay," I say. My internship at Dad's office doesn't start until the Monday after next. The only thing I have is kickboxing tomorrow, but I wasn't planning to go because of Brie.

"Dad is leaving to get the car in a few minutes," Mom says. "He's already called the garage so you should go pack. We'll stay until Sunday."

As I start toward my room, Mom says, "Did you turn your essay in?"

"Yeah." I smooth my skirt around my thighs. My *chubby* thighs. Just this morning I was thinking my skirt looked awesome. I had a fantasy about meeting Sebastian in a different neighborhood, like down on the High Line, and wearing this exact outfit.

"Congrats on finishing sophomore year," Mom says, sighing. "You're midway through high school now. That's a significant milestone."

We listen as Dad knocks on Byron's door. Three hard, fast raps, like he means it.

"I'm leaving for the garage," Dad says through the door.

"I said I'm not coming," Byron mutters back.

"Son, we've been over this. I told you it's not a choice." Dad's voice is just short of yelling. "Pack your bag and be ready in thirty minutes."

I suck in my breath. I've never heard Dad talk to Byron like that. In our house, Byron has carte blanche to do what he wants and no one ever gives him a hard time. I scurry into my room, slip off my skirt, kick it under the bed, and pull on some loose capris. My tote is still packed from last weekend, so I throw in a few novels and my phone charger.

A half hour later, we're on the West Side Highway heading north. Dad is driving. Mom is googling. I know because I peeked over her shoulder and saw that she's looking up who has posted the news about my brother. Byron and I are buckled in the back, headphones on, listening to music. He hasn't said a word since he emerged from his room. He looks like hell, pale and unshaven with deep circles under his eyes.

**Hey.**

The text from Fry pops up on my phone.

**Hey,** I write back. I angle the phone deep into my hand. My heart is thumping hard. We shouldn't be doing this. I shouldn't be texting with Annie Mills's brother.

**I saw,** he writes. **The articles. I'm sorry.**

**You shouldn't apologize,** I write back. **It's not your fault.**

He sends me a frowny face. **We probably shouldn't be texting.**

I glance up at Mom and Dad, and over at Byron.

**Agreed,** I finally say. **I'm in the car with my family.**

**Okay.**

And that's it. After a minute, I delete his texts and stare out my window, watching the city streak by until it succumbs to the Bronx and Westchester and finally Connecticut.

# 14

Tree Babe is working in the backyard. I'm reading in the hammock on the other side of the yard. I can see her up on a ladder using long clippers. She's wearing olive-colored shorts, a white T-shirt, and a Green Arbor baseball cap. Her long blond hair is in a loose braid and she's got headphones on as she clips and saws at the branches.

It's Saturday afternoon and really hot, like over ninety. I want to offer her something to drink, but I'm remembering how Dad kept trying to push seltzer on her last week and she kept saying no.

I'm reading *The Great Gatsby*, which is making me think about social class, like how Gatsby is new rich versus Tom Buchanan's old money. That makes me think about Mom and Dad. It's no secret that my family has money. We have an apartment in Manhattan and a country house in Connecticut, and

I go to private school. Dad comes from a wealthy New England family, and he inherited money when his parents died. Mom grew up working class in Ozark, Arkansas. She doesn't talk much about it, but from what I've pieced together, she reinvented herself when she went to Dartmouth and met Dad. Not that meeting a rich guy solves everything or makes you a better person, but it definitely helped Mom put distance between her poor past and her privileged present.

We've been on lockdown since we got to Connecticut on Thursday night. This might be the first warm weekend ever that my parents aren't golfing from sunup to sundown. I assume they're avoiding their golf friends in case anyone has seen the news about Byron.

As for me, I've been reading my book, and at least three times a day, I pace our property and then over the stone wall into our neighbor's yard with my phone raised above my head. I'm trying to get a fraction of a signal. No luck so far. Cell service is patchy in this part of Connecticut.

I just want to see if Sebastian has texted me again. I know we shouldn't be in touch. I know it's wrong. And yet.

"What are you reading?"

I look up from my book, squinting into the sun. It's Tree Babe, standing near my hammock. She has her headphones around her neck, and she's wiping her forehead with the back of her hand.

"*The Great Gatsby*," I say. I push up to sitting position and swing my legs over the side of the hammock.

"Is it for school?"

I shake my head. "School's over."

"Already?"

"Private school lets out early," I say. I feel weird talking to her while knowing the sleazy comments Dad made about her body. I wish I could erase them from my brain.

She nods and offers me a small wave. "I'm Frances, by the way."

"I'm Virginia."

"Nice to meet you." She rolls her head from side to side and then examines her fingernails. "I hated high school."

"You?" I ask.

I'm shocked for two reasons.

1. Her name is *Frances*??? I would have assumed Tree Babe would be a Crystal or a Lola.
2. Her type is built to peak in high school. If you have big boobs and long blond hair and you're super skinny and you didn't love high school, what hope does that leave for people like me?

Frances shakes her head. "I didn't fit in. I'm sort of ADHD, and that didn't help. Even now I run into people I knew from high school, and they're like, *You trim trees*? Like I'm a lumberjack. I'm a certified arborist! The thing is, I actually like my job. I listen to music. I get to be outdoors. I don't know. It still bothers me."

"If you like your job," I say, pushing my feet against the

ground so the hammock swings back and forth, "then who cares what other people think?"

Frances laughs. "You should tell my parents that. I'm a disappointment to them."

I stare at her. If I looked like her, my parents would love me unconditionally. They wouldn't care that I'm a crappy driver and I can't speak French and I swing a golf club like it's a baseball bat.

"My parents are business-mogul types. According to them, I should be done with my MBA by now. My older sisters have both finished theirs."

"Want some iced tea?" I ask suddenly. "I can run in and get it."

"I'd love it. It's so hot today." Frances hoists up her ladder and gestures across the yard. "I need to get back to work. I'll be over there."

"Okay, I'll just be a second."

As I stand up, she says, "Virginia, right?"

"Yeah?"

"Sorry to complain. My boyfriend says I should let it go, all the high school stuff and the parent stuff, too. He's obsessed with being mindful and present."

"But it's hard," I say. I'm talking about her, but I'm also thinking about myself.

"Hell, yeah," Frances says, smiling at me. "It's really freakin' hard."

ⓖ ⓖ ⓖ ⓖ

On Sunday morning I walk forever down our street, searching for a signal, and then trek forever in the other direction. We're way out in the country, on a long windy road lined with old maple trees. I walk for an hour, but I can't find any cell reception.

When I return home, Mom hands me a glass of water. "It's nice to see you starting a summer fitness routine. We could all use an endorphin boost right about now. It's really hot out, so make sure to hydrate."

Petty Observation: After Byron exercises *he* gets Vitaminwater. But not me. Just plain water for me.

"How many miles did you go?" she asks.

"I don't know . . . maybe four or five."

"Wonderful. Good for you."

I sip the water and smile because, hey, I rarely receive compliments from Mom. It's not like I'm going to tell her that I'm only walking in order to find a cell signal so I can see if Thursday's texts with Sebastian were good-bye for now or good-bye forever.

I'm not usually this phone obsessed. With Froggy, I was fine with text vacations when I was in Connecticut. But Sebastian feels different in every possible way. Those two times we met, I could be myself around him and make him laugh and he made me laugh. Not to mention that he's so cute. And even though I'm a mountain of self-doubt around this topic, I think he might be attracted to me.

Mount Kilimanjaro of Doubt: He's just a chubby chaser.

On the other hand: He drew me. He drew me beautiful.

Back when we were in the city, I read a description of *Futurama* and the Fry-Leela relationship. They're on-and-off attracted to each other for many seasons, but they don't get together until the very end.

Mount Everest of Doubt: It's a television show, Virginia. Don't be delusional. Don't read into it.

On the other hand: He called me Leela. He told me to put him in my phone as Fry. How can I not read into that?

Welcome to my morning. Mountains of doubt followed by valleys of justification. And, worst of all, valleys without the slightest flicker of cell reception.

Finally, I've had enough. I find Dad under the sunshade on the back porch.

"Can you take me driving?" I ask. "I need to go to the bookstore, and that's practice, right? Like with intersections and traffic lights?"

There's a bookstore called Words on Pages in Lincoln Township. I know they have cell reception. And for a signal, I will brave intersections.

Dad looks up from his magazine. "Not now," he says gruffly.

I'm shocked. Dad loves nothing more than Dadsplaining the mechanics of driving to me.

"What about Mom?" I ask.

"She's upstairs. She's got a headache."

"But I have to buy something for a project," I plead. One

perk of having a dad who is oblivious about my life is that I can use school as an excuse when necessary. I don't think he's even aware that Brewster has let out for the summer.

"Byron?" Dad calls into the house.

Oh, great. Just what I need. Quality time with the one person I am most betraying by checking to see if Sebastian has texted.

"Take Virginia to Words on Pages," Dad says. "The keys are on the counter. Let her drive. Practice who yields to whom at an intersection."

"Am I even allowed to?" Byron asks from inside.

"Yes," Dad says. "You're twenty and you've had your license for four consecutive years without any violations."

Dad took serious notes at that parent-teen safety class.

"Now?" Byron asks.

"Now," Dad says.

Before the arrest, Byron would have said *Sorry . . . I can't*, but he's on thin ice right now and he knows it. It's not just about the bail money and the fact that my parents are paying for his expensive lawyer. It's that Byron's entire life is on the brink of wreck and Mom and Dad are trying to right the ship.

"Do you need money?" Dad asks, opening his wallet and offering me some bills.

"No, that's okay."

Byron and I don't say anything as we get into the car, me in the driver's seat, him in the passenger seat. The car is pointed forward, so at least I don't have to turn it around. I position my hands on the wheel and press the gas. We jerk clumsily down the driveway. I won't let myself look over at Byron to see if he's smirking. I hate this. I hate driving. I don't see the point. My fingers are sweaty on the wheel as I nose closer to the road. I study the lanes, remind myself to cross over the yellow line, and then pull out.

"Want me to just drive?"

Upon hearing Byron's voice, I ram the brake and the car slams to a stop. Luckily I was only going three miles an hour and no one was behind me.

"Yeah," I say quickly. "That'd be great."

"Shift into park and turn on your hazards," he says. "We can change here. Just don't tell Dad."

"What are hazards?" As I hold my foot on the brake and shift into park, I scan my mental database for everything I learned in driver's ed.

Byron reaches over me and presses a button that makes a rapid clicking sound. Oh, right. Those lights that flash if you stop in the road to yield your seat because you suck at driving and should never be behind a wheel.

"Let's go," he says, unbuckling his seat belt and hopping out.

A few minutes later, Byron pulls into the parking lot of the bookstore.

"I'm going to wait here," he says. "You're not going to take too long, right?"

"Probably about ten minutes."

Byron nods and reaches for his phone.

Speaking of phones, I won't let myself peek at mine until I'm safely huddled in the empty cookbook section. Alyssa sent four texts on Thursday night and Friday morning asking if I'm okay. She's also texted that she's leaving for New Jersey. A girl from kickboxing wrote on Friday night asking where I was. And then there's Fry.

Yes, Fry. Sebastian.

On Friday, he wrote, **Want to meet in person? Enough with the texts. Let's kick it old school.**

On Saturday morning he wrote me again: **Have you decided we shouldn't be talking?**

A few hours later he added, **I understand and respect if you think we shouldn't be in touch. I wanted to tell you that I read When You Reach Me last night. I finished it in three hours and didn't get up the whole time. SO GOOD. Loved the Wrinkle references.**

I smile as I read his texts, commit them to memory, and then delete them. I pluck a cookbook about kale off the shelf and stand in line to buy it. In the off-chance that Dad asks what I got, I need something to show for myself. He and Mom are obsessed with the health benefits of leafy greens, so this might karmically offset my wrongdoing.

Before I leave the bookstore, I tuck into a corner and quickly respond to Sebastian.

**Yes. I'd love to meet. I'm out of cell range until tomorrow. I'll write when I get home.**

I send the text and then delete it like it never happened.

When I get back in the car, Byron starts up the engine. I'm trying not to smile. I can't believe Sebastian wrote three times. I can't believe he read *When You Reach Me* because I recommended it. I can't believe he wants to meet up.

"Don't worry so much about your road test," Byron says as he pulls out of the parking lot. "I know Dad is making it into a big thing, but his expectations are low. It's not the end of the world if you don't pass."

I glance at him. "Is that supposed to be a good thing?"

"I'm just saying you have it easy. They've pinned all their female hopes on Anaïs and all their male hopes onto me. You can just be . . . you."

I shrug. I decide not to tell Byron that he's oblivious about the many ways I've let our parents down.

"Believe me," Byron says, "it's better than being a big hope and fucking everything up."

Now is the moment when I'm supposed to tell Byron that he hasn't fucked everything up, but that would be a lie. Instead I roll down my window and rest my head against the side of the car. The trees are bursting with green, and there are pastures, fences, and tidy Colonial houses with black shutters. The soft summer air is blowing on my face. I think about Sebastian, and how he wants to meet up. I think about how school is out and I don't have to see any Brewster people for almost three months. Maybe I really will look into public school. Maybe I'll learn to cook with kale. Maybe I'll take some money out of savings and buy business-casual clothes to wear to my internship at Dad's company. Maybe things don't have to be so bad—

Suddenly there's a wet splash on my cheek. I jolt forward, only to be slammed back into place by the seat belt, and raise my hand to my face. It feels slimier than water and smells like a chemical.

"I have no idea what just—" I start to say when I notice that Byron is laughing.

"What's going on?" I reach in the glove compartment for a tissue. "What happened?"

"You didn't know our car could do that?"

"Do what?"

"When you spray the windshield-wiper fluid, it's at a weird angle and can peg the person in the passenger seat. If the window is open, of course."

I'm aghast. "You sprayed me with *windshield-wiper fluid*? *On purpose*? That stuff is toxic. You could have gotten it in my eyes."

"I only did a little bit."

"You're an asshole," I tell him.

"I've done it to other people and they thought it was funny. You should learn to take a joke."

I wipe at my cheek some more. I'm too mad to respond. Is this how it all starts? Someone thinks it's funny to spray windshield-wiper fluid on someone else. Everyone thinks that person is so great that no one tells him it's an asshole thing to do. All the while, he gets praised for taking no prisoners when he plays rugby even though he's leaving a trail of sprained ankles and black eyes. So he keeps on being an asshole. And the next thing you know, he's inviting a friend into his dorm room and forcing her to have sex even though she's saying no.

When we pull into the driveway, I don't wait for the car to come to a complete stop. I unbuckle my seat belt, grab my bag, and run into the bathroom where I wash my face until the chemical smell is completely gone. And then I wash my face some more.

☙ ☙ ☙ ☙

We leave on Sunday night to avoid the traffic back to the city. It's after nine but still dusky out. In a few days it will be the longest day of the year. Dad is driving and Mom is in the passenger seat. It's weird the way Dad lectures me about the importance of being a driver, yet he dominates the wheel and rarely yields it to Mom. I've been noticing things like that recently, sexist things, and they've been bothering me.

Mom and Dad decided to have Byron stay in Connecticut this week. There's a fence that needs painting, and the deck could use a coat of sealant. They figured it would be more therapeutic for Byron to fill his week with physical labor than to languish around the apartment. They left him with a fridge full of groceries, and there are bikes in the garage in case he needs to go anywhere.

We're getting closer to Manhattan when Dad turns down the radio. "Gin, there's something we need to talk about."

"What?"

Mom takes out her Altoids case and pops a few in her mouth.

"I'm sorry to tell you this," Dad says, "but the internship at Ciel isn't going to work out."

"Why not?" I ask, suddenly worried that Dad has lost his job.

Dad clears his throat. "Because of Byron's situation and

how the news got out . . . I need to maintain a boundary between my work life and my home life. It's not the time to have my daughter at my workplace."

"Oh," I say.

There goes my dream internship with my fantasy rock star boyfriend, or at least a cool summer job with a pool table and concert tickets.

"The good news," Mom says, "is that I called the manager at Whole Fitness today. You know Gerri, right? She can offer you a part-time job this summer. It'll be good for you. Get some work experience."

"No way," I say. Whole Fakeness? No thanks. "No offense, but that's not my kind of place."

Mom shakes her head. "That's a rash judgment. You haven't even given it a chance."

"Do I have a choice here?" I ask.

"The alternative is that we could look into Outward Bound," Dad says. "Maybe they still have room on one of their hiking expeditions, or even white-water rafting."

I don't say anything. We both know he's got me.

"Tomorrow," Mom says, snapping her Altoids tin shut. "Gerri is expecting you at nine."

# 15

"Fill out this application," Gerri says as she curls hand weights from her hip up to her shoulder, "but it's just a formality. I love your parents. I would do anything for them."

We're in the brightly lit office that's off to one side of the lobby at Whole Fakeness. *Whole Fitness.* I have to start thinking of it as Whole Fitness. Gerri is sitting on a yoga ball behind her desk, and I'm in a plastic chair. I've seen Gerri here before, when Mom has dragged me to the gym with a guest pass, but I've never talked to her. Other than the fact that she's been pumping hand weights the entire time and other than the fact that she looks like she wears workout clothes morning, noon, and night and other than the fact that she's conducting an interview from a yoga ball, she doesn't seem that bad. She's not even as skinny as I thought a Whole Fitness manager would be. She's more of the muscular type.

I write my name, address, and phone number on the application. For the question about previous work history, I write that I've done cat-sitting for neighbors. When the application asks about previous workout history, I write that I go to kickboxing every Friday. I don't mention that I bailed on my last class and will most likely never go again. At the bottom of the application, one question sends a chill up my spine.

Do you consent to Whole Fitness running a background check? We are required to do this for all potential employees.

As I select "yes," I think about my brother. For the rest of his life, when anyone runs a background check on Byron, it will reveal that he's been arrested for sexual assault. For a second, I feel sorry for him. But then I remember yesterday. I know in the big picture, being squirted with windshield-wiper fluid isn't the worst thing. But I've been thinking more and more about how it's small things that add up to the sum total of who people are.

When I'm done, I push the application across the desk to Gerri. She scans it, sets down her weights, and reaches over to shake my hand.

"Welcome to Whole Fitness," she says. She has a tight grip. I practically expect her to start pumping my arm up and down, curling me like a barbell. "Pending the background check, which I'm sure will be fine, you'll be on the morning shift. Don't kill me, but we need someone Monday to Friday from six to noon. Our regular morning person is waitressing at Yellowstone

National Park this summer. You'll be at the front desk swiping IDs and handing out towels. We offer one half-hour break midmorning, and a lot of our staff uses it to work out. But no pressure. Do you want direct deposit or a check? We pay every other Thursday."

I'm staring at her, not sure how to respond. I SO didn't picture my summer going this way, but I'm actually a little excited. My first real job with a real paycheck! Of course, I wish I didn't have to get up before six during summer vacation and I wish my first workplace wasn't a place I hate, but it's not like I have much choice.

"I guess a paycheck?" I say. I have no idea how direct deposit works.

"I'm going to grab some shirts for you," Gerri says as she rises from her yoga ball. "I'll give you a five-day supply so you can wear one every day. Come a little before six tomorrow, and I'll show you the ropes."

I follow her to a supply closet where she pulls out a stack of red shirts with the Whole Fitness logo on the front, a Whole Fitness water bottle, and a Whole Fitness baseball hat. I didn't bring a bag, so I cradle the gear in my arms. As we cross the lobby she says, "Your parents are awesome, by the way. They're some of the first people here every morning. It's so impressive."

"Thanks," I say.

"It's uncanny how much you look like your mom. She's so attractive and smart and has this amazing career. She's told me about her book proposal. I've said to remember us little people when."

I guess Gerri hasn't heard about Byron, and how Mom's career and book proposal are falling apart.

Gerri pauses at the doorway. Now is when I'm supposed to say, *Yeah, my parents are great, my mom is wonderful, I wake up every morning grateful to be in the Shreves family.*

Instead I say, "Okay . . . thanks . . . see you tomorrow."

It's only once I'm on the sidewalk that I realize she said Mom is attractive and I look like Mom. No way. Gerri's brain must be scrambled from so much bouncing on that yoga ball.

🌀 🌀 🌀 🌀

I should text Sebastian. I told him I'd text him when I got back to the city, but I was too nervous last night. Instead I watched a movie on my bed, consumed a bag of Swedish Fish, and promised myself I'd text him in the morning.

Which is now.

I'll just drop off the Whole Fitness stuff at the apartment and then text him.

Once I dump everything on my bed, I realize I need to send a package to Shannon. She told me the resupply stations where she could receive mail along the trail and the approximate dates she'd be there. If I want to reach her at Tuolumne Meadows, then my package has to go out today. I went to Walgreens last night and bought her deodorant, waxing strips, and butt wipes. It's supposed to be a joke, but I figure by the time it gets to her she'll be desperate for sanitation.

I grab a blank notecard from my shelf and try to figure out what to say. I could just say *Hey, how are you, how's the wilderness?* But Shannon and I have our honestly pact, and so I write to her that Froggy and I broke up and I met a new guy. I listen to make sure no one's home and then write who Sebastian is. I seal the letter quickly and then go into my sister's room to get a padded envelope.

Mom's office area is tidy as usual. The book proposal is still on her desk. There's a stack of new white sheets on the bed against the far wall. I'm guessing it's for Anaïs, who is flying home in four days. I wonder if Anaïs is moving back home for a while, or just for the summer so she can take her MCAT prep course. On the phone, she said she wasn't staying long, but she didn't give me any details.

The line at the post office is slow, making it the perfect time to text Sebastian. I already have my phone in my hand because Mom has been texting me about Whole Fitness. She seems thrilled that I'll be working at her gym, like maybe the fitness bug will burrow under my skin and transform me into a workout maniac.

When I get to the front of the line, I hand the package to the postal worker, pay, and walk outside.

It's ten fifteen on a sunny June morning. I have nearly twelve hours of daylight ahead of me and nowhere to be.

And yet I can't text Sebastian.

The thing is, I'm nervous. For one, he's Annie Mills's brother. But it's more than that. It's that I always want to have *this*. *This* being the fact that Sebastian sketched me and called me pretty and asked to see me. What comes next could be good. On the other hand, I could have read the situation wrong and Sebastian just wants me to be his tour guide while he's visiting the city. Or he could see me again and realize he's not attracted to me and he's twenty-thousand leagues out of my league. And then I'll never have this perfect moment again.

But then I'll never see his sea-glass eyes again.

And I'll never see. I'll never see what it could have been. What it could be.

I open my contacts and hit *Fry*.

Hey, it's Leela. Want to meet? I'm free today.

Hey you, he writes back a few seconds later. Welcome back. Yes! Where?

I was thinking a different neighborhood, I write.

I was thinking the same thing. I'm the tourist. You name the place.

My brain flashes to the High Line. That's a mile-and-a-half-long park that runs along the west side of downtown Manhattan. It used to be an elevated train track in the early 1900s but went out of service and eventually became a run-down mess. Around the turn of this century, people got money together and transformed it into a gorgeous elevated park, with wooden walkways interspersed with train tracks, sculptures, and sweeping views of Manhattan. Whenever I've been to the High Line, usually when my parents are showing it to out-of-town guests, I've seen couples holding hands and it always seems so romantic.

Have you heard of the High Line? I write to Sebastian. We could meet at the 23rd Street entrance. There are benches across from the glass elevator.

Glass elevator! Very Willy Wonka. How's 11?

I glance at the time. That's in forty-three minutes. It's not like I was planning an intricate beauty routine, but I thought maybe a shower and some lip gloss.

**Eleven thirty?** I write.

**See you there,** he says. **Across from the great glass elevator.**

I love that he's name-checking Roald Dahl. For some girls it's sexy when a guy bench-presses or throws a football, but he's slaying me with the book references.

ⓖ ⓖ ⓖ ⓖ

"Full disclosure," Sebastian says as soon as I step off the elevator and walk across the wooden pathway.

It's 11:40 and I'm just arriving. It took me longer to get ready because I changed outfits six times, and then the downtown trains were delayed. I had *The Great Gatsby* in my bag, but I was so distracted I read the same paragraph over and over and finally gave up.

"Full disclosure about what?" I ask. I'm trying not to gawk at him, but I totally am. He's even taller than I remembered, like over six feet. He's wearing a T-shirt that shows off his wide shoulders. His blond hair is tucked behind his ear on one side and spilling over his forehead on the other. And his eyes. Out here, in the sunshine, they are blue-green like the Caribbean Sea.

"Can we sit?" he says to me. He crosses his arms over his chest, then uncrosses them, then crosses them again. "I have to say this sitting down."

"Okay . . . ," I say as I sit on a bench next to him.

"For the sake of full disclosure, I'm going to put this out there. I think we should kiss."

My stomach flips over. I totally didn't see that coming.

"Let me explain." He lets out a slow breath. "We have this messed-up family situation, right? Like we have a shitload of awkward between us. And that's making me nervous already. Add to that that I want to kiss you and I'm hoping you want to kiss me. That's making me even more nervous, because you're this attractive, cool New York City girl. So what if we made a decision to get it over with and then we can go on to have a nice afternoon?"

I stare at him. I seriously can't believe this is happening.

"Listen, Leela. *Virginia*. I don't usually talk this much." Sebastian runs his finger up and down the slope of his nose. It's crooked, like maybe he's broken it before. When we met at Absolute Bagel he said he'd broken his wrist twice and cut his face. Maybe he really is clumsy. Which is cute. Everything about him is cute. Even his compulsive talking.

"Okay, that's not true," Sebastian continues. "I do talk a lot. Do you know the Myers-Briggs personality types? I'm an ESFP. Which probably explains why I'm talking so much, so could you please say something to shut me up?"

I don't say anything.

Instead I lean in and kiss him.

As our lips touch, he makes this sound like *mmmmm* and holds the back of my head with his hand, pulling me in. My body goes limp, and I press my lips against his. It flickers through my head that he tastes like ChapStick. Then my brain goes blank and I'm not thinking about anything at all.

"I can't believe we just did that," he says as we pull back.

Our faces are close, and we're both smiling.

"I know."

"Now that that's checked off the list," he says, exhaling loudly, "let's start again. I'm Sebastian Mills. I'm from Regina, Saskatchewan. That's the capital. I just finished high school. And, no, I don't play ice hockey or even ice skate."

"Horrible Things?"

"Exactly. Horrible Things. Sharp blades on the bottom of boots should never have been invented, much less taken onto ice." He pauses and then says, "Anyhoo, tell me about you."

I laugh out loud. He remembers that anyhoo is on my list of Horrible Things! That's what I told him when we were saying good-bye for the first time at the bagel store, before we walked to the cathedral.

"Anyhoo," I say, grinning, "I'm Virginia Shreves."

As soon as he hears my last name, the smile drops from his face.

"Shit," he says.

I know exactly what he's thinking. He's thinking *Shreves*. Byron Shreves. His sister's rapist.

I stare into my lap. I shouldn't be here. We shouldn't be here.

He reaches over and touches my hand. "We could just shut up and kiss all day."

"You said one kiss."

"One kiss for starters," he says. "One to get it over with."

I have to laugh, and when I do, he laughs, too. I wonder if this is how it felt when Lotto and Mathilde met at that party during their senior year at Vassar. Or Jay Gatsby and Daisy Buchanan. No, Virginia! This isn't fiction. This is real life. My life.

"Let's walk." He grabs my hand and pulls me up from the bench. "Let's talk about other things."

"Do you have a dog?" I ask as we start heading south. "I saw it on your phone that time."

At the exact same moment, he says, "Have you ever taken the Myers-Briggs test?"

"What's that?"

Sebastian trips on some raised train tracks and lunges forward. I reach out to catch him, but he grabs a railing to stop himself from falling.

"Are you okay?"

"Story of my life," he says, pushing his hair behind his ear. "The dog is my nana and pop pop's. His name is Buster. They live in Saskatoon, but they're originally from Norway."

Norway. That would explain his size. He's big like a Viking.

I suddenly love Leif Eriksson and Erik the Red and all those other tall Viking people. Also, I love that he has a nana and pop pop. Dad's parents were cold and formal, with a sitting room and a cocktail hour. And other than the obligatory Christmas phone call, Mom barely has contact with her family.

"Last summer, my grandparents drove to Alaska, so Buster came to stay with us. But then my sister was really allergic to dogs, so—" He stops abruptly at the mention of Annie and then says, "Shit."

As we walk on in silence, I point out raised railroad tracks and he maneuvers over them. Conversation is feeling like a minefield. There's just so much we can't say.

"Myers-Briggs," he finally says. He takes some ChapStick from his pocket and slides it across his lips. "It's a personality test where you answer tons of questions and it determines whether you're an introvert or an extrovert, someone who is driven by thinking or feeling. Things like that."

"Oh, I've done that!" I say. Shannon and I used to take personality tests in middle school. "It said I was an introvert."

"But you're so funny," he says.

*I am?* In my head I think of myself as funny, but I've never been able to connect that with what comes out of my mouth.

"No, I get it," Sebastian says. "Being an introvert isn't about how funny you are. It's about getting energy from being alone instead of being around people. A lot of famous comedians are introverts."

"For me, it's definitely alone." I think about how I walk across Central Park to and from school most days just to detox from all the noise and chaos.

"Should I take offense?" Sebastian asks.

I shake my head. "No. I like this." I point out another raised train track, and he steps over it. "I'm guessing you're an extrovert."

"Extroverted Sensing Feeling Perceiving," he says.

"I have no idea what that means."

"Life of the party," he says, grinning. "And the friend to have if you're feeling sad."

"I'll keep that in mind."

Sebastian checks out a sculpture that has strips of red metal swirling into a bell, and I show him where you can see the Statue of Liberty down in the New York Harbor. He pulls out his phone and takes a picture. Then he takes a bunch of pictures of the Empire State Building presiding over the skyline. I guess that's how it is when you don't live in New York City. It's all cool and new.

When we start walking again, I say, "How long are you in the city?"

I'm hoping he doesn't say until tomorrow morning. If he does, I might burst into tears.

"That's the thing," he says.

"What thing?"

"The answer to that question brings us back to the stuff we don't want to talk about." Sebastian pulls out his phone and takes a picture of a New York Water Taxi zipping across the Hudson. Then he takes a few more of the Empire State Building. "Let's move on. Do you have a boyfriend? I'm guessing no because of . . . well . . . before."

"Before?" I ask. I know he's referring to the kiss, but I'm teasing him.

"Anyhoo."

"I did," I say. "We broke up."

"Recently?"

I clear my throat. It's weird to think that Froggy and I were together when I first met Sebastian. But it also feels like the bagel store was a million years ago, before Byron got arrested, before school ended. "We broke up last Monday. A week ago."

He grins. "So I'm the rebound guy. That's cool. I'll take it."

"I didn't say that!" I say, swatting his arm. "So what about you?"

"I had a girlfriend. It's over."

"When?"

He shrugs. I decide not to push it.

A couple stops us and asks if we'll take their picture. They're probably in their twenties and wearing dresses and Birkenstocks. As Sebastian snaps a few pictures, it hits me that they probably think we're a couple, too.

"Want us to take yours?" the taller one says in a thick German accent as Sebastian hands her phone back.

Sebastian and I both shake our heads. We can't be in pictures together. Too risky. Annie knows what I look like.

As we walk on in silence, I decide that it's a shitload of awkward but it's worse not to talk about it.

"My brother doesn't remember doing it," I finally say. "He was really drunk that night. His name is Byron, but you probably know that. I also have an older sister. Her name is Anaïs. She's been in Africa for the past two years, and she's getting home Friday. Honestly, I don't know what to say about my brother. He's self-centered and sort of an asshole, but it's still awful. Like, he could go to jail and have to register as a sex offender. I'm not saying he shouldn't be punished, but it's awful."

"You're right." Sebastian nods. "It's awful."

I can't say how grateful I am to hear that. Because it's a terrible situation and I wish I could turn back the clock and make it not happen. But I couldn't control the fact that Byron got drunk and forced a friend to have sex with him. Neither could Sebastian. And yet we are somehow pulled into the mess.

Then again, we wouldn't have met again if I hadn't gone to the Hungarian Pastry Shop and I wouldn't have gone to the Hungarian Pastry Shop if Annie hadn't pressed charges. So we have THAT to thank for being together today. Which is bizarre.

After a long silence, Sebastian says, "I'm supposed to go to Columbia in the fall. I got in and got offered a lot of financial aid. There's a fine arts teacher I really want to work with, and I've always wanted to go to the school where my sister went. She'll be a senior when I'm a freshman." Sebastian pushes back his hair, and then says, "My parents are both teachers who have the summer off. The plan was that we were all going to spend the summer in New York City, help me get settled in. We sublet a place in Morningside Heights for two months. But then Annie started having a really hard time and she went to the police and things have changed."

"Like how?"

"We're definitely staying for the summer to support Annie during the legal stuff, but my parents are pushing hard for me not to go to Columbia after all. Annie has a year left, so she has to finish. But they're done with Columbia. They want me to go to the University of Saskatchewan next year and then transfer if I want."

"Wow."

"I know," he says. "We've been fighting a lot. My mom is making us go to family therapy. The thing is, my sister has a history of anxiety and depression, and it's gotten bad this year because of . . ."

As he trails off, I don't say anything. I can't believe Sebastian is supposed to go to Columbia in the fall. Columbia is thirty blocks from my apartment. Then again, he could go to the University of Saskatchewan, which may as well be thirty thousand miles away.

"Shit." Sebastian punches one hand into the other.

"What?"

"I shouldn't have told you about my sister and the depression."

"Why not?"

"What if you tell your brother's lawyer and he uses it against my sister, like she's mentally unstable and might not be telling the truth?"

"And I shouldn't have told you anything about Byron when what I say could result in him going to jail." I shake my head. "Besides, I'd never tell anyone what you said."

"Neither would I." Sebastian takes my hand. "I really like you, Leela, but I honestly don't know what the hell we should do."

We're standing in front of a low wooden lounge chair. I sit on the edge and tug Sebastian's arm. He falls down after me, practically tumbling onto my lap.

"We should kiss," I say.

And so we do.

# 16

I know what's going on," Gerri says grimly. It's a little after six on Tuesday morning, my first day of work. She's just shown me how to swipe IDs, how to greet members, and where to book sessions with personal trainers. Right after the laundry guy arrived to unload the towels behind the front desk, Gerri gestured me into her office and closed the door.

"I want you to know that I know what's going on," she adds, "and I'll keep it between us. I won't talk about it with your parents."

I freeze, my stomach in knots. I can't look at her, so I stare at the yoga ball. It says *Property of Gerri Goldberg!!!!* on it in Sharpie. I have no idea how Gerri found out about yesterday with Sebastian. We didn't take pictures together, and we stayed downtown the whole afternoon, and we even rode separate subway cars back to the Upper West Side. Even if she *did* see us together, how could she know he's forbidden?

"I can tell you're upset," Gerri says. She picks up her weights but holds them steady at her waist. "It's just . . . I googled your name yesterday. I do that for all potential employees to make sure nothing horrible jumps out on social media, and the articles on your brother came up. On what happened."

I fill my cheeks with air and slowly exhale. She's talking about Byron's arrest, not Sebastian and me. Phew. I guess.

"I can't imagine what your family is going through," Gerri says. "I know your mom values family so much. This must be really hard for her."

I nod even though it's more like Mom values the *image* of family. The news leak on Byron's arrest is messing up the whole image thing.

"That's why I wanted you to know that I won't discuss it with her," Gerri says. "A gym should be a safe place for every member."

"Thanks," I say.

Again, not entirely in agreement. A gym feeling safe? Too many full-length mirrors and toned thighs and empty treadmills taunting me like, *WE are the equipment standing between you and a better body.*

Gerri curls her weights up to her shoulders. "Moving on?"

I nod gratefully.

"Let's talk towels. We've got a towel-inventory problem

161

here. All gyms do. We figure that for every twenty-five people who walk through the door, two will walk out with a towel. And it adds up, you know? We buy high-quality towels here. Thick and plush."

I nod like I know, even though I don't. I've never given much thought to towels other than to hate the little ones that don't make it around my body.

"I'd love to eliminate our towel service altogether and have members bring their own," Gerri says. "We lose a lot of money on this. But we're a high-end private gym, and people want their towels."

As Gerri talks, she's pumping her weights harder and harder. She's really passionate about this towel thing.

I take a sip of water from my Whole Fitness bottle.

"I've looked into towel trackers," she adds, "but we think members would take offense at that. So basically you should just give each person one towel. Two if they request it. And when they leave you smile brightly and hope they don't have a towel stuffed in their bag."

"Can I ask them?"

Gerri shakes her head. "People pay a lot for membership here. They don't want to feel accused."

"Okay," I say, shrugging. Whole Fakeness all over again. People steal towels but take offense at being accused of it.

Gerri sets down her weights. "Ready to start work?"

I nod and follow her out to the lobby. A few minutes later, I'm perched on a stool behind the front desk when my parents come through the door. Dad waves and Mom breezes over and air-kisses Gerri, who is signing invoices on a clipboard.

"How's Virginia doing?" Mom asks, smiling brightly.

Looking at Mom now it would be impossible to see that she just spent the weekend holed up in her bedroom in Connecticut. Whenever she emerged, somber and serious, she'd embark on hours of downward dogs and sun salutations on the living room rug.

"She's wonderful," Gerri says as she hands them both a towel.

"May I have two?" Dad asks.

"Of course!" Gerri passes him a second towel.

Looking at Gerri, you would have no idea about her towel woes or that she knows of Byron's arrest.

As I swipe my parents' IDs, I say, "Welcome, Phyllis and Mike."

"Perfect," Gerri says, nodding.

Dad takes a picture of me, and Mom leans in and kisses my forehead. I smile back at them. Maybe whole fakeness is okay every now and then.

ⓖ ⓖ ⓖ ⓖ

As soon as I finish my shift, I dodge into a bathroom, stuff my shorts and Whole Fitness shirt into my bag, pull on a sundress, and then walk to the downtown train. I transfer to the R at Times Square and take it to Canal Street. I told Sebastian to meet me on the corner of Canal and Mulberry. I'm going to show him Chinatown.

I climb the crowded stairs from the subway, my stomach churning. What if yesterday was a fluke? What if Sebastian sees me again and he's no longer interested?

But then I see him. He's wearing sunglasses and a straw hat, and he's reading a subway map, all huge and unfolded. I didn't even know they made paper subway maps anymore.

"Leela!" he says, smiling as he sees me. He attempts to fold the map, but it's not cooperating, so he crumples it messily and stuffs it in his pocket.

"Hey," I say, grinning at him. "Are you trying to look like a tourist with that map?"

He takes off his sunglasses and hooks them over the collar of his shirt. "I'd like to see you get around Saskatchewan without a map."

"There are these things called phones," I say. "They actually have subway maps in them."

"Snob." He lifts my chin up with his hand, leans down, and kisses me.

I kiss him back. Cars are honking and people and bikes are streaming by us. I think about that German couple from the High Line yesterday. If they saw us now, they'd definitely think we are a couple.

Sebastian takes my hand, and we start walking. We cross over Canal Street, and I lead him down Mulberry. I point out windows with pinkish-brownish duck carcasses hanging suspended from the ceiling and trinket shops with cheap fidget spinners and plastic frogs swimming in tubs of water.

"It's like going to another country," he says in awe.

"I know. That's what I love about Chinatown."

We stop in a candy store, and I buy some chewy ginger candies and Sour Patch Kids. I've decided that my next care package for Shannon will be sweets instead of bathroom-themed items. Sebastian gets a bag of cola gummies that we share on the walk over to Tasty Dumpling. When we get to the counter, I order us fried pork dumplings and scallion pancakes.

"Okay, these are incredible," he says as he plunges his second dumpling in soy sauce. "And I'd say these scallion pancakes are the best ever, but I've never had them before so I have nothing to compare them to."

"You've never had scallion pancakes?" I ask incredulously. Scallion pancakes are one of life's great indulgences, and it's a tragedy to go eighteen years without ever having them.

I tell him this.

"Seventeen," he says. "I turn eighteen in September. What about you?"

"I'm sixteen," I say. "March."

"Barely legal," he says jokingly.

We both freeze. I hug my arms around my middle. Definite conversation minefield for us.

As he pops another dumpling in his mouth, I dip a triangle of scallion pancake into soy sauce. While part of my brain is here with Sebastian, another part is thinking about rule number 2.5 from the list I made up called How to Make Sure Skinny Girls Aren't the Only Ones Who Have Boyfriends. Sebastian isn't my boyfriend and I'm not his girlfriend, but kissing means we're something. And my rule number 2.5 was that I'm not supposed to eat in front of a guy I'm having something with. But as I'm simultaneously enjoying the Chinese food and being here with Sebastian, I'm also creating a new version of rule number 2.5 in my head.

## WHY RULE NUMBER 2.5 SUCKS AND SHOULD BE IGNORED AND I SHOULDN'T STARVE MYSELF (EVEN IF THE BOY IS REALLY CUTE AND A GOOD KISSER):

1. I'm hungry. I've been up since 5:20 this morning and just had a banana and I need to eat.
2. Torture = watching someone else eat scallion pancakes at Tasty Dumpling and not having one. Or three.
3. I'm sick of pretending to be someone I'm not (i.e., a person who doesn't eat). I want to be myself (i.e., a person who eats) around Sebastian.
4. I wrote How to Make Sure Skinny Girls Aren't the Only Ones Who Have Boyfriends so I can edit it. Better yet, I can delete the whole thing. Fuck How to Make Sure Skinny Girls Aren't the Only Ones Who Have Boyfriends. And while I'm at it, I'm sick of thinking in terms of skinny and fat. What about being a curvaceous chick? Much better. Sexier. More luscious.

When we leave Tasty Dumplings, we cross into the park. The old Chinese women are line dancing. A boom box is plugged into speakers and blasting disco music. The women are holding colorful fans, and it looks like they're doing the electric slide.

"What's up with the dancing ladies?" Sebastian asks.

I shrug. "They're always here. I don't think it's a class. I think they just meet up and dance."

We watch them for a few minutes. They must be seventy or eighty years old, with short hair, no-nonsense T-shirts, and sweatpants. None of them are smiling as they step from side to side, swiveling their fans in the air.

"Are they even having fun?" Sebastian asks.

"I think so. I think it's a cultural thing. Americans feel like they always have to smile to show they're happy or even when they're not happy to show that they're pretending to be happy. Down here, it's different. That's why I like it."

I tell him my Chinatown theory, about how I feel more comfortable here where I'm obviously different than uptown in the elite private-school culture where I'm supposed to fit in but totally don't.

"Why don't you fit in up there?"

"Isn't it obvious?" I say. Yes, there's the purple-and-green hair and the eyebrow ring. But that's not the big reason. Emphasis on "big."

He watches me, waiting for an answer.

I cross my arms and quickly say, "I don't exactly have the ideal body type."

"Is there an ideal type? And who's making that decision?"

I don't answer. It's not like I'm going to spell it out for him, how Brie routinely mocks my body, how Cole could only be attracted to me if he's a chubby chaser, how Mom wants me to eat salad for every meal, how Dad only compliments skinny women's bodies.

"I think you're awesome," Sebastian says. He takes my arms and unwraps them, placing my hands on his shoulders. "When I first saw you I thought you looked like a superhero. I still do. Besides, you're talking to a Canadian who thinks winter sports are Horrible Things. Talk about not fitting in."

"But that's hardly—"

"No buts." He leans over and plants a soft kiss on my lips. As he does, he slides his hand along the back of my dress, lower and lower. "Actually this butt. I'll take this butt."

I tighten my arms around his neck and kiss him back, hard and deep.

☙ ☙ ☙ ☙

When I get out of work on Wednesday, we decide to meet in Brooklyn Heights and walk across the Brooklyn Bridge to Manhattan. Sebastian is wearing his straw hat again. He told me he bought it from a street vendor yesterday morning. He seemed proud about that fact, like he's a real New Yorker. As we're walking, I tell him how when the bridge opened to the public in 1883, it was the longest-ever suspension bridge and the first bridge to connect Brooklyn to Manhattan. Back in elementary school, teachers devoted half of every year to the history of New York City. Back then, it felt tedious, but it's actually fun to be a tour guide. I can tell Sebastian is impressed.

Partway across the bridge, he whips out his phone and starts taking pictures of the Empire State Building.

I take his elbow so he doesn't trip while he's walking and shooting. "What's with you and the Empire State Building?" I ask.

He laughs. "Total tourist moment?"

"Sort of."

"Here's the thing. My whole life I've seen the Empire State Building as this symbol of New York City, and now I'm here looking at it." He takes another picture. "Remember that children's book *Olivia*?"

"I think so," I say.

"Remember how Olivia's mom takes her to the beach and she sculpts her sand castle into the Empire State Building? And remember how King Kong climbs the Empire State Building? And Spider-Man, too. And even *Futurama*! They call it the Vampire State Building, but it's obvious that's what it is."

I touch a padlock clipped to a gate on the side on the bridge. "What's with you and children's books? Like *Olivia*? And you mentioned Willy Wonka before and Winnie-the-Pooh and *A Wrinkle in Time*."

He tucks his phone back in his pocket and takes my hand. "I'm obsessed with all children's books but mostly picture books. I think they're the perfect art form. The good ones, that is. I love the way the words complement the illustrations and the illustrations complement the words."

"I never thought of it that way," I say. "Almost like a movie."

Sebastian nods. "I'd love to illustrate picture books someday. Maybe write my own. That's one of the reasons I want to go to Columbia. There's a fine arts professor there who's also a children's book illustrator. He's seen my portfolio. He thinks I have potential."

"Seriously?" I ask. That has to be the coolest thing in the world. And to think that he drew me! I have proof on my phone. "That's amazing."

"Yeah. Well." He frowns and squints into the sunlight. "It may not happen, though. Columbia."

"Oh. Right."

We walk quietly for a bit. We're halfway across the bridge, with Brooklyn behind us, Manhattan in front of us, airplanes above us, and boats in the East River below us. It's pretty extraordinary to take in all at once.

After a few minutes, I say, "I think I want to be a writer. I'm not sure what kind, like fiction or nonfiction. Honestly I've never said it out loud before, so if I become an accountant or a dentist don't hold it against me."

"No, that's awesome. Do you write stuff now?"

"A little. Lists mostly. Rants." I tell him about the blog I started with Alyssa over the winter. That's where I used to write some of my lists. I haven't written any down since we put the blog on hold to focus on schoolwork. Now I just think the lists in my head. I don't mention that Froggy was the graphic designer for the blog. It's not a secret, but I don't feel the need to bring Froggy into the conversation. Sebastian still hasn't talked about his ex-girlfriend, so I haven't asked.

"More than anything," I say, "I'm happiest when I'm reading. And maybe it sounds random, but I feel like I have stories to tell."

I can't believe I'm sharing this. It's been in my head for so long, these vague shadowy thoughts that I've never exposed to daylight.

"I can totally see that," Sebastian says. He takes his Chap-Stick out of his pocket and slides it across his lips. I'm starting to think he's addicted. Not that I mind. Anything having to do with his lips is fine with me. "You're an introvert. You could be like Virginia Woolf, just without the depression."

I giggle. "No stones in the pockets."

"No wading into rivers." Sebastian tips his hat forward so it's shading his eyes. "Speaking of children's books, you know what this reminds me of?"

I shake my head. I have a sudden urge to grab on to Sebastian, to kiss those ChapSticked lips, to press my body into him. Just thinking about it gives me a pulsing feeling between my legs.

"You're going to think *this* sounds random," Sebastian continues, oblivious that I'm mentally undressing him, "but remember *The Very Hungry Caterpillar*?"

I force myself back to reality. "Like where the caterpillar crawls around and eats something every day?"

Sebastian nods. "Yeah. Like on Monday we went to the High Line. That was our apple. On Tuesday we went to China-town. That was two pears."

"What did the caterpillar eat on Wednesday?"

Sebastian scratches his chin. "Today was three plums, I think."

"How do you remember that?"

"I told you. This is my thing." Sebastian fixes his eyes on me and takes both of my hands in his. When he speaks, his voice is low and sexy. "Remember how every day, after his meal, he was still hungry? That's how I feel every time we say good-bye."

We smile at each other. Maybe he *did* know I was mentally undressing him, because he's running his fingers across my shoulders, down my bare arms, up my sides toward my breasts. I can see he's looking at my cleavage, so I press my chest into him. As I do, he takes me in his arms and kisses me.

When we finally come up for air, I say, "Didn't the hungry caterpillar go into a cocoon after all that eating?"

"Yep," he says.

I stand up on my tiptoes, and we start kissing again. It would be nice to go into a cocoon with Sebastian. No Byron, no Annie. Not my parents or his parents or the lawyer Mark Levy or the district attorney or any of the reasons we should have no contact with each other. Not even Shannon, who'd probably say it's stupid I'm hooking up with Sebastian, or Alyssa, who'd tell me to call Froggy and see if he'll take me back.

As we continue walking, I steal Sebastian's straw hat and wear it the rest of the way across the Brooklyn Bridge.

ⓖ ⓖ ⓖ ⓖ

On Thursday morning, as I'm swiping IDs and greeting members by name, I attempt to count the towels that I hand out. Gerri is right. There's a definite hemorrhaging of fluffy white towels. Some members ask for two or even three. When I see them exit the gym ninety minutes later, all shiny cheeked and showered, they rarely toss a towel into the bins outside the locker rooms. Of course a lot of people are putting wet towels in the bins stationed near the showers, but they could also be adding them to their fluffy white towel collection at home.

Gerri sighs heavily as a bald guy wearing a pinstriped suit walks out of the gym.

"He took two towels when he came in," she says grumpily.

I watch him go. His name is Richard. He comes in every morning in track pants and leaves in a suit. "Don't you think he put them in the laundry bin?"

"Probably, but who knows?" Gerri pumps fast at her hand weights. "It's not like he even has any hair to dry that would justify the two towels."

I start to laugh but then cover my mouth with my hand. This towel thing is really irking her.

As soon as I get off work, I walk down to Fairway and buy a baguette, a block of cheddar cheese, and some hard salami. Before I left the apartment this morning, I smuggled a cutting board, a knife wrapped in a dish towel, and a picnic blanket into my backpack. Sebastian is bringing fruit, drinks, and dessert and we're going to meet at the Botanical Garden and have a picnic.

When Sebastian proposed the idea of a picnic it sounded

like something out of a fairy tale in the English countryside. He told how he read about the Botanical Garden, and thought it would be a good place to hang out, sketch, and be anonymous.

It's a forever train ride up to the Bronx, and then I take a city bus to the garden. When I mapped it out last night I was tempted to suggest we meet at the subway station and travel there together. But then I heard Mom and Dad in the living room having a conversation about Byron's legal woes and I decided no. I have to keep these worlds apart.

Even though Byron has been in Connecticut all week, it hasn't taken the problem away. When my parents were talking last night, Dad was telling Mom that he talked to Mark Levy. Mark told him that the district attorney still hasn't responded to our lawyer's request to settle out of court. If they don't work out a plea bargain, Byron will go to trial for sexual assault.

Then I heard Dad say that Mark Levy told him that the Mills family could also pursue a civil suit against Byron. If he's found guilty in a civil suit, we'd have to pay them a large financial sum to cover damages.

I put my knuckle in my mouth and tried not to listen to the part about the Mills family. They were talking loudly, though. It was hard to tune it out.

"What kind of damages?" Mom asked nervously. "Do you think she's doing this because she wants our money? Can Mark figure out what her parents do for a living?"

*She*. Sebastian's sister. *Her parents*. Sebastian's parents.

It's weird how I know that his parents are teachers. It's weird how I know they're in New York City for the summer.

When I took my hand out of my mouth, I had bite marks on my knuckles. I reached for my headphones, slid them on, and blasted the music.

᪥  ᪥  ᪥  ᪥

"My sister is getting home from Africa tomorrow," I tell Sebastian. "Well, officially from London, but before that she was in Burkina Faso for two years. We're picking her up from the airport in the morning."

We've finished eating the bread and cheese and salami and drinking the bottles of iced tea. Now we're resting on the picnic blanket on a sloping hill above the rose garden. The sweet scent of lilac is in the air. I swear, I could close my eyes and be in the English countryside. Not that I've ever been to the English countryside, but I could easily picture it to be like this, complete with a beautiful guy wearing a straw hat.

"Anaïs, right?" he asks.

I nod. "As in Anaïs Nin, the French poet. My mom is a literature snob. And a francophone snob, too."

"Another snob," Sebastian says, laughing. "Like mother, like daughter."

I swat his arm with my hand. "Don't even say that! My mom and I are polar opposites."

Seriously. If there were geographic locations farther apart than the North and South Pole, that would be Mom and me.

Sebastian rolls over on his side so he's facing me. His hair is hanging over his face. I reach up and tuck it behind his ear and then touch the scar on his cheek. He told me the other day that he got it during a snowboarding wipeout and had to be taken down the hill on a stretcher.

"What's your sister like?" Sebastian asks.

"It's been so long since I've seen her," I say. "She's really pretty. Like people used to say she should be a model. She was premed at Brown and wanted to go to medical school but decided to take time off and do the Peace Corps. Also—" I watch some clouds drift by, all wispy like cotton candy. There's something I want to tell Sebastian, but I can't think of how to say it without it sounding weird.

"What?"

I shake my head. Sebastian's hat is on the blanket next to my shoulder. I grab it and put it over my face so he can't see me.

He quickly snatches off the hat. "You may be cute with your obsession with my hat, but if you don't tell me what you were going to say I'm going to have to tickle it out of you."

I giggle and attempt to wriggle away, but he's rolled part way on me, pinning me down. He waggles his fingers over my underarms like he's about to tickle me. I'm laughing and shrieking. Eventually he slides off me and kisses me hard. I kiss him hard right back.

After a few minutes, Sebastian says, "What were you going to tell me before? About your sister?"

I shake my head. "It's just that when I met *your* sister last year she reminded me of Anaïs. That's all."

The other day, I told him about how I went up to Columbia in December to apologize to Annie for what happened. I wasn't sure how much he already knew, but I wanted him to hear it from me.

"How does she remind you of Annie?" he asks curiously.

I nibble at a strawberry, thinking. He brought a container of berries and shortbread cookies, too.

"Long hair," I finally say, dropping the green strawberry top onto a paper towel and rubbing off my fingers. "Confident. Independent."

Sebastian opens his sketch pad and grabs a few pastels out of a pencil bag.

"What?" I ask.

"It's just weird, that's all."

I think about how Dad told Mom that his family might sue my family. It's not his family and my family, though. It's Annie and Byron. But what if my parents run out of money paying them a large financial sum and can't send me to college? Then it *is* me, too.

I sigh heavily. "I know."

"We're doing this family therapy session tomorrow," he says. He begins swirling light green across the page, punctuated by streaks of brown. "I'm dreading it. Annie's having a really hard time. She says there's no point in talking about it, that nothing will make it better. My parents want to meet with Columbia about getting a refund on my tuition, but they're also saying they'd consider forfeiting the money they've put down for me. No one but me can see how Annie's issues and my going to Columbia aren't related."

Sebastian picks up a white pastel but then sets it down

again. "Annie's like how you described. She was the first girl in our high school to skate as well as the guys and to describe herself as a feminist. I was a freshman when she was a senior."

I nod. Anaïs also identifies as a feminist. I am, too, though I don't go around declaring it. It just means you think women deserve the same rights and privileges as men. Putting it that way, I can't imagine a woman not being a feminist.

Sebastian glances across the sloped lawn at a lilac bush and then reaches for a pale purple pastel. "But my sister's also . . . she can be prickly. She's not this tragic victim who is only nice and sweet and good. That's not real life." He shakes his head. "We shouldn't talk about her, I guess."

As Sebastian goes back to drawing, I pull *The Great Gatsby* out of my bag and lie on my side with the book propped on the blanket next to me. It's been such a hazy few days that I'm rereading the early chapters to remember what's going on.

"What?" Sebastian asks.

I touch my finger against the page to hold my spot. "What *what*?"

"You said 'wow.' "

"No, I didn't," I say. I totally didn't.

"Need another tickle to prove it?"

I glance at him. He's smiling, which makes me realize that I must have said "wow," because I thought "wow" in my head. I point to a line in the book. Sebastian leans in, and we read it together: *It was one of those rare smiles with a quality of eternal reassurance in it, that you may come across four or five times in life.*

"Nick is describing Gatsby, but when I read it I thought of you," I tell him. "Of your smile. Of how it makes me feel."

He sets down his sketch pad. "Virginia."

"Yeah?"

"You're awesome."

"I know," I say, laughing uncomfortably.

"I'm serious. You're not like the girls back home. Okay, that sounds stupid. But you're not. You're real. I know we're not talking about my sister, but I love that you went up to Columbia to apologize to her even though you didn't do anything wrong. You think deeply about things. You're not scared to say what's on your mind. I don't know, it's just . . ."

As he trails off, I nod. Even though this is totally not how I am with the rest of the world, I feel like I'm my best self around Sebastian.

"What about your ex-girlfriend?" I ask. It just came out. Or maybe I wanted it to. After all, I'm the girl who's not scared to say what's on her mind.

"Maddie." Sebastian flops down next to me and covers his face with the straw hat. His fingers are smudged with several shades of pastels. "She cheated on me with a guy she went snowmobiling with. She singlehandedly obliterated my ability to ever trust again."

"Wow."

"Yeah. Atomic. Especially for a clumsy ESFP who couldn't snowmobile to save his life."

I lace my fingers through his. After a minute, he lifts the hat off his face.

"I feel the same way about you," he says. "Your smile of eternal reassurance."

Since I'm on an honesty kick, I blurt out, "After we pick up my sister tomorrow, we're going to Connecticut. I won't be back until Monday. I'm going to miss you."

"Three days?"

"Three and a half."

"We're on strawberry, by the way," he says.

I glance at the container of berries, trying to make sense of what he just said.

"The very hungry caterpillar," Sebastian adds. "Today is the day when he eats four strawberries."

"Then what?"

"Then there's an epic food binge coming."

I giggle. "Sounds fun."

We stay at the Botanical Garden for the rest of the afternoon, wandering around, sketching, reading, kissing. On the bus to the subway, he gives me his straw hat to borrow for the weekend. We take the subway to 125th Street together, but then I get out and switch to a separate car for the rest of the ride back to the Upper West Side.

# 17

My sister's plane is landing at Kennedy airport around noon. Gerri lets me do a half shift and leave the gym at nine. After finishing at Whole Fitness, I quickly swing by the post office and mail a package to Shannon. I address it to a place called South Lake Tahoe. It's about 150 miles from the Tuolumne Meadows stop, where I sent her last package. This time I'm sending the Chinatown candies, a few packs of gum, and orange Tic Tacs. I wait until I'm in line at the post office to scribble a note on the back of a flyer for a personal trainer who works at the gym.

Dear Shannon,

Hey there, pooping-in-the-woods woman! How's the hike? Have you been chased by any bears? Anaïs is getting home today! We're picking her up from the airport as soon as I mail this. My dad says I can't do the internship at Ciel because of the Byron stuff so I'm working at Whole Fitness instead. Before you die of total shock I'll tell you that it's actually not so bad. Sometimes, during breaks, I take a small walk on a treadmill. Not 150 miles of rugged terrain like you, but still. Being on workout equipment hasn't caused me to barf in disgust.

Also, remember that guy I wrote about in my last letter? Sebastian? I'm going to write this and then send it before I can take it back.

I might be falling in love with him.

Now, eat this letter. Or burn it in a campfire. Or, no! Use it for much-needed toilet paper.

Love,

Virginia

I write that one sentence really tiny, like if she doesn't look hard enough she might not see it, like if I write it full size then it might be full-size true. And it's hard to imagine that full-size thing truly happening to me.

On the drive to the airport, I keep imagining the moment we see Anaïs. I wonder if I'll feel comfortable around her. My big sister was the one who told me about boys and what sex is actually like versus what it says in the puberty books Mom gave us. Yet thinking about her now, she seems like a stranger. Also, I hope she doesn't let it slip that I told her about Byron's arrest. I know she wouldn't intentionally, but like she said on the phone last week, she's out of practice with the way we keep secrets in our family.

I push my seat belt to the side and wiggle my phone out of my shorts pocket. I consider texting Sebastian but decide not to with my parents so close. In the front seat, Mom is typing furiously at her phone. Dad is entering something into GPS. I open the Notes app and start writing. Ever since I told Sebastian I want to be a writer I've been jotting lists on my phone, in my computer, on random scraps of paper at the gym. Maybe someday I'll publish a book of lists and it will become a bestseller and I'll go on a book tour. Now that Mom's "Purple Hair and Piercings" proposal has been scrapped, I am my only hope for fame and fortune. Anyway, here goes for today:

## A CURVACEOUS CHICK'S MUSINGS ON FULL-SIZE LOVE

1. When I think about S., I smile with eternal reassurance.
2. I love that I can be myself around him and he makes me laugh and I make him laugh.
3. I love that he's a klutz.
4. I love kissing him, ChapStick and all.
5. I clutched his straw hat while I was falling asleep last night. I'm guessing it's the only time in history that a straw hat has been tenderly hugged.

"Gin," Dad says sharply. "Enough with the phone. It's not becoming of your generation the way you're always texting or playing video games. Just look out the window and be in your head for a while."

Stunned, I drop my phone into my lap. "I wasn't playing a video game."

"Well, then texting. Your generation is never going to learn the art of conversation if you're on your phones all the time."

I stare out the window, my hands clenched, my fingernails digging into my palms. At first, I think *it's no use trying to explain myself.* Then I remember what Sebastian said, about how he likes that I'm the kind of girl who speaks her mind.

"Did you know I actually hate video games?" I say to Dad. "I think they're a waste of time, and I never play them."

Dad glances quickly in his rearview mirror and then shifts lanes.

"Besides," I add, "look at Mom. She's on her phone. And you're always on your phone. How is that different? Also, I didn't realize I represent the unbecomingness of my whole generation."

Mom sets her phone in the center console but doesn't say a word.

"Are you talking back?" Dad asks.

Just then, a van slows in front of us and Dad hits the brakes too hard.

"Mike, easy," Mom says as she loosens the seat belt from her neck area.

"Don't be a back seat driver," he mutters.

"I don't think it's talking back to say that you guys are on your phones a lot," I say. "Don't you want me to have an opinion? Also, what if I told you that I want to be a writer and I'm actually doing creative writing on my phone, not texting and playing games?"

We pass a sign for Kennedy airport. Dad flicks his signal and then says, "Listen, I'm sorry. I'm under a lot of stress right now. We all are."

I'm about to say "it's okay," but the truth is that it's not okay. I hate the way I'm the punching bag whenever my parents are stressed. Instead, I open Notes and add one final line.

6. Forget what Dad said about how I'm NOT becoming. I want to think about what I am becoming. About what we are becoming.

⸰ ⸰ ⸰ ⸰

A few minutes after noon, Anaïs emerges through the doors of customs. When we see her long brown hair and beaming smile, we hop up, waving and running toward her. She's wearing a floor-length white dress and she looks as beautiful as always, with her big brown eyes, high cheekbones, and lean elegant body.

Mom gets the first hug, then Dad, and then me. As she squeezes me tight, I breathe her in and I'm transported back to Anaïs helping me with my eighth-grade science fair project or teaching me how to ride a bike when everyone else in my family gave up.

"Look at you, all grown up with your purple-and-green hair," Anaïs says.

My face is pressed tight in her shoulder and my eyes are teary. "I did it myself."

"I love it."

When we let go, I can see that Anaïs is crying, too, and so are Mom and Dad. They didn't want her to go into the Peace Corps because it delayed her medical school plans, but I know they were also worried about her safety being in a remote village in Burkina Faso.

"Sweetie." Mom clasps my sister's cheeks with her hands and leans in close. "You look gorgeous. How's your health? I love your dress."

"We're so glad you're home," Dad says, smiling. He looks genuinely happy for the first time since Byron's arrest, or possibly for the first time since before the dean of students called last fall to say that Byron was getting suspended from Columbia.

Anaïs wipes her eyes and then looks to her side. That's when I notice that the whole time we've been hugging, a woman with curly red hair has been standing next to my sister, backpack on her shoulders, smile on her face.

"Guys," Anaïs says, "this is Lindsey. Lindsey, this is my family. Except for my brother. Where is Byron, anyway? Wasn't he going to come?"

"He's in Connecticut," Mom says quickly. "You'll see him tomorrow."

Lindsey sticks out her hand. "Nice to meet you. Ana has told me so much about you."

Dad shakes her hand first, then Mom, and then me. She has

one of those smiles that reveal her top teeth and a pink strip of gums, too. I wonder what she's heard about us, the real story or the picture-perfect variety. I have a feeling Mom is wondering the same thing because she's watching Lindsey closely, studying her jeans and tank top, her sneakers, the freckles across the bridge of her nose.

"Were you in the Peace Corps together?" Dad asks.

At the same time, Mom says, "Anaïs, you didn't mention you were bringing a friend home."

Anaïs says, "We were both in the Gurunsi region but in different villages."

At the same time, Lindsey laughs and says, "Oh, no, I'm not coming home with you. My aunt lives in Brooklyn. I'm going to her place. Ana and I were in London visiting my parents and we flew in on the same flight."

Mom visibly exhales. She likes houseguests when she can be in show-off mode, flaunting our beautiful apartment and her successful children. But now, with everything going on with Byron, it's not show-and-tell time.

I, on the other hand, am still holding my breath because I just realized that Lindsey calls my sister "Ana." But it's more than that. It's the way they're smiling at each other. I know that smile. It's a smile of eternal reassurance.

Mom must be picking up on it, too, because she says, "You said you're friends from the Peace Corps?"

Anaïs takes Lindsey's hand and holds it up to her chest. "Lindsey is my girlfriend from the Peace Corps."

Enter: Utter silence. Pin-drop silence. The most silence that has ever occurred in the baggage claim area at Kennedy airport's international terminal.

⑥ ⑥ ⑨ ⑥

Mom and Dad are pros at the fakey-nicey thing, so they quickly recover. They hug Lindsey and ask her all these questions like how long she and my sister have been together, and whether she grew up in London, and where she's staying in Brooklyn.

Lindsey tells them that she and my sister have been friends since they entered the Peace Corps, but have only been together for three months. She grew up in California with her mom and stepdad. Her dad and stepmom live in London. Her aunt has an apartment in Park Slope. That's where she stays when she comes to New York City.

As we lug Anaïs's and Lindsey's enormous duffels off the baggage carousel and heave them onto carts, Lindsey compliments my hair and tells me she can't wait to get to know me more. She's definitely talking a lot. I wonder if she's nervous, or if she's an extrovert, or both. Ever since I met Sebastian, I've been thinking more about personality types.

We walk Lindsey to the taxi line and then give them some space to say good-bye. I watch Lindsey rise onto her toes to kiss Anaïs on the lips, and I see other people looking, too. I wonder if they're staring in a homophobic way or a curious way, like it's not every day you see two women kissing in public. I'm definitely in the curious camp.

Once we're in the car, with my parents in the front and Anaïs and me in the back, Mom says, "You could have given us some warning."

"Warning makes it sound like a bad thing," Anaïs says. "I wanted to surprise you. We did the same with Lindsey's parents, and they were thrilled."

I glance sideways at my sister. Her dress is embroidered with tiny cream-colored flowers and she's wearing leather sandals. Her face is tan and she has creases around her eyes. Seeing her close up like this, she definitely looks older. I can't believe she's twenty-four.

"Good for Lindsey's parents," Mom says. "So you're a lesbian now?"

"I don't feel the need to identify with one particular sexual orientation," Anaïs says. "I'm in love with Lindsey. Love is love is love. I don't have to categorize it. That's so your generation."

"Oh, right," Mom says, laughing sharply. "Our generation and every generation that came before us for thousands of years."

"Phyllis," Dad warns. "Take it easy."

"Now you're the back seat driver," Mom mutters.

It's funny how on the ride here Dad dissed my generation for being on their phones and now my sister is dissing Mom's generation for pigeon-holing sexual orientation. I wish people wouldn't lump together whole generations. Honestly, it's about individual people. Also, I'm struck by what my sister just said, that *love is love is love*. It makes me think about Sebastian and

189

how we're falling for each other even though we totally shouldn't.

"This actually has nothing to do with you," Anaïs says. "This is my life."

"When will you learn"—Mom takes a slow breath—"that this has everything to do with us? We are your parents. If you're an actual lesbian, it's one thing. But if it's just a passing phase . . . then . . . don't you realize that passing phases can affect your entire life?"

"That doesn't even make sense," Anaïs says. "Besides, what's up with Byron? Why didn't he come?"

I clench my jaw tight. I'm trying to send subliminal messages to my sister not to mention what I told her about Byron's arrest. As far as my parents are concerned, all Anaïs knows is that Byron was suspended last fall.

"This has nothing to do with Byron," Mom says. Her voice has an icy edge as if to say, *Conversation over.*

We drive on in silence. I reach into my bag for my water bottle. I'm sipping water and looking out the window at a massive cemetery, endless rows of graves, when Mom blurts out, "Did you know that Virginia has a boyfriend?"

I choke on a mouthful of water. As Mom glances at me in her mirror, I realize I'm an idiot, that she meant Froggy. For a horrible second, I thought she was talking about Sebastian.

It's been such a crazy few weeks that I haven't filled her in on the fact that Froggy and I are over. Mom and I don't have cozy fireside chats, but I do tell her the bare bones of my personal life, mostly so she doesn't worry that I don't have a personal life and then harass me to get one.

"Oh, that's great!" Anaïs says. "Who is it?"

"No," I say quickly. "We broke up."

"You didn't tell me that," Mom says. "When did you and Froggy break up?"

"It was an end-of-the-year thing," I say. "He's going to band camp in Maine for eight weeks."

Dad chuckles when I say "band camp," which annoys me. Dad is in his fifties, for God's sake. When will he get over shaming the band geeks? Dad was probably an asshole just like Byron back when he was in high school, one of the popular guys who called their friends "chubby chasers" if they checked out curvaceous chicks.

As we near the city, Dad glances briefly at my sister. "Are you still a vegetarian? Mom made a reservation at Strip House tonight, but Virginia was reminding us how you were a vegetarian before you left."

"Not anymore," Anaïs says. "It was too hard to get non-meat sources of protein in Burkino Faso."

"So *that* passing phase is over," Mom murmurs.

Anaïs doesn't grace that with a response.

⑥ ⑥ ⑥ ⑥

When we get home, Anaïs goes into her old room and closes the door. Dad leaves to put in a few hours at the office and says he'll meet us at the steakhouse. I eat a nectarine in the kitchen and lie on my bed. Between waking up at five in the morning, working so much at the gym, and having long afternoons with Sebastian, I'm exhausted.

Around three, a text comes in. I yawn and pull my phone out of my pocket. It's from Tisha, my kickboxing teacher. Oh yeah. Today is Friday.

**We missed you last Friday, she's written. You didn't mention you're away this summer, so I assume we'll see you today? Let me know.**

I think about Brie showing up at kickboxing and how awful she made me feel that day and every day. I'm tired of feeling awful. This positive self-image stuff is definitely superior.

I ignore the text from Tisha.

I can hear Mom and Anaïs having a heated conversation in the living room. They're talking in French, which is the official language of Burkina Faso and Mom's preferred tongue even though she's from Arkansas. Since I don't do French, I have no idea what they're saying. I hope they're not on round two of fighting. I smooth my shirt around my stomach and head out to the living room to see what's up.

I'm shocked to find them both in shorts and jog bras, stretching their hamstrings and laughing.

"Hey, Ginny!" Anaïs says, switching to English. "Were you sleeping all this time?"

I nod. "Where are you going?"

"For a run," Mom says.

"I got really into running in Kensington Gardens last

week," my sister says. "I might do a half marathon at the end of the summer."

Mom brightens at the mention of torturous amounts of exercise. "Let me know when and I'll sign up, too. We can train together."

"Wonderful!"

I watch, confused, as they pull on racer-back tanks, lace up their sneakers, and jog out of the apartment.

# 18

I wear Sebastian's straw hat on the drive up to Connecticut and also the red-checkered tank top I had on the first time I met him. For most of the ride, Anaïs is telling us about life in Africa. No, not Africa. She was very clear about her annoyance at people who refer to Burkina Faso as the entire continent of Africa. Also, I'm noticing that most of what Anaïs says starts with "I can't believe" followed by "in Burkina Faso."

For example:

"I can't believe you guys leave the water running while you brush your teeth," she said as we were getting ready this morning. "In Burkina Faso we transported drinking water from another village five kilometers away."

Or, as we were walking to get the car:

"I can't believe the way Americans hurry so much. In

Burkina Faso I spent hours sitting under a tree with my host mother pounding millet and chatting."

After Dad pulls over to use a restroom at the little stone building off the highway, my sister says:

"I can't believe the way you guys can just go in and use the bathroom. In Burkina Faso, it was a big deal when we dug ten new latrines. That's what Lindsey's crew was doing."

"She was digging latrines?" Mom asks.

I know from her letters that Anaïs was doing health-care education and also helping in a women's clinic. I somehow assumed Lindsey did that, too.

"In Burkina Faso, at least in the remote villages, latrines are a big deal. When we didn't have a latrine, we had to go aboveground."

"You're going to have a requisite adjustment period," Mom says in her TherapistVoice. "I've had several patients return from developing countries, and it takes a while to get used to being back."

"Pooping outside." Dad nods like he's impressed. "Like in your Outward Bound days."

Here we go again. I have no idea why pooping outside is such a point of pride. I feel no shame that I prefer to take care of business on a toilet.

"Burkina Faso is nothing like Outward Bound," Anaïs says. "That's a country club for spoiled rich kids. This is real life."

I want to steer the subject away from Outward Bound, so I ask Anaïs about Lindsey and how they fell in love. She tells me that they were friends for a long time but realized in the past few months that it was something more. Since Burkina Faso is a socially conservative country, they didn't tell anyone until last week in London.

"How's Caleb doing?" Mom asks. He was Anaïs's boyfriend back at Brown. Mom's biggest dream in life was that Caleb would become her son-in-law.

"I got a few letters from him while I was there," Anaïs says. "He's just finished his second year at law school. Cornell."

Mom sighs. "I miss Caleb."

"Mom," Anaïs warns.

"I know, I know," Mom says. "I'm sure I'll love Lindsey, too. Just give me a few days for it to sink in."

"In Burkina Faso," Dad says, "the mother sits for hours and pounds millet with her daughter's new girlfriend."

"Shut up!" Anaïs shrieks.

But she's laughing and so is Mom and so am I.

6 6 6 6

When we get to the Connecticut house, Byron isn't home. Mom sends me to the garage to look for his bike. It's gone, which means he's out for a ride. When I see my parents' skis and Anaïs's and Byron's snowboards lined up on the far wall of the garage, I have to smile. I'm thinking about the first time I met Sebastian and told him that skiing and snowboarding are Horrible Things. That was before I knew him and before I knew that strapping someone like Sebastian to a snowboard and sending him down a mountain is a terrible idea.

After they carry their totes inside, Mom and Dad get back

in the car. They're going to the farmers' market to buy vegetables to grill tonight, and they're also swinging by the golf club. I know they're nervous about whether their golf buddies are going to shun them because of Byron's arrest, but a summer without golfing is an even worse prospect.

Anaïs and I are chatting in lounge chairs on the back porch when Byron comes through the sliding doors. He's still wearing his bike helmet and he's super tan, several shades darker than when I saw him last Sunday.

"Hey," he says, hugging Anaïs. "Welcome back to civilization. I hear you're a dyke now."

I suck in my breath, but before I can tell him not to be an asshole, Anaïs shoots back, "And I hear you're a felon."

"Touché," he says.

I stare hard at Anaïs like *please don't give away our secret.* She nods reassuringly at me. I'm guessing Mom told her about Byron's arrest on their run yesterday.

"Hey, Gin," Byron says to me. "What's up with that straw hat?"

I raise my hand self-consciously to Sebastian's hat. All along, I've been thinking it looks nice, but maybe I'm wrong. I quickly take it off and drop it on the picnic table.

"It looks nice," Anaïs says to Byron. "Leave her alone."

Byron unclips his helmet and swings it around his wrist. "I'm going to go take a shower. Welcome back from Africa."

"Burkina Faso," she calls after him.

Once the sliding doors are closed, Anaïs turns to me. "I guess he's the same dick as always."

I nod gratefully, relieved to finally have a family member with whom I can discuss Byron.

"But he's our dick," Anaïs says.

As she goes inside to call Lindsey's aunt's house from the landline, I consider what she said, that Byron is *our* dick. The thing is, I'm not sure I agree. Saying he's our dick means we have to put up with him however he acts.

I carry Sebastian's straw hat inside and try it on in front of the mirror. It's not perfect and maybe it's a little small for my face—

Stop.

I like it and Sebastian likes it and that's all that matters.

ⓖ ⓖ ⓖ ⓖ

That evening, at dinner, everyone is in a good mood. My parents got in four hours of golfing, and it sounds like Byron's arrest wasn't an issue at the club. Plus, while Dad was grilling chicken and zucchini, Mom got a voicemail from the parent of one of her patients who canceled, booking an appointment for next Tuesday. So maybe her career isn't over after all.

As we gather at the picnic table on the back porch, Dad raises a wineglass.

"To the five of us," he says.

We all clink. The four of them are drinking white wine and I'm drinking water. Dad offered me wine, too, but Mom shot it down. I wasn't sure whether it was the underage-drinking thing or the fact that wine has calories. I'm guessing it's the calories because my brother isn't the legal drinking age either and yet my parents usually offer him wine.

"To the five of us," Mom says as we set down our glasses. "Together again."

Dad offers me butter for my corn on the cob, but I shake my head. It'll just get Mom started. I opt for salt and pepper instead.

As Mom passes the chicken to Dad, she points to the backyard. "I was thinking of having a yoga studio built. Something small. Can we get a contractor over here to price it out?"

"Where?" Dad asks.

"Over there," Mom says, "by the pine trees."

"Since when do you do yoga?" Byron asks.

"I've always done yoga," Mom says. "Virginia has seen me come in for classes at Whole Fitness. Right, Virginia?"

I nod and help myself to a skewer of zucchini. I don't want to get pulled into a conversation about Whole Fitness. I don't see that going anywhere productive, especially if they start asking me if I've been using my free time to work out.

"When is that tree woman coming back?" Mom asks. "I'll ask her about taking down a few small trees, making room to build a yoga studio."

"Frances," I say.

"I have the tree woman set up for next Saturday," Dad says. "She has to prune the rest of the medium-height branches on the sugar maples."

"Frances," I say again. "That's her name."

"It's so different here," Anaïs says. "It's like you guys have

199

nothing to worry about, so you talk about yoga studios and golfing and tree women. In Burkina Faso we had to work hard for water and food and all our basic needs, but it made everything so much more meaningful."

I glance at Mom, assuming she'll be offended, but instead she smiles at my sister. "As I said, it's going to take time to adjust. But soon you'll be taking the MCAT prep course and applying to medical school and it will all start feeling normal again."

"I foraged for vegetables at the farmers' market," Dad says, grinning. "Doesn't that count?"

As Mom and Byron laugh, Anaïs stares down at her plate. She butters her corn, sprinkles on some salt, and eats quietly for the rest of the meal.

❻ ❻ ❻ ❻

In the morning, everything goes south.

Byron is still sleeping, but the rest of us are in the kitchen having breakfast when Anaïs informs us that she's not taking the MCATs because she's not applying to medical school.

Mom and Dad stare at her in shock. I'm shocked, too. Ever since I can remember, Anaïs has wanted to be a doctor.

"The thing is," Anaïs says, "Lindsey and I want to continue giving back. We've talked a lot about it. We're going to look into volunteer programs in refugee camps for Syrians."

"No way," Mom says. "I already paid for that MCAT prep class. It wasn't cheap. And how can you be 'Lindsey and I' already? You've only been together for three months."

"Aren't you listening to me?" Anaïs asks. "I'm telling you I don't want to go to medical school. I didn't ask you to sign me up for a class."

Dad clears his throat. "You have to think about your safety. About terrorism. That's a dangerous part of the world."

"I knew you'd say that," Anaïs says. "But life is more than your immediate wants and needs."

"Anaïs!" Dad says. "That's enough."

"I agree," Anaïs says, grabbing Mom's phone off the table. "It is enough."

She slides her feet into her sandals and starts toward the door. I stand up and hurry out after her. At the end of the driveway, my sister is pacing back and forth, staring at Mom's phone, trying to dial a number.

"No signal," I tell her.

"Still?" she asks. "Not even down here?"

I shake my head and sit cross-legged on a big boulder. We have a row of large rocks in the front yard with flowers planted around them. I remember when Dad hired a rock guy to deliver them in a dump truck. *Tree woman. Rock guy.* Maybe our existence really is trivial.

"You're going to a refugee camp?" I ask. "What about medical school? And Dad's right about terrorism. I don't think it's very safe there right now."

Anaïs shakes her head angrily. "You sound just like them," she says, gesturing her chin toward the house.

I bite the inside of my cheeks to keep from crying. I'm not like them. I'm nothing like them. I can't believe she would ever say that.

"Listen," Anaïs says as she twists her hair in a knot on the top of her head. "I'm sorry, okay? I'm freaking out about being back, and I shouldn't take it out on you. I've changed so much these past two years, and everyone here is still the same."

I don't happen to agree with that. I've changed a lot these past two years, too. Even these past two weeks.

"I'm guessing Mom told you about Byron," I say, trying to swallow the lump in my throat.

"Yeah, she told me yesterday. She said that Byron's lawyer is making progress with the district attorney. It sounds like they might be able to settle on some kind of plea bargain without going to trial."

"Really? No one told me that."

"I think on some level Mom and Dad want you to believe that everything is perfect and normal."

When she says that, my stomach rolls nervously. That sounds like the old Anaïs, cutting through the bullshit and talking to me about how it really is. But then I remind myself that a minute ago she was accusing me of being just like them. Honestly, I have no idea what to think of anything right now.

"What plea bargain are they settling on?" I ask. "And did Mom say anything about a civil suit? Like, you know, the girl's family suing us?"

My face flushes when I say "the girl's family," and I dig my toes into the grass, trying to act as nonchalant as possible.

"Mom didn't say anything about a civil suit or them suing," Anaïs says. "She just told me that the lawyers are in preliminary discussions, but the plea bargain might be something like weekend jail time and no SORA. That means he wouldn't have to register as a sex offender and he could still go to school on weekdays."

"Weekend jail time?" I shudder, thinking about Byron in jail on weekends. I hadn't even realized people do that. Would he have to change into an orange jumpsuit every Friday night? Would he write his papers and study for exams from a jail cell? "Does Byron know about all that? He seemed fine at dinner last night."

Anaïs shakes her head. "They're going to have him meet with the lawyer on Thursday and that's when he'll find out. *Shit*."

"What?"

"Don't tell Byron or even Mom and Dad that you know. *Shit*. I'm home two days and I'm already back into the secrets."

With that, Anaïs tosses me Mom's phone. "Can you give this back? I'm taking a walk."

I sit on a boulder for a long time before going into the house.

6 6 6 6

The fun morning isn't complete without a few hours of driving practice.

"Less than two weeks until your road rest," Dad says as I'm making my way to the parking lot.

"I know," I say, sighing.

"It's the Friday after next," Dad says.

"I know."

"And it's not just about passing the road test," Dad says. "Driving is an essential life skill."

"I know," I say for a third time. "Like what if I were stranded in the Sahara Desert and the person driving got eaten by a camel?"

Dad ignores my commentary. "How are you feeling about the road test?"

"Well, you know. Not great. How much do self-driving cars cost?"

Dad takes this as an invitation to do some Dadsplaining. As I loop around and around the parking lot, he goes on about using the screen for reverse and who yields to whom at a four-way stop. I nod like, *yeah, wow, thanks.* The truth is, I know all of this. I aced the test for my learner's permit. The classroom teachers in driver's ed loved me. But when it comes to the real thing, I have a total block.

Today's lesson is more of the same. As I press the gas and the car jerks forward, Dad says, "I think the problem is that you need to stop thinking and let your instincts take over."

"But you said a few weeks ago that I don't have instincts."

"Did I say that? Well, you'll just have to make up for that with a lot of practice. Let's go, and this time we'll add in parallel parking."

⑥ ⑥ ⑥ ⑥

That evening, we all cram into the car for the drive back to Manhattan. Byron wanted to stay in Connecticut for another week, but my parents told him they have a meeting with Mark Levy on Thursday so he needs to come home. It was weird to realize that I know about the possible weekend jail time before he does.

I'm in the seat behind Mom. I'm looking out the window and trying to figure out the last time the five of us were in a car together. I think it was the spring before my sister went into the Peace Corps, when we went on a vacation to the Dominican Republic. We were staying at a fancy resort, and my parents and Anaïs and Byron spent most of their time on the golf course. While they were golfing, I walked on the beach or read by the pool.

I'm thinking about the huge pool with the hot tub and the bar that served virgin piña coladas and I suddenly remember.

*Towels.*

Whenever I wanted a towel from the cabana I would give our room number to a guy in a white polo shirt. He would write it down and record on a piece of paper how many towels I took. But when I returned the towels later, no one asked what room we were in or marked off that I returned them. I questioned Mom about this, and she explained that people's psychology is such that if they think someone is watching, they will do the right thing. Therefore if a person knows that someone is aware of how many towels they took, they will return that many towels without being asked. In fact, as Mom explained, not only will they do the right thing but they'll actually feel good about doing it.

# 19

love it," Gerri says to me the next morning. "Basically when we greet people by name we'll show them that we're jotting down how many towels they took."

"Right," I say. "But we won't check to see if they returned them. They can put them in a bin in the locker room or the shower area or wherever they want. That way, they won't feel tracked."

Gerri nods. "We let them feel ownership."

"Yeah, I guess. We'll just throw away the chart at the end of the day."

"Resort-style," Gerri says. "It's worth a try."

As Gerri carries a stack of invoices into her office, I print out blank charts. The left column is to write down the members' names, and the column on the right is to record how many towels they took. I'm sticking the charts in a clipboard when Mom and Dad walk in the front door.

"Hello, Mike and Phyllis!" I smile at them as I swipe their IDs. "How many towels would you like this morning?"

I can see Gerri standing in the doorway of her office, watching us.

"Two each," Mom says.

"Two each," I repeat. I hand them a stack of four neatly folded white towels, then jot their names and the number of towels on the chart. They don't ask about it, or even seem to notice a change in the routine. They just wave and Mom goes to her yoga class while Dad hits the machines.

"So far, so good," Gerri says, grabbing her hand weights and giving them a few pumps.

⟲ ⟲ ⟲ ⟲

By Tuesday, Gerri is feeling hopeful.

"I told the laundry service to do a detailed inventory," she tells me after I get back from my break. "We'll compare it with the numbers from every day last week. We don't have any data yet, but judging by the number of towels they loaded into the laundry truck yesterday afternoon it seems like people returned more."

I nod happily. I'm feeling all-around happy today. Sebastian and I met at Astor Place yesterday afternoon and explored the East Village. I was worried that things would feel awkward after three and a half days apart, but as soon as we saw each other, we hugged and kissed and were right back to where we were last Thursday. I brought Sebastian's hat for him, and he surprised me with my very own straw hat. It's got a wider brim and a thin purple ribbon and I love it. We ended up walking all the way to Strand Book Store where he looked at children's books and I bought some novels to read this summer like *Americanah*, which my Humanities teacher told me about, and another novel by the same person who wrote *Fates and Furies*.

"I have a good feeling about this," Gerri says as I print out more blank charts and add them to the clipboard. The evening staff filled up all the ones I put in there yesterday. "I can feel in my bones that this is going to work."

I smile at Gerri. I like that she cares about towels so deeply that she feels it in her bones.

Sure enough, when I get to Whole Fitness on Wednesday, Gerri is beaming.

"You are a hero!" she says, offering me a high five. "According to preliminary data, resort-style counting has resulted in a thirty percent reduction in lost towels. People don't feel blamed. They don't feel accused. They watch their behavior more and listen to their moral compass if they think someone is aware of it."

When she says that, I think of Byron.

If my brother knew that someone was aware of what he was doing to Annie, would he still have forced her to have sex? Or is his moral compass so skewed that when he got drunk he lost all sense of right and wrong?

Whatever it is, he's definitely gloomy this week. Monday

was the day he was supposed to leave for his summer-study program in Paris. He got a few calls from Columbia friends who were making plans to meet at the airport. I heard him tell them that he was pulling out. Ever since then, he's been in his room with the door closed and he's refusing to join us for meals. When he didn't come to dinner on Wednesday night all I could think was, *wait until Thursday*. That's when Anaïs said my parents are taking him to see the lawyer to go over the settlement terms. If not going to Paris is making Byron feel miserable, wait until he finds out about weekend jail.

ⓖ ⓖ ⓖ ⓖ

When I get out of work on Thursday, I meet Anaïs and Lindsey at Brookfield Place. Anaïs has been staying at Lindsey's aunt's apartment in Park Slope since Tuesday night. We decide to meet at Brookfield because there's a hand-rolled bagel shop there that Lindsey wants to try. I wonder if Lindsey appreciates butter-to-dough ratios. I sort of feel like she might.

"How're things at home?" Anaïs asks as we're sitting down with our bagel sandwiches. "Is Byron still sulking?"

I glance quickly at Lindsey. It's one thing to discuss Byron with Sebastian, who is obviously aware of the situation. But I've only met Lindsey for five minutes in the airport and this is really personal stuff.

"It's about the same," I say vaguely.

"Don't worry about talking about it," Anaïs says, taking Lindsey's hand. "She knows everything."

Lindsey nods and smiles at me. I can tell she's nice and

friendly and that I'll probably like her a lot. But as of now, she feels like a stranger. In some ways, Anaïs does, too. She and Lindsey are laughing and talking about people from the Peace Corps and about their Burkinabé friends. By the time we toss our bagel wrappers in the trash, I'm exhausted trying to keep up. I'm actually relieved when they head back to Brooklyn. I pop in some gum, pull on my wide-brimmed straw hat, and walk over to the river to meet Sebastian.

☙ ☙ ☙ ☙

"What's your school like?" Sebastian asks. We've been stretched out on a grassy pier in the West Village all afternoon. He's sketching and I'm watching the clouds, and we're talking about whatever random things come up. "You said it's called Brewster. Is it full of purple-haired Leela superheroes like you?"

"Hardly," I say, laughing. "It's the kind of place where the popular people rule and the rest of us scurry around scared. I've got my best friend, Shannon, who's been away this year, but she's coming back. And my friend Alyssa. And there are some good teachers, especially when they're not obsessed with college prep."

"How many popular people are there?"

I squint at him. "How many? Like, in my grade?"

Sebastian nods. As he adds streaks of silver to his sketch of the Hudson River, I count the main popular people. Brie, of course, and her bitchy core group, which number about five. Then there's Cole and Josh and Russ and a few other guys who cycle in and out of the royalty circles.

210

"Maybe ten key people," I say. "More come and go. Let's say twelve for sure."

"How many people are in your grade total?"

"Eighty," I say. "It's a small school."

"So about fifteen percent of the total people in your grade are popular and yet they rule?"

I stare out at the river. Even though it's late afternoon, the sun is still high in the sky. Sebastian is right. It doesn't make sense. And yet there it is.

"I'm not saying it's not true," he says. "My school wasn't much different. It just shouldn't be that way. There should be a revolution. The nonpopular people should take over and subvert the paradigm."

"Now you sound like Hamilton," I say. "Young, scrappy, and hungry."

Sebastian grins and tucks his hair behind his ears. I love his grin. I'm going to miss his grin. July Fourth weekend is coming up, and Sebastian's family is going camping in the Catskills. In fact, he needs to pack up his pastels in a few minutes and meet his parents in Union Square to buy camping supplies. He cracked up when I asked if he's staying in a campground with a bathroom. He thought I was joking, but I told him no way. I don't joke about pooping in the woods.

"What was your school like?" I ask.

"It's a big public secondary school. My parents are teachers there, so that gave me some advantages. Then again, I suck at hockey, so that took me down a few notches. Hockey was the big thing. That and snowmobiling."

*Snowmobiling.*

As soon as he says it, he visibly flinches. His ex-girlfriend, Maddie, was a snowmobiler. She cheated on him with another snowmobiler.

"How long were you together?" I ask. "You and Maddie?"

"Over a year. But who knows how much of that year she was cheating on me? All winter, I'm guessing. Snowmobile season."

"I'm sorry."

"Yeah, well, it was hard. Especially for a ESFP."

"Why?"

"We're loyal to a fault. We give someone our one hundred percent."

I slide closer to him and lace my hands through his. We stay like that for a long time, our heads touching, our shoulders touching, his leg splayed over mine. I've never felt this close to anyone before. I feel like he has my heart. He has my one hundred percent.

ⓖ ⓖ ⓖ ⓖ

After we say good-bye, I'm walking to the subway when Alyssa calls. Alyssa and I mostly text, so I'm surprised to see her call come in.

"Can you talk?" she asks. Her voice sounds faint and far away.

"Yeah . . . what's up?"

"You have no idea how hard this call was to make," Alyssa says, sighing heavily.

"What do you mean?"

Alyssa sighs again. I hear kids shrieking in the background and bugle music playing.

"Are you at camp?" I ask.

"Yeah, it's pickup time. I got another CIT to cover for me. I can't talk at my uncle's house because my cousins are snooping around all the time. And I can't talk at camp because we're not supposed to have our phones out. But there's something I need to tell you. I've been holding it inside, and it's eating me up."

Alyssa sniffles like she's crying. The thing is, Alyssa is one of those perennially peppy people who doesn't have dark moods. She's scaring me right now.

I glance up and down West Eleventh Street looking for a quiet place to talk. The Village is more crowded than the Upper West Side, especially on a warm summer afternoon. "I'm sure it's okay. I'm sure whatever you have to tell me is—"

"I kissed Froggy."

I stop in my tracks on the sidewalk. Seriously, my legs lock in place.

"Are you still there?" Alyssa asks. "Did you hang up? I'd understand if you hung up."

"No, I'm here." My legs are wobbly. I sit on the stoop of a nearby brownstone and run my fingers along the rough texture of the stairs. I'm thinking about Maddie and how she cheated on Sebastian. Was Froggy cheating on me while we were together? Were he and Alyssa fooling around behind my back?

"It was after you guys broke up," Alyssa says quickly, like she's reading my mind. "We went for a walk after Field Day that Thursday. Remember how you left early? We were talking for a long time and, well, we kissed."

Okay. So he didn't cheat. Alyssa didn't sneak around with my boyfriend.

"Virginia, I promise you that I didn't even know I liked Froggy until that afternoon. Once we kissed, it all came to me. I liked you guys together because *I* liked Froggy. He seemed like the perfect boyfriend because I wanted him to be *my* boyfriend. But honest. I wasn't thinking about it until that day."

I take a deep breath. There's a line wrapping around the block to get into Magnolia. I bet Sebastian would like to try a cupcake there. He's always getting excited about New York City food.

"Are you together?" I ask after a second. "I mean, is he your boyfriend now?"

"I don't know. Maybe. I really, really, really like him. He's in Maine for the summer and doesn't have access to technology, but we're writing letters." Alyssa pauses before adding, "If you hate me for this, then I'll never talk to Froggy again. It will make me sad, but I'll do it."

"I wouldn't ask you to do that," I say quickly.

Now that I'm over the initial shock that my first boyfriend and my friend are getting together, I can actually see it. They're right for each other. Much more right than Froggy and me.

"Oh my God!" Alyssa shouts all of a sudden. "I'm going to pee my pants! I've been so upset that I couldn't pee all day, but now that I've told you I'm going to wet my pants right here in the middle of day camp."

"Go pee," I tell her. "It's okay. We can talk later."

"Virginia?"

"Yeah?"

"Thanks."

After we hang up, I go into a store and buy a bottle of water. As I'm taking sips, I realize that Froggy deserves to be really, really, really liked. I never felt that way about him, not like how I feel with Sebastian. But Froggy deserves it and Alyssa deserves it, and it's not my place to get between them.

⊚ ⊚ ⊚ ⊚

We drive back to Connecticut on Friday night. On Saturday morning, I'm reading *Americanah* in the hammock and thinking how, after Lotto and Mathilde's debacle, Ifemelu and Obinze are renewing my belief in true love. Also, even though *Americanah* is set in Nigeria and my sister has been very clear that she hates when people lump all African countries together, it's still interesting to read a novel set in the continent where my sister was living. I'm deep in the book when I hear a shriek from across the yard. At first I think someone is being attacked. As I toss down *Americanah* and bolt out of the hammock, I realize three things in rapid succession:

1. Frances's ladder is on the ground under the sugar maple.

2. Two seconds ago, her ladder was up in the sugar maple and Frances was on it.

3. Frances is on the grass, curled in the fetal position.

My heart is pounding as I run across the lawn and kneel by her side. "Are you okay?"

I notice that her long clippers are twenty feet away and there's no blood anywhere. So that's good, I guess. Except she's looking really pale and her eyes are scrunched up tight.

"Ladder was unsteady . . ." She whimpers and shakes her head. "I fell . . . my foot . . . maybe my ribs."

I glance desperately toward the house, even though I know that no one's home. Anaïs is staying with Lindsey this weekend, and Mom and Dad forced Byron to go golfing with them. Ever since the meeting with Mark Levy on Thursday, Byron has descended into an even deeper funk. He's barely talking, and he has a terrible, hacking cough. I'm not sure what my parents said to convince him to go golfing, but I heard Dad's chief operating officer voice, loud and firm, and then they got in the car and left two hours ago.

"Want me to call 911?" I ask Frances. "I can get you some ice."

"No phone signal," she manages to say.

"We have a home phone," I offer.

"Can you just . . . drive me to the . . . hospital?"

"Me?" I ask, shocked. "I only have my learner's permit."

Frances digs in her shorts pocket and hands me a car key. No, not a car key. A truck key. Frances has a blue pickup truck that is currently parked in our driveway.

I'm looking at the truck key and looking at Frances and trying to figure out what the hell to do when she says, "Please. It's really hurting. I'd have you call my boyfriend, but he's bartending at a July Fourth party and probably wouldn't hear his phone."

Her lips are pale, and there are tiny beads of sweat on her forehead. I lean over and hoist her up. She slings one arm around my shoulder, and we slowly make our way across the lawn. She's hopping on one foot and wincing and clutching her rib cage with her free hand. Even though she's sweaty, her body feels cold. After I help her into the passenger seat, I pull the seat belt over her, careful not to touch her ribs. Before I get into the driver's seat I run into the house and grab my phone, a few ice packs from the freezer, and the throw blanket off the couch, which I drape over her.

"Thanks," she whispers.

As I climb into the driver's seat, I slide the seat forward, tweak the mirrors, and turn the ignition. The truck is facing toward the house. I try not to think about being so high up or how I've never driven a truck or how I have no natural driving instincts. I shift into drive, reverse, and drive as I manage a three-point turn and then make it down the driveway and out onto the street.

"Do you know how to get to the hospital?" Frances asks. "Like, in New Milford?"

New Milford. Hometown of my dreaded driver's ed class.

"Yeah," I say. "I've seen it."

I'm not saying it's the best-ever drive to the hospital, but I stay in my lane and I stop at intersections and I avoid oncoming cars and I manage to ease my foot gingerly onto the gas and brakes so I don't hurt Frances. Mostly she's quiet in the passenger seat. Every now and then she rocks back and forth and moans and I tell her it's going to be okay, that we're almost there.

Twenty minutes later, I pull up to the entryway leading to the emergency room. I leave Frances in the passenger seat while I run in and ask for help. A few hospital workers rush out with a stretcher and lift her onto it. I follow her inside and ask her for her boyfriend's number. Luckily there's a phone signal here, and after a few tries, he finally answers. I explain who I am and what happened. He says he'll get there as soon as he can. Since some nurses are hovering around Frances, I go outside and park the pickup truck. And then, finally, as I'm walking back across the parking lot, I call Dad and tell him where I am.

# 20

That afternoon, my parents and I are sitting on the back porch drinking unsweetened iced tea and eating cherries. They're marveling about how I drove Frances to the emergency room.

"It's amazing," Dad says, spitting a cherry pit into a paper towel. "I just talked to Green Arbor, and they asked what they can do to thank you."

I overheard Dad on the phone with the tree-pruning company. I think he was reviewing the liability waiver to make sure Frances wouldn't sue us for getting injured on our property, and then I heard him telling Mom that she can't. That was good news. The last thing we need is another lawsuit.

"Green Arbor is sending you a gift certificate," Dad says. "I said you love to read, so they're getting you one from Words on Pages."

Mom nods. "You were cool under pressure. Especially the

way you gave her a blanket. People go into shock with that kind of pain. A broken ankle and two broken ribs. How awful."

"How did you even know how to drive a pickup?" Dad asks. "We've never talked about adjusting to different-sized vehicles."

I tip my straw hat so it's shading my eyes from the sun. "I did what I had to do."

"That's my girl," Dad says.

"Thanks," I say, squeezing some droplets of lemon into my iced tea. I have to admit I'm soaking up the praise. Even Frances's boyfriend was impressed that I drove her to the hospital with only a learner's permit. When we met him at the emergency room, he went on and on to my parents about how her truck is not the easiest vehicle to handle.

Byron comes out to the porch and grabs a few cherries. It's the first thing I've seen him eat since Thursday. His sunken cheeks are coated with a few days' worth of stubble.

"I don't understand why you didn't call an ambulance," he says. "Wouldn't that have made more sense?"

"She was in a lot of pain," I say. "She asked me to get her to the hospital quickly."

"I just can't picture it." Byron coughs a few times. "I can't picture Virginia driving someone to the hospital."

He says it like he wants Mom and Dad to agree that, yes, it's hard to picture me doing something strong and bold and brave. But they ignore his commentary and he goes back into the house.

An hour later, I'm reading on the couch when Mom says, "Gin."

"Yeah?" I ask, folding over the page.

"Mike, come in here," Mom calls to Dad. "I've got some news about Virginia, and I want to say it in front of you."

Dad turns off the water in the kitchen sink. "Did she rescue someone from a burning building as well?"

I grin. I have no idea what Mom is going to tell us. Even so, this hero stuff is pretty nice.

"I was just in town checking my e-mail, and I got your grades from Brewster," Mom says when Dad appears, wiping his hands on a dish towel. "You made high honor roll."

"Wow!" I say. I knew my grades were strong this semester, but I'm surprised I did so well on finals. That week wasn't exactly the best of my life.

"Anaïs and Byron always made honor roll," Mom says. "But never *high* honor roll. Also, I got a personal note from the college counselor. With your grades this year and your score on last fall's PSAT, she thinks you've got a solid shot at Harvard. She wants to set up a meeting in the fall for all of us to discuss what steps you can take junior year to further strengthen your candidacy."

"Harvard," Dad says. "Imagine that."

"I sort of want to go to Vassar," I say.

"You've mentioned that before," Mom says. "Why Vassar?"

"A lot of my favorite writers went there."

"You don't say no to Harvard," Mom concludes. "I'm sure Harvard has wonderful writing classes, too."

"It's not like Harvard is saying yes," I tell her. I don't add that, for one, I'm a year away from applying to college. And for two, I've never seen Harvard. I don't even know if I want *it*.

"Let's celebrate," Mom says. "Dad got a few bunches of kale at the farmers' market this morning. We can make something out of that new cookbook you bought. I was flipping through it, and it looks great."

Dad tosses the dish towel over his shoulder and heads back into the kitchen.

"Some of my colleagues have read *Americanah* and say they love it," Mom says, eyeing my book. "Very impressive."

❀ ❀ ❀ ❀

It's not like I wanted a gold medal from Sebastian for driving Frances to the emergency room, but he doesn't seem excited about it at all. It's Monday afternoon and we're in line at Magnolia down in the West Village. Sebastian is sketching the corner of Bleecker and West Eleventh as we wait, complete with the awning and the cursive script spelling out *The Magnolia Bakery*. As we wait, we're chatting about our weekends. Actually, it's mostly me. All he's said is that they came home early from camping and his nana flew in from Saskatchewan last night.

"How far was it again?" he asks. We're getting closer to the front of the line. He zips his pastels into his pencil case and puts them in his messenger bag. "You said fifteen miles from your house to the ER? Like twenty-four kilometers? That's not too far."

"The point is, I'm a terrible driver."

"Maybe you're not," he offers.

"That's the thing," I say. "I always thought I was, but when I actually *had* to drive, I just did it."

The people in front of us step into the bakery.

"Everyone in Regina drives when they turn sixteen," he says. "It's not even an option. You don't get to decide you're a bad driver. You just get your license and that's it."

I'm not sure what to say. When I texted Alyssa about it last night, she wrote me a congratulatory note full of caps and exclamation points and emojis with balloons. Maybe she did it out of guilt for getting together with Froggy, but I'm honestly not mad at her. I was sure to tell her that in a text before I described my heroic drive.

"Some people even start driving at fifteen," Sebastian says. "For snowmobiling, there are kids doing that at twelve."

"It's not like it's a big deal." I shuffle my feet along in the line. I suddenly want this conversation to be over. "It was just a good story."

When we get to the front, Sebastian orders a vanilla cupcake with chocolate buttercream frosting. I ask for vanilla with vanilla buttercream and point to the one with purple frosting. Sebastian insists on paying, so I grab napkins and save us a table near the window.

But then, as soon as we're sitting down, I have no interest in eating. Partially, my mouth has gone dry. But also, Sebastian's snowmobile comment made me think about Maddie, and thinking about his ex-girlfriend is making me feel fat. The last thing I need is to stuff a cupcake down my throat.

At first, Sebastian is oblivious. He peels off the paper and takes a bite from the side. "Wow, that's amazing. Really good."

But then, three bites in, he's like, "Aren't you eating yours?"

I shrug. I'm wearing a short sundress with spaghetti straps, and I'm suddenly aware of my upper arms being exposed. I yank my dress farther down on my thighs and hug my stomach. Back in middle school, kids told me I looked pregnant when I wore a dress. I bet I look pregnant now, maybe even with twins.

And just like that, my worst self comes out.

"Is Maddie thin?" I ask.

Sebastian looks up, confused. "That's a messed-up question."

"She must be thin," I say. "Otherwise you would have answered me."

Sebastian shakes his head. His eyes are narrowed in a way I've never seen before.

"She's regular," he says after a second.

"What's regular?" I know I'm pushing it, but I'm on a roll and I can't stop.

"Regular," Sebastian says sharply. "I guess thin. I don't know."

I nod. Regular is thin. Of course it is. I knew that and I led him into the trap.

"What's going on?" Sebastian asks.

I stare at my hands, folded on top of the table. "Why are you even attracted to me?"

"What are you talking about?"

"Are you a chubby chaser?"

Sebastian pushes his chair back like he's going to leave but then shakes his head angrily. "That's a horrible thing to say."

I grab my untouched cupcake, drop it in the trash, and hurry out onto the street. There's still a line weaving around the corner, so I walk the other way on Bleecker. Halfway down the block, I lean against a building and bury my face in my hands. A second later, Sebastian shows up.

"Hey," he says, touching my shoulder. "Are you okay?"

"What's wrong with you?" I wipe my nose with the back of my hand. "You could have anyone, so why are you attracted to me?"

"I'm attracted to you because I am."

"No way," I say, shaking my head.

"Listen," Sebastian says. "I don't have some big flaw, if that's what you're wondering. I like you. I may even love you. There doesn't need to be something wrong with me to be attracted to you."

I shake my head harder. I'm not buying it.

"Whatever," he says. "I'm not going to argue about this. Look me up when you believe me."

Sebastian hurries to the corner, trips on the curb, and nearly face plants onto the pavement. He quickly recovers and disappears into a park on the other side of the street.

For a few minutes, I stand there crying. Then I go back into Magnolia, lock myself in the bathroom, and cry for several more minutes. As I'm walking out to the sidewalk, my phone rings.

"I can see you," Sebastian says when I answer. "I'm sitting on a bench in the park across the street. Come on over."

⊚ ⊚ ⊚ ⊚

First we hug. I breathe him in, touching my lips against the soft cotton of his T-shirt. Once we start talking, I tell him I'm sorry for the things I said and for bringing up Maddie and for not believing him when he told me he's attracted to me. He apologizes for being a jerk about how I drove Frances to the emergency room and for being in a bad mood in general.

"Our weekend camping trip was awful," he explains.

"Awful how?"

Sebastian shakes his head. "I don't know for sure, but I think my sister is having a breakdown."

"A breakdown?"

Sebastian shrugs. "The first night of camping she started crying and couldn't stop. She said she thought that reporting what happened with Byron to the police would help, but it's not helping. Now she's freaking out that if it goes to trial she'll have to testify, and she doesn't think she can do that. It got so bad that we had to pack up early and drive back to the city."

"I'm so sorry," I say.

"That's why my nana flew in. She's always been able to get through to Annie." Sebastian bites down on his bottom lip. "This is only strengthening my parents' case that they don't want me to go to Columbia. It's just . . . I'm sorry I'm taking it out on you."

"It's okay," I say. "I understand."

"No." Sebastian looks me in my eyes. "It's a big deal that you drove someone to the emergency room."

"I'm sorry I asked about Maddie," I tell him. "I know she hurt you. That wasn't fair of me to bring her up."

"She's one person and you're another," he says. "Maybe some guys find only one body type attractive, but that's not me."

I stare at him, at his blue-green eyes, his long hair, his crooked nose. My heart is swelling with how much I care about him. I nestle closer to him, and he slings his arm around my shoulder.

"Can we make a deal?" he asks, kissing the top of my head. "How long was our fight?"

"Ten minutes. Maybe less."

"Okay, so let's make a deal to cap fights at ten minutes. That's as long as we'll go without talking."

"What if we just agree not to fight?" I ask. I can't imagine ever having to go through this again.

"Not realistic," Sebastian says. "People fight. Let's just not exceed ten minutes."

"Deal," I say.

We lean in and start kissing.

227

After a few minutes, I pull back and smile. "Before . . . when we were fighting . . . did you say you might . . . ?"

"I did," he says, nodding. "I do."

"Me too."

❺ ❺ ❺ ❺

I'm in the elevator when I see Mrs. Myers hobbling across the lobby. I consider pushing *door close* so she can't get on the elevator with me, but then I see Alberto watching and my moral compass kicks in.

"Hello, young lady," she says in her scratchy old voice as she steps inside. She taps her cane on the elevator floor a few times. "I noticed that your beautiful sister got home from Africa."

A million thoughts ping through my head. I could tell her that beauty comes in all shapes and sizes. I could tell her that an amazing guy loves me. I could tell her that, sure, men like their bank accounts big, but they also like curvaceous chicks. Or I could simply tell Mrs. Myers to fuck herself.

Instead I decide to ignore her. I step out of the elevator, letting the door close with her alone inside.

❺ ❺ ❺ ❺

The next day, I put together another package for Shannon. I'm sending her a shirt because I read that clothes get ratty on the Pacific Crest Trail and having something new to wear is like Christmas morning. This time I write a short card.

Dear Shannon,

Hey there, hiker. New clothes! Yay! Now you won't stink anymore. Remember how I said that I might love Sebastian? Well, I do. He does. We've said it.

# We love each other.

Your clean and showered friend,

Virginia

I don't write it small. I don't even write it medium. I write it full size. Bold. Black Sharpie.

# 21

Two days later, I wake up with my period. It's five in the morning. As I'm scrounging around for tampons and getting dressed for work, I think about how when I got my period a month ago, Byron had just been arrested. I had just figured out the Annie-Sebastian connection. It was the day Froggy broke up with me.

It's amazing the difference a month makes.

My cramps are bad today. I keep hunching over and pressing my fists into my abdomen. Gerri can see I'm feeling like crap, so she urges me to take a break from swiping IDs and do some gentle running on the treadmill. I look at her skeptically, but she explains that exercise can ease cramps. The crazy thing is, she's right. After a few minutes, I start feeling remotely human again.

The resort-style towel counting is still going well. When Mom comes in for a yoga class on Wednesday, Gerri raves about how I've solved the towel situation at Whole Fitness. Mom must have texted Dad immediately because, by noon, he writes to me.

I heard you're the towel hero at the gym. #BelieveInYourself

That's been his thing this week. He's been texting me cheesy hashtag affirmations. On Monday, he wrote: To my strong, brave daughter. #AlwaysRespectYourself

My favorite so far was the text he sent me on Tuesday afternoon. I was walking to the subway to meet Sebastian at the Bronx Zoo when Dad texted: Follow your heart and you can't go wrong. #BeTrueToYourself

When I saw that one, it made me think about Sebastian and me. Obviously our being together is an example of #BeingTrueToMyself. Because if I were being true to my family, then I wouldn't have contact with the brother of Annie Mills. Then again, my brother made his own choice when he forced Annie to have sex with him. And I'm making my choice, too. I'm choosing Sebastian.

🌀 🌀 🌀 🌀

That evening, Mom is still excited about the towels. We're in her bathroom. She's drying her hair, and I'm borrowing some of her makeup. Alyssa is on break from camp and texted me that she's in the city for twenty-four hours. We made a plan to meet for dinner at Dojo down near NYU. It'll be good to see each other again after everything that happened with Froggy. At least I hope so.

"I hadn't even realized there was a towel problem at the

gym," Mom says. She shuts off the hairdryer and leans into the mirror, examining the hair around her temples. Mom gets honey-blond highlights every four weeks. If it goes even a day over she starts complaining that she looks like a senior citizen and coerces Talia to bump up her appointment.

I take a dab of Mom's fancy foundation and rub it on my face. Along with my period, I've gotten a lovely crop of chin zits. "Gerri didn't want to do a towel-tracking system," I say. "She didn't want members to feel judged."

"So you solved it by letting people know they're being watched and assuming they'd make the right choice." Mom nods proudly at me. "It's called the Hawthorne Effect. A lot of research has been done on it."

"Like at that resort in the Dominican Republic."

Mom shakes her head. "You know, I completely forgot about that."

As Mom continues blowing out her hair, I wonder what she's thinking. Anaïs hasn't given me any legal updates on Byron, so I'm guessing nothing has changed there. Mom made him go to the doctor yesterday for his cough, and he came home with a prescription for antibiotics and an order to sleep and eat better.

"The doctor talked to me about self-care," Byron muttered as he was telling her about the doctor's appointment. I was collecting laundry from my room, but I froze to listen. "Just like all that self-care I'll be able to do in weekend jail."

"Nothing's been decided yet about weekend jail," Mom said. "Besides . . . doing that might allow you to avoid SORA, which would be worth it. The sex-offender registry would follow you forever."

That's the update I give Alyssa as we sit down at Dojo. It's an airy Japanese restaurant full of college students. Alyssa and I decide to split a soy burger and a plate of edamame, and get our own lychee drinks as a treat.

"But your parents hired a good lawyer?" she asks after we order. "I mean, they'll make sure he doesn't get, like, full-time jail?"

"Hopefully," I say, "but you never know."

As the waiter brings our drinks, we both go quiet. I'm wishing I could tell Alyssa about Sebastian. I also want to ask her about Froggy, how things are going, if they're really together. But I somehow can't think of how to say any of it. The thoughts are there, fully formed in my head, but I can't transform them into words.

She must be feeling the awkwardness, too, because she shrugs and sips her drink and checks her phone. I check my phone. She turns her phone over. I turn mine over, too. We smile uncomfortably at each other.

Finally, I decide: *fuck it*. If I want our friendship to be real, then we have to talk about Froggy and about Sebastian, too. Not who his sister is, of course, but the fact that he exists at all.

"Maybe it sounds crazy," I say as the edamame arrives, "but I've been hanging out with this guy. Sebastian. He's an artist. He's just finished high school. No one in my family knows. It's sort of . . . secret."

"Ooooh! I love his name." Alyssa sucks on an edamame

and spits out the shell. She's grinning hard, and she looks genuinely happy. "Where did you meet?"

"In line at the bagel store. He's visiting the city this summer." Before she can ask anything else, like if he's related to someone who is pressing charges against my brother, I pivot over to her. "What about Froggy? How's that going?"

Alyssa smiles. No, she doesn't smile. She beams. "Good. I mean, it's just letters for now. Really long letters." She pauses and then says, "Are you sure you're not mad at me? Like, if we get together for real?"

I lick the salt from an edamame and chase it with a sip of my lychee juice. "I'm sure. For real. I'm happy for you."

"Not that we should go on any double dates," Alyssa says, giggling mischievously. "You and Sebastian, Froggy and me."

I crack up. "At least not yet."

The soy burger arrives. We're still laughing as we push aside the edamame and Alyssa cuts the burger in half.

⑥ ⑥ ⑥ ⑥

On Friday, Mom picks me up outside Whole Fitness at noon and we drive straight to Danbury. Mom brings me a Caesar salad with chicken and actual, real dressing on the side and actual, real croutons. Despite the shocking caloric windfall, I take a few bites and push it away. Partially it's hard to eat salad in the passenger seat of a car. Partially it's hard to indulge in carbs and creamy dressing with Mom two feet away. But mostly I can't eat because today is the day I've been dreading and fearing and hoping would never arrive.

Yep, it's here. July tenth.

The appointment for my road test is at two thirty. We arrive twenty minutes early and pull into a line of cars waiting at the DMV. Mom is in the driver's seat. She shifts into park and taps her fingernails on the steering wheel and checks her phone and pops a few cinnamon Altoids.

She's nervous. I think she might be more nervous than I am. My stomach is fluttery, but I've decided I'm going to do my best and #MyBestIsTheBestICanDo. Also, if I fail my road test, then I can take it again. Or I can take it never. One thing I'm glad about is that Dad isn't here. Originally he was going to bring me, but something came up at work. Which is good. If Dad were here he'd be Dadsplaining until the very last drop.

A tester steps into the passenger seat of the white Honda in front of us. After a few minutes, the car takes off.

"We're next," Mom says. "Why don't I get out and you get in the driver's seat?"

I nod, my hands instantly clammy. Okay, maybe I am a little nervous.

Mom wishes me luck, climbs out, and sits on a green metal chair in the waiting area. I slowly walk around the car, get into the driver's seat, and adjust the mirrors. I wipe my palms on my shorts and place my hands at ten and two.

A full-figured woman holding a clipboard opens the door and slides into our car.

"I'm Silvia," she says, buckling her seat belt. "May I please see your permit?"

As she scans my permit, I decide it's a good sign that Silvia's got some curves. Us curvaceous chicks stick together. Or maybe she doesn't give a damn about my body type and just wants to see if I can drive.

Holy shit.

This is my road test.

"Pull out whenever you're ready," Silvia says, jotting something on the clipboard and gesturing to the exit. "And take a right up there."

I shift into drive and press the gas. The car lurches a little. Shit. Breathe. I try to imagine that Silvia is Frances, wrapped in a blanket and rocking back and forth in the passenger seat. That helps a little. So does breathing.

Over the next ten minutes, Silvia instructs me to turn right and turn left. I remember to signal every time. She has me parallel park behind a Prius, and I somehow do it. The three-point turn takes four points, but I slow at stop signs and yield to an SUV that arrives at the four-way intersection before me.

When we get back to the DMV, I shift into park. Silvia hands me a slip of paper and is just turning to get out when I say, "How did I do?"

"Look down," she says.

I glance at the paper in my hand. It clearly reads *Pass*.

"*Seriously?* I passed?"

Silvia nods and smiles. "Your permanent license should arrive in the mail in two to four weeks. You're a good driver, Virginia. You have all the skills. You just need more confidence. Practice and time on the road will get you there."

So now it's official. If I get stranded in the Sahara or

Saskatchewan or anywhere in the world with a road, I can get myself home.

⑥ ⑥ ⑥ ⑥

That night, Dad takes the train up from the city. Mom goes to the station to pick him up. She offered for me to get him, but I need a little break from being in the driver's seat.

When Mom and Dad arrive from the train station, I meet them at the door. Dad presents me with a bouquet of white roses and a card. As Mom carries the flowers into the kitchen, I tear open the card and read it.

*Dear Virginia,*
*Congratulations on getting your license. I'm so proud of you, but I'm also not surprised. After all, no Shreves has ever failed their road test.*
*Love,*
*Dad*

I thank him for the card and for teaching me how to drive. A few months ago, a note like that would have pissed me off to no end. But right now I'm too happy to care.

⑥ ⑥ ⑥ ⑥

On Monday evening, Dad's phone rings. We're back in New York City. Dad, Byron, and I are watching the Yankee game. Mom and Anaïs are at the dining room table reading up on training regimens for half marathons. I think they've struck a careful peace. My sister and Lindsey still haven't given up on their plan to volunteer in a refugee camp, but Anaïs has agreed to look into master's programs in nonprofit administration for the year after next.

"I don't recognize the number," Dad says as he lifts the phone to his ear. "Hello?"

Byron and I watch as Dad stands up, walks into his room, and closes the door. I glance over at Mom, but she just shrugs and says, "No idea."

"I wonder if it's Mark Levy?" Byron asks, coughing into his elbow. His face has gone pale and he looks terrified.

"No," I offer, "because Dad didn't recognize the number."

A few minutes later Dad emerges from his room. He goes into the kitchen, pours a glass of vodka, and joins Mom at the dining room table. Byron reaches for the remote and mutes the volume on the game.

"That was Dean Briggs," Dad says, sipping his drink. "The dean of students at Columbia."

"I know who that is," Mom says quickly. Her eyes are wide and she looks scared, too. "Should we go in the other room and talk about it?"

Dad massages his temples with his thumbs. "This is going to affect all of us, so I may as well say it. Columbia is asking Byron not to come back next semester."

Mom sucks in her breath.

"What the hell?" Byron says.

"But he already completed Columbia's punishment," Anaïs says. "He was suspended last fall."

"Now he's been arrested and there's a potential trial pending," Dad says. "The dean said he's gotten a lot of e-mails from worried parents. They read about Byron's case, and they're threatening to pull their children and demand refunds. The dean was polite and expressed his concern about Byron's situation. He said that if the case is dismissed they'd be happy to have him back."

Byron is slumped over on the couch, his head slung between his knees, his hands laced behind his neck.

"What if we agree to a lesser charge?" Mom asks.

"I'm going to call the lawyer about that now," Dad says. He takes the remote from the couch, shuts off the game, and disappears back into his room.

An hour later, I get a text from Sebastian.

**Amazing news**, he writes. **Can you meet?**

I'm in my bedroom with the door closed. I watched some Netflix, and now I'm googling public high schools in New York City. It sounds nice to have a fresh start without Brie or Cole or any of the other popular kids who feel justified making fun of me. Unfortunately, I quickly realize that the application process was last fall. Damn. Brewster it is.

**Meet where?** I text back, glancing at the time. **Like downtown?**

It's after nine. I'm not even sure my parents would let me go downtown at night without a plan. Well, without a plan they know about.

**I was thinking West End Avenue**, he writes. **You can walk up and I'll walk down.**

Do you really think it's safe?

It's dark out. No one will see us.

I stare at my phone, trying to figure out what to do.

Please, Leela, he adds. I've got some really good news. I want to tell you in person.

Okay, I write, smiling at the "Leela." Walk on the west side. The side closer to the river.

Leaving in five.

Me too.

I slide my feet into my Converse, glance in the bathroom mirror to make sure my chin zits are concealed, and shout that I'm taking a walk. Anaïs and Mom are in the kitchen cutting up a watermelon. Seeing them in there, chatting and slicing fruit, reminds me of how Anaïs said that she and her host mother in Burkina Faso would pound millet together. In a weird way, it's not all that different.

I walk from Riverside over to West End and start heading uptown. As I'm walking, I try to figure out what Sebastian is going to tell me. We've been talking about wanting to be alone together, not just outside in a park, so maybe he got keys to an apartment that's not his and not mine and is five hundred miles from anyone we know.

Ten minutes later, I see him coming toward me on West End Avenue.

"Hey," he says, grinning.

I wave at him. "Hey."

We stand there, two feet apart, smiling stupidly at each other. We're hungering to kiss, but we both know we shouldn't.

There aren't any doorman buildings on this block and there's just one guy walking his dog. But still. We are way too close to home.

"Want to walk down?" he asks.

"Sure."

We walk side by side. It feels weird not to hold hands, but it's still nice to see him. It's nice to be in our neighborhood, not hiding in the Bronx or down in Chinatown. Also, West End is sort of enchanting at night. It's a wide avenue without stores or banks or bus stops. It's lined with grand prewar buildings. If there weren't traffic lights or cars, it would feel like we've gone back in time a hundred years.

"So guess what?" Sebastian says as we pause at the corner. Before I can answer, he continues. "My parents just told me that they're going to let me go to Columbia this fall."

"What?" I ask, shocked. "For real?"

"For real." Sebastian takes my hand and gives it a quick squeeze. "Virginia, I'm going to Columbia. It's happening."

We stare at each other. We both know what this means. He gets to study with that children's book illustrator. But also, we'll be thirty blocks from each other. And not just that. We'll be thirty blocks from each other and he'll have a dorm room.

"Do you know what changed their minds?" I ask.

The second I ask it I know exactly what changed their minds.

"No clue," Sebastian says. "They just sat me down a half hour ago and told me they talked to the dean of students today and he reassured them that Columbia supported our family. I think it's—"

Sebastian stops midsentence and stares at me. I'm frozen on the street, my mouth hanging open.

"What?" he asks.

I tell him about the phone call from the dean and how my brother isn't allowed to return to Columbia this fall.

"Oh shit," Sebastian says, his forehead creasing.

"It's not your fault," I say. "You didn't know."

"But I'm directly benefiting from your brother's expulsion."

"Suspension." I pause before adding, "It's okay. I mean, it's okay to be happy."

"I am," Sebastian says. "But it still sucks."

We start walking again. After a block of silence, Sebastian points to a building. "I love how there are so many windows up there and all the windows are full of light and behind each of those windows is a home with a family and a story."

I follow his gaze upward. I try to imagine a family in one of those windows and what their life is like, all the problems and challenges and the good things, too.

"And this is our story," Sebastian says, putting his arm around me and kissing the top of my head.

We stay like that for a second and then we step apart, both of us looking around guiltily, making sure no one saw us together.

# 22

This is her," Mom says, taking my hand. "Our younger daughter. Virginia."

"Lovely to meet you," the woman says. She has the exact same honey-blond hair as Mom's, and she's wearing a similar cocktail dress, just pale pink where Mom's is pale blue. "I'm Margaret. Our house is over in Sharon. Your mom and I golf together, and she gives me free parenting advice. My twins are a little younger than you."

"Virginia just passed her road test two weeks ago," Mom says, smiling. "And she got high honor roll at Brewster. They want to talk to her about applying to Harvard."

Margaret nods, obviously impressed. The diamond ring on her right hand is practically the size of a golf ball. "That's fabulous. Peter went to law school there, and I know they don't take just anyone."

I glance sideways at Mom to see if she's flinching at the mention of law school, like if it's reminding her that Byron once dreamed about Harvard Law School. If Columbia won't let him finish college, then the law school plan is going to be a challenge. But nope. Mom's smiling and chatting it up like she's having the time of her life.

It's early evening and we're at a fundraiser for my parents' golf club. The party is at a super-rich member's house in Roxbury. They have an enormous backyard with a pool and a tennis court and a koi pond full of red and black fish. There's a band playing, an open bar staffed by bartenders wearing tuxedos, and catered stations offering everything from grilled meats to strawberries dipped in dark chocolate.

**HYPOCRISY ALERT:**

This party must have cost a fortune to put on. Why didn't they just take all that cash and give it to the golf club instead of spending money to have a fundraiser?

No one else seems to find that baffling. As I glance around the landscaped yard, I see my parents' friends, the Lowensteins. Other than them, it's a sea of strangers. The women all have shiny blown-out hair in honey-blond, auburn-brown, or black, sparkling diamond rings, and pastel cocktail dresses. The men, with their khaki slacks and pink or lime-green shirts, all have closely cut hair.

I didn't want to come to this golf club fundraiser, but Mom and Dad donated enough money to get four tickets.

Lindsey is flying to California to see her mom on Sunday, so Anaïs is spending the weekend with her. That got my sister off the hook for the party. Which meant it was up to Byron and me to represent the Shreves offspring. The one good thing about coming is that Mom took me shopping for a dress at Torrid. I was shocked when she suggested it because, in Mom's opinion, there's only one place to buy plus-size clothing and that's Saks. Otherwise known as "Sacks" because their idea of fashion is putting curvaceous chicks into burlap sacks. But Mom announced the other day that one of her patients was saying that Torrid has stylish clothes for all shapes and sizes. I decided not to tell her I've been shopping there since last year. We found two awesome dresses, a shorter one that's silver and a black one that's low-cut in the front. Mom shocked me a second time by declaring, "Let's get them both!"

And then, when I was changing back into my jeans and Mom was outside the dressing room, she dropped the third shock:

"Both of those dresses show off your chest," she said. "Very flattering."

I stood with my jeans bunched around my ankles and tears in my eyes. It was possibly the first time ever that Mom has said anything nice about my body.

So, yeah, I'm feeling good at the golf party in my silver, boob-flattering dress with my new silver sandals. I'm saving the black dress for next Thursday when Sebastian and I are going to the Met. We've already been to the Guggenheim one day when it was too hot to be outside. We've also ridden the Staten Island

Ferry and the Roosevelt Island Tram. I've honestly never seen as much of New York City as I have in the past month. I love it, but I'm also happy just walking on West End at night. We've done that a few more times, and we're always careful not to hold hands or kiss if anyone's around.

Mom's friend Margaret air-kisses her on both cheeks and then drifts away to find her husband. As soon as she's gone, the smile slips off Mom's face and she sighs heavily. I wonder if she's finding this as exhausting as I am. That makes me feel sad for Mom. I have a feeling my parents donated a lot of money to the fundraiser so their golf buddies won't judge them about Byron.

Mom walks off to greet a friend. A few minutes later, she returns with a petite Indian woman wearing a shimmery turquoise dress. She has the same hairstyle as Mom, just black with brown lowlights. "I was just talking to my friend Divya about your hair," Mom says. "Her daughter wants to dye her hair blue and needs advice."

Divya nods, sending her diamond earrings swinging back and forth. "I offered to take Mira to my salon, but she said it's more authentic to do it herself."

"That's right," Mom says. "It's not as cool if it's done professionally. Virginia's hair is the real deal."

Color me shocked. What about Mom trying to coerce me to go to Talia and get rid of my purple and green because it doesn't reflect well on the family?

I explain the process of bleach and tinfoil and what brands of dye are the best, but the ironic thing is that I've been letting my color wash out. Every time I shampoo, I see more and more of my natural blond. It's not like I have a game plan for my hair, but I'm thinking about going natural for a while. When I asked Sebastian if he'd still like me without purple hair he took me in his arms and said, "You will always be a Leela, no matter what."

"Virginia," Dad says as I'm wrapping up my lesson on home hair coloring. He's brought over two men, one white with spiky hair and one tall and Asian. "I want you to meet Brian and Andrew. Their daughter, Madison, is starting at Brewster in the fall, and she's nervous. Sixth grade. Can you reassure them it will be okay?"

I smile at the men and open my mouth to speak when I realize my tongue has gone dry. I excuse myself to get water and hurry over to the bar area. On the way, my breathing feels tight. After sixteen years of being the Shreves sibling who didn't inspire bragging, I'm feeling the full weight of it tonight.

"How do you like it?" Byron asks as I arrive at the bar to get my water. Byron is standing with one hand pressed on the edge of the table, finishing a glass of something that looks like whiskey.

"How do I like what?"

"The Mike and Phyllis pressure machine. It's on you now, Gin. You're their only hope."

Byron has a lopsided grin, making it fairly obvious that this isn't his first drink of the night. It's no secret that Byron isn't a teetotaler. He was a popular jock in high school. That's synonymous with partying. And he played rugby at Columbia, which landed him squarely in the kegger scene there, too. But ever since the arrest, Byron hasn't slipped into the apartment in the middle of the night reeking of beer, and I've also noticed that Mom and Dad have recently stopped offering him wine at dinner. I think a big part of that is the fact that he was drunk when he forced Annie to have sex. Not that being drunk excuses sexual violence *ever ever ever*, but maybe he wouldn't have been such an asshole if he were operating with a few more brain cells.

As Byron orders another drink, I glance around the backyard in search of my parents. They definitely wouldn't want Byron getting drunk in front of their golf friends when all they want is to prove that we are a functional family, dealing with the arrest, righting the wrongs, back on the path to perfection. Just as I spot the back of Dad's head, Byron thanks the bartender for his drink and walks over toward where the band is playing. I watch him go. At least he's not stumbling.

I turn to ask the bartender for water when I look at his face and realize I know him. It's Frances's boyfriend! We met at the emergency room a few weeks ago.

"Hey!" I say. "Dylan, right?"

He stares at me like he has no idea who I am. I suddenly wonder if we all look alike to him. Here I am, feeling so different from this shiny-haired, pastel-dressed crowd, but to an outsider maybe I'm just another one of them.

"I drove Frances to the emergency room," I tell him, "when she broke her ankle and ribs."

"Oh, right!" His face breaks out in a wide smile. "Totally. It was just, you know, out of context."

Dylan pours me some water and fills me in on Frances, who he says is doing much better. He tells me how she's taking classes to get into an arboriculture society, which will keep her busy until she can return to the trees. I'm about to tell him that I got my license when Mom comes over, touches my elbow, and says, "Can I talk to you privately?"

"Sure," I say, nodding good-bye to Dylan.

"That's Frances's boyfriend," I tell Mom as we're walking over to the side yard. It's empty here and shaded by oak trees. "You know, the tree woman?"

Mom nods absentmindedly. "Listen, Virginia, we need you to drive Byron home."

I stare at her.

"He's had too much to drink. It's not appropriate for him to be here. Dad has already walked him to the car. We'd take him home, but it would look strange if we left so early. We'll catch a ride from the Lowensteins in a bit."

"But—" I start to say but then pause. I'm trying to think of all the reasons I can't do it, like I've never driven without a parent in the evening and I've never driven from Roxbury to our house, but then I think how driving Frances to the emergency room made me feel strong and brave and bold. And I want to do more things like that. Not necessarily in crisis situations involving broken bones. Just in my real life.

"Byron shouldn't have had alcohol. He's underage, and he doesn't need that kind of trouble right now. Plus, he's on antibiotics," Mom explains. "And also, well . . ." She trails off, her fists clenched at her sides, her face contorted.

"Okay," I say quickly. "Sure."

"Thanks." Mom sighs. "Honey, this is really hard for me. It's breaking my heart."

Mom looks like she's about to cry. I touch her arm to comfort her, but she flinches away.

"Let's go," she says brusquely, tugging my elbow in the direction of the car. "Dad has the keys."

⑥ ⑥ ⑥ ⑥

Halfway home, Byron nods off. It's actually easier to drive with him sleeping. I roll down the windows and carefully listen to the directions on my phone. I'm the slowest driver to exist in Connecticut, and every car on the road is passing me, but who cares? Fuck it.

I've been feeling all-around *fuck it* recently. Maybe that should become my motto. In the best possible way, of course.

As I get closer to home, I flick the blinker for our street and suddenly remember the windshield-wiper trick. Before I can ponder whether it's a stupid idea, I tug at the wiper-fluid stick and spray a squirt onto Byron's cheek. He squirms a little but doesn't wake up. I turn into our driveway, park, and reach in the back seat for the paper towels.

The thing is, it's not funny. It doesn't feel in any way good.

I dab at my brother's cheek, poke him awake, and help him onto the couch. As he's falling back asleep, he rips out a loud fart. In the past, I would have been delighted to witness Byron doing something so gross and *un*perfect. But now I just feel sorry for him.

# 23

Whole Fitness has become Whole Momness. She's here all the time. She goes to yoga classes and spins on the bikes and has appointments with trainers. When she's not exercising, she's seeking me out on my breaks and inviting me for iced tea or showing me shirts that she ordered for me from Torrid.

It's almost a relief on Wednesday when Mom leaves after her regular morning workout because she's seeing patients until midafternoon. I'm refilling the dispenser of hand sanitizer when I hear someone say, "Virginia? I was wondering what happened to you. Do you work here?"

*Shit.*

It's Tisha, my kickboxing teacher. I've totally been blowing off her classes and her texts. A few weeks ago she even called my phone and I didn't answer.

"Yeah," I say quietly. "Summer job."

I glance around to make sure Gerri or a trainer isn't in earshot. I have a feeling Tisha is about to stick it to me, and I don't want witnesses.

"So you're not away this summer?" Tisha asks sharply. Her cornrowed hair is twisted high on her head, and she's wearing a tiny gold locket shaped like a heart.

As I set down the jug of Purell, I bite my bottom lip. I can feel the tears coming.

"I've got a training session in six minutes," Tisha says. "I'm working with a member in the kickboxing studio. But what happened? I thought you loved kickboxing. Did you lose interest? That happens . . . but you should have told me."

I slowly shake my head. The tears are pushing farther up my throat. Unlike Mom, I suck at sweeping things under the rug.

"What is it?" Tisha says, tipping her head to one side. "Is everything okay?"

Like a tsunami hitting the shore, it all comes crashing out. I start crying and sniffling. I tell her about Brie and how Mom told Brie's mom about kickboxing and how Brie has always been mean to me, like calling me fat and humiliating me in public.

Tisha hands me a tissue. "I can see that. Brie has a sweet side, but I can also see what you're saying."

I blow my nose. I'm not so sure about Brie's sweet side, but I'm glad Tisha believes me about her mean side.

"The thing is, you can't let her drive you from class," Tisha says. "That way, she wins. She gets the class and you lose it."

*Easier said than done.* I put away the Purell and swipe a member's ID. "Welcome, Lila," I say, smiling at her. "How many towels today?"

She asks for one. I write her name and *one towel* on the clipboard.

Tisha glances at her phone. "Here's what we're going to do. I'm going to talk to Brie. She seems to like kickboxing, but I'm going to let her know that that kind of bullshit is not allowed in my class. If she can agree to those terms, she's in. If not, she's out."

"But how will I know what she agrees to?" I ask, wiping my eyes.

"I'll text you. This time you answer me!" Tisha smiles and gives my arm a light punch. "There's no perfect solution, but we have to try. We have to deal with it."

"I think I see what you're saying . . ."

"Trust me, I've been there." Tisha hoists a gym bag onto her shoulder. "The most powerful thing you can do is walk back into that class."

⑥ ⑥ ⑥ ⑥

Sebastian can't get together on Wednesday afternoon, so I decide to go home and relax after work. As I'm heading back to the apartment, I have a light feeling inside. Maybe it's actually all going to be okay. Maybe Brie will agree to Tisha's terms or she'll leave the class. When I think about going to kickboxing again, with or without Brie, my stomach flutters excitedly.

And maybe Tisha's right about how the most powerful

thing I can do is walk back in. Not just for kickboxing but for Brewster, too. Instead of fantasizing about transferring to another school, I'll walk in in September and I'll have Shannon with me and Alyssa and I'll take an elective writing class and I'll kick ass on the SATs. Thinking about it that way, Brie and Josh and all the other jerks seem insignificant.

When I get to our lobby I check the mail, and like a sign from the universe, there's a letter from Froggy. The return address is his camp up in Maine.

JULY 26
DEAR VIRGINIA,
    I HOPE YOU'RE HAVING A GOOD SUMMER. BAND
CAMP IS FUN, THOUGH IT'S HARD TO SURVIVE
WITHOUT MINECRAFT OR MY PHONE. I WANTED TO
WRITE AND TELL YOU THAT I'M SORRY THE END OF
THE YEAR WAS HARD FOR US. I MEANT IT WHEN I
SAID THAT I WANT TO BE FRIENDS. EVEN THOUGH
WE'RE NOT TOGETHER, I DON'T WANT TO THROW
AWAY OUR FRIENDSHIP. ANYWAY, WRITE IF YOU FEEL
LIKE IT AND I'LL SEE YOU IN THE FALL.
YOUR FRIEND (FOR REAL),
FROGGY

I make a ham sandwich for lunch and go into my room and write Froggy a note. I tell him that I'd be happy to be friends, and I also tell him I'm sorry for how I acted in June. I'm not sorry I fell out of like with him, but I feel bad for the way I blew him off. I add a PS that I'm excited about him and Alyssa. I'm just sealing the letter in an envelope when Mom gets home.

"Hey," she says, standing in my doorway. "Want to go for a walk in the park? It's so pretty today. The air feels clean."

I eye her suspiciously, trying to locate the hidden agenda. Does "walk" actually mean "power walk," and before long she's going to be sprinting, urging me to step up the pace and burn some evil calories?

"Gin," Mom says, smiling. "Just a walk. Promise."

"Do you have a stamp?"

She nods. "Sure . . . how many do you need?"

"Just one. I guess I'll come. I have to mail a letter."

I grab my straw hat, slide my feet into sneakers, and we head toward the park. On the way, I drop Froggy's letter into a mailbox, turning it upside down so Mom can't see his name. No need to invite an inquisition.

Once we're in the park, Mom mentions that we're staying in the city this weekend because she and Dad have tickets to a play on Saturday night. That's fine with me. I think Sebastian is going to be here, too. When she asks about my morning at the gym, I opt for honesty. I tell her that Tisha came into Whole Fitness and it was awkward because I've been avoiding kickboxing since Brie joined the class.

Mom shakes her head. "I'm so sorry I told Simone Newhart about your class," she says. "I've thought about it a lot. Actually, I've thought about a lot of things. I've been so focused on helping other teenagers that I haven't watched out for my own kids first. Sort of like the cobbler's children not having shoes."

"Well, I do have those new silver sandals you got me," I offer. I make that bad joke to cover for the fact that Mom is deep diving into emotions and apologies and that simply doesn't happen, like, ever.

As we're looping toward home, I ask, "How're things going with Byron?"

"Better, actually," Mom says. "It seems like Mark Levy and the district attorney are close to agreeing to a plea bargain for a lesser change. We're hoping harassment, which wouldn't be a criminal offense."

"So no weekend jail?"

"If they agree to it." Mom pauses as the light changes on Riverside Drive. We're a block from our building now. "Hopefully it would just entail community service and probation."

"What about Columbia?"

"We've decided to hold off on Columbia either way. Byron is going to register for a few classes at City College fall semester. Then we'll talk about him transferring somewhere else, maybe out of state where he can start over. But that's getting way ahead. He's got a lot to deal with first."

"Like what?" I ask. I can guess what he needs to deal with, like the fact that he got drunk and forced someone to have sex with him, but I'm curious to hear it from Mom, to see if she'll gloss over it or actually address it straight on.

Mom stretches her neck from side to side, lifting her shoulders so they're touching one ear and then the other. After a minute, she pushes up her sunglasses, looks right at me, and says, "This is Byron's business, so I don't want to share too much. But . . . he's going to see a therapist. A really good one. He needs to understand what happened that night last fall, and he also needs to figure out where things went wrong so that doing what he did was even in his realm of possibility."

Wow.

I stare back at her, totally speechless. She didn't gloss it over. She didn't call it a "we" problem. She didn't say what he "may have done."

I mean, wow.

"There's something else I want you to know," Mom adds. "I don't want you to think that we believe your brother should be off the hook. But Dad and I feel the entire arrest nightmare, plus being kicked out of Columbia, is punishment enough. Jail won't help. It rarely does."

The light changes. Mom and I start across the street. We're sweaty when we get back to the apartment. She pours herself a glass of seltzer. I reach into the back of the fridge, past the water and the orange juice, and I grab a bottle of Byron's Vitaminwater. I don't ask Mom or look to her for approval. *Fuck it*. I just unscrew the cap and lean against the counter and start drinking.

⑥ ⑥ ⑤ ⑥

That night, I can hear Mom and Dad watching a show in the living room. I think Byron is with them and maybe Anaïs, too. The funny thing is, the image of the four of them on the couch actually makes me happy. I've always pictured them as this beautiful French-speaking, skiing, golf-playing unit, and I was pushed off to one side of the frame, the ugly-duckling, switched-at-birth child. What I didn't realize until this summer is that I actually like it this way. I may share a gene pool with my family, but I want to be a Shreves on my own terms.

I lean back on my bed and open my computer to a folder called "Lists." A new list has been on my mind, and I want to write it down.

## THE UNIVERSE IS EXPANDING AND SO AM I

1. They say the universe is expanding, and now I finally get it. Over the past six weeks, my universe has become full with more love and friendship and meaning than I ever thought possible.
2. Speaking of full, my heart is full of Sebastian.
3. Speaking of full, my butt is also full. And if it expands a little, fine. Curves are good. Curvaceous chicks rule.
4. From here on out, I'm going to fuck it all and embrace my expanding universe and my expanding heart and my expanding butt.

⑥ ⑥ ⑥ ⑥

On Friday evening, Sebastian and I are walking together on West End Avenue. We met halfway and then he walked me down toward my place. Then we turned around and now I'm walking him up toward his apartment.

I'm in the best mood. I'm feeling giddy about kickboxing. I went this afternoon and Brie was there and Tisha greeted me with a squeal and a hug. As I walked into the studio, I thought about my expanding universe, and, for real, Brie didn't even matter. I barely even looked at her as I kicked and punched and sweated for an hour.

Yes, I took a shower before meeting Sebastian tonight.

As we're walking, we're talking about art. When we went to the Met yesterday, Sebastian sketched a Renoir and then he did a sketch of me in my new dress in front of an ancient Egyptian temple. Something about the sketches inspired him, and that's what he's explaining now. He's telling me how he wants to take his sketches of New York City from this summer and turn them into a children's book. The drawings will be the backdrop, and the story will be through the eyes of a young boy visiting the city for the first time.

"I was thinking I'd find a boy to photograph, like a real kid," Sebastian says, "and superimpose the photos of him over my sketches."

He's so excited about this he's practically skipping. And when Sebastian skips he's three seconds from crashing hard on the sidewalk. As a safety precaution, I take his hand and hold on tight.

"Sort of like Mo Willems did in *Knuffle Bunny*," Sebastian says, "but the opposite. He did sketches of people over real photos of New York City."

"I thought it was 'Knuffle' with a silent 'K.'"

He laughs. "I've always said it with a hard 'K.'"

A second later, Sebastian drops my hand.

I see them a moment after he does.

We've just crossed the intersection a block from Sebastian's apartment, and there, approaching on a side street, is Annie Mills and two extremely tall parent-looking people. Annie gapes at us, her mouth open in shock. The parent-looking people smile when they see Sebastian and raise their eyebrows at me, a little confused.

"Who's this?" the mom-looking person asks Sebastian.

"I didn't realize you were out with a friend," the dad-looking person says.

Sebastian and I are frozen. Utterly speechless.

"Virginia Shreves," Annie says quietly. "Byron's little sister."

Sebastian's parents stare at me, their expressions morphing from confusion to comprehension to complete fury.

# 24

I can't believe it.

The text comes in at midnight. This is the first I've heard from Sebastian. I haven't written to him in case his parents have confiscated his phone.

I know, I write back. I'm in my room. I've been hugging the straw hat he gave me and crying on and off for hours.

My parents are really mad, he writes. They're saying I've let down the family.

I'm sorry.

Don't be sorry. I have no regrets.

When he writes that, I upgrade to full-fledged sobbing. My face is pressed into my pillow so I don't wake anyone up. All I can think about is how, after we ran into the Mills family, Sebastian and his parents and sister walked up West End and I walked down. But then, a few seconds later, we turned around and caught each other's eye. We weren't smiling or waving. It's more like we were saying good-bye.

⑥ ⑥ ⑥ ⑥

I hadn't even realized I'd fallen asleep, but it's light out when Mom comes into my bedroom. Her hair is pulled into a messy ponytail, and she has on ratty yoga pants and the pajama shirt Dad wears when he's sick. My first thought is that the police carted Byron off again.

"Get up," she says flatly. "We need to talk. Now."

As Mom walks out, I check my phone. Nothing from Sebastian. I don't have a mirror in my room, which is good because I don't need to see the bags under my eyes. I wriggle into a bra and trudge out to the living room.

Mom, Dad, and Anaïs are on the couch, and Byron is in the chair next to them. Their faces are solemn, their mouths pressed tight. I move toward an empty chair and sit down.

"Imagine my surprise," Mom starts.

"Not surprise," Dad says. "Shock. Horror."

Mom nods. "Imagine my shock and horror when Dad got a call from Mark Levy at six this morning. Mark got a call from the district attorney at eleven last night because he received a panicked message from the parents of Annie Mills about their son. Who even knew Annie Mills had a brother?"

My arms and legs go weak, and my teeth start chattering.

Mom hunches forward like she's having a hard time breathing, so Dad takes over. "Mark tells me that it turns out the Mills family is in the city for the summer, which you of course

262

know, and that they have a seventeen-year-old son, which you also know. And then Mark says, 'So it looks like your younger daughter is having a relationship with their son.'"

Anaïs and Byron are frowning at me. I stare down at the rug. The toes on my left foot are prickly with pins and needles.

"We thought we knew you," Mom says, wiping under her eyes. "Now you've betrayed our trust, not to mention that you've put Byron's plea bargain in jeopardy."

There's a pillow on the chair. I wriggle it out from behind me and hug it to my stomach. I didn't mean to betray my family or make things worse for Byron. I just met a guy and he sketched me and we fell in love.

"Do you have anything to say for yourself?" Dad asks.

I open my mouth. Before I can speak, my sister jumps in.

"Do you have any idea about the implications of this?" she says. Her hands are clenched tight over her knees. "The reason the district attorney is agreeing to a less-than-criminal charge for Byron is because Annie told him she wants to drop the charges. Not that she has the ability to do that, because the charges have been made and now it's the People of New York versus Byron. But the prosecutors will take Annie into consideration, like if she's a reluctant witness then they may not want to go to trial."

I stare at Anaïs. It's a lot of information to take in with my current state of mind.

"What Anaïs is saying," Dad says, "is that your relationship with this brother may appear that we've been getting in with the Mills family to coerce Annie to drop the charges."

"But I didn't even—" I start.

263

"I'm not done," Dad says.

I glance at Mom. Usually she's the one who leads family meetings, but she's wiping her nose with a tissue and shaking her head in disbelief.

"Because of this," Dad says, "we could be back at square one with the negotiations."

There's the "we" again. As if "we" got drunk and forced Annie Mills to have sex.

"I don't know what we're going to do about the play tonight," Mom says all of a sudden.

I have no idea what their play tonight has to do with any of this.

"It's not like we can give back the tickets." Dad shoots her a sideways glance. "The *tickets* are coming."

I dig my fingernails into the edges of the pillow. "Can I say something?"

"Fine." Dad crosses his arms over his chest. "Go."

"His name is Sebastian," I say. My voice feels surprisingly strong. "We met at the bagel store, and I didn't know who he was, and he didn't know who I was. We found out pretty quickly but . . . ." I shrug. "I love him. We love each other."

Mom looks up in alarm.

"I was getting a bagel for Dad," I tell her.

The irony is not lost on me that in this moment of extreme crisis, Mom is monitoring my past carb intake. Or maybe not. Maybe she doesn't care about bagels. Maybe she can't believe I'm in love, that something so amazing has happened to someone like me.

"Remember, Dad?" I ask. "That day you went to Connecticut to meet Frances about the trees and you brought me along for driving practice? Remember how you were going to pick me up from the bagel store but you came really late? That was when I met him. It was before . . . you know . . . the arrest."

Dad doesn't say anything. Neither do Mom or Byron. Anaïs is the one who speaks next.

"But then the arrest happened and you stayed with him?" she asks. "And he's your boyfriend now? That's not how these things work. You don't fall in love with the brother of the person who is pressing charges against Byron."

I chuck the pillow onto the ground and jump to my feet. "I can't believe you would say that," I tell my sister. "You, of all people. What about *love is love is love*? Doesn't that mean anything?"

Anaïs stares at me, her mouth open.

"Virginia," Mom says softly. "You're only sixteen."

"And?" I ask.

"This is your brother's life," Dad says.

"It's my life, too," I say, storming toward my room.

I'm about to slam my door when I hear Byron speak for the first time all morning.

"She loves him," he says quietly. "It's not her fault."

I close the door and topple face-first onto my bed.

I'm still in my room when I hear Mom leaving the apartment. Byron and Anaïs go out soon after. I can hear Dad in the living room talking to the lawyer on the phone. I chew at my thumbnails. I knew my parents wouldn't be happy about my relationship with Annie Mills's brother, but I had no idea it would be a problem from a legal standpoint.

I'm sitting cross-legged on my bed. My computer is open to "Lists," but I can't think of a single word to write. There's a mosquito lazily circling my bedroom. Every time it drifts close to me, I swat at it but it always gets away.

I want to talk to someone so badly. I text Alyssa but then remember she's tubing on the Delaware River today. Shannon is still hiking through the wilderness. I wish I could call Sebastian because he's the only person who truly understands how horrible this is, but I don't want to make things worse for him.

I can hear Dad hanging up with the lawyer and leaving the apartment. Just as the front door closes, I feel burning on my knee. I slap my hand on it, but it's too late. I grab a tissue from my bedside table and wipe off the mosquito carcass and a smear of blood.

I try to cry and I try to nap. No luck on either front. I'm out of tears and I'm too upset to sleep. I decide to take a walk.

It's sunny and warm out, and people are chatting and drinking iced coffee and walking their dogs. It's hard to imagine that the world is still turning when mine has been shaken upside down. My phone is in my pocket. I keep hoping it will ring, and Sebastian will be calling to tell me that he still loves me and let's run away into the sunset together.

Hang on.

My world has only been shaken upside down if I let it be

that way. And if I'm strong and bold and brave—which I definitely *want* to be—then why should I wait for Sebastian to invite me to run away?

I stop at the curb, take out my phone, and call him. He answers on the first ring.

"Leela," he says. His voice sounds quiet and tired.

"Remember that day on the High Line when you were telling me how you're an ESFP, which means you're the friend to have if someone is feeling sad?"

"Yeah," he says.

"And remember how we made a deal not to let fights go for more than ten minutes?"

"The problem is," he says, "we're not even in a fight. My parents just said they couldn't believe I would do that to Annie."

"You didn't do anything to Annie," I say. "I didn't do anything to Byron."

"And it's been longer than ten minutes," he says.

I lean over to scratch the mosquito bite on my knee. "Do you have a sleeping bag?"

"Yeah . . . why?"

"And a tent? Like from that camping trip you went on a few weeks ago?"

"Why? Are we going somewhere?"

I give him the address of the garage where we park our car. I tell him to meet me there in thirty minutes.

# 25

"It's not really running away if we're going to your country house," Sebastian says, grinning at me from the driver's seat. He has circles under his eyes like he didn't get much sleep last night either.

"So let's just call it a vacation from the drama," I say.

"And it's not like they've forbidden me from seeing you. They just said it made them very unhappy."

I nod. "Exactly."

"I left them a note saying I was going away overnight and would be fine."

"Me too," I say. "So it's not like we're causing unnecessary worry."

"Have we justified enough?" Sebastian asks.

"We have an hour and a half. I'm sure we can come up with more justifications."

We're on the Saw Mill River Parkway, heading toward Connecticut. Even though we're in my family's car, Sebastian is driving. I have to wait six months before I'm allowed to drive with anyone who is under twenty in the passenger seat. They told us that practically every week in driver's ed.

I navigate Sebastian onto 684 and then rest my head against the door. We've got seventy miles until he needs me to copilot again, so I close my eyes and fall asleep.

ⓖ ⓖ ⓖ ⓖ

"Let me get this straight," Sebastian says. We're nearing our house. I've woken up, and I'm giving him directions. "We're going to camp out in your backyard, right?"

"Way in the back of the backyard," I explain. "We'll be far away from everything."

"But with a bathroom in walking distance," he says.

"Yep," I say. I decide not to go into my anti-pooping-in-the-woods speech. I think he gets the point.

It's early evening when we pull up to the house. We park the car in the garage so neighbors don't see it. For that same reason, we're careful only to put on the downstairs bathroom light. I don't even turn on the light when I grab cheese and salami from the fridge, a box of crackers, and a few flashlights from the drawer in the kitchen.

When I get back to the yard, Sebastian is setting up the tent. I try to help, but, seriously, whoever invented tents was an idiot. There's this lump of fabric, and then there are all these poles that have to fit into other poles to make one big pole that

269

you slide into sleeves along various sections of the fabric. I attempt to bend a pole at an angle to slide it in, but it snaps backward and nearly slashes Sebastian's face.

Camping = Definitely stupid.

Camping with Sebastian = Definitely worth it.

Once the tent is up and our sleeping bags are inside and we've eaten our picnic dinner, we swing together in the hammock, looking up at the stars.

"What are we going to do?" I whisper to Sebastian. He's so quiet I thought maybe the rocking put him to sleep, but he rolls his head toward me and kisses me gently on the lips.

"How about we figure it out tomorrow?" he asks.

"Do your parents hate me?"

"They can't hate you . . . they don't even know you."

"I guess . . ."

"Annie said you're pretty," Sebastian says. "She also told me you seem really nice."

Wow. Seriously. Wow. Just thinking about Annie saying that makes me tear up.

"But your parents are still mad?" I ask.

"It's not you. It's all the other stuff they're mad about."

We take turns using the bathroom and brushing our teeth. Sebastian is inside the tent when I crawl in. I can see with my dim flashlight beam that he's unzipped our sleeping bags so they're spread out like a big blanket.

"Hey," he says as I flop next to him and turn off the flashlight.

"Hey," I say.

This is the first time we've been inside somewhere together that's not a museum or a restaurant. Sebastian must be thinking that, too, because the next thing I know we're kissing and our hands are all over each other. He's sucking on my lower lip, which is sending tingles up my spine, and I'm running my hands over his chest, tugging his shirt over his head.

I want to feel my bare chest against his, so I pull off my shirt and unhook my bra, tossing them both into a corner of the tent.

"Mmmmm," he says, pulling me in. "That feels amazing."

"It does."

Real intimacy is not about trying to get up shirts, trying to get down jeans. It's about being close to someone and loving them and wanting to touch them and be touched by them.

"How about we save more for later?" Sebastian whispers into my hair. "Take it slow."

"That sounds good," I say. I can feel his hands trembling, and I think about how his ex-girlfriend cheated on him and destroyed his ability to trust. I wonder if he's starting to rebuild that with me. I hope so.

"I like the idea of us having a later," he murmurs.

I pull the sleeping bags over our shoulders, and we fall asleep in each other's arms.

6 6 6 6

It's weird to wake up next to Sebastian. Not bad weird. More like cool weird. His eyes are a little puffy, and he has a sheepish smile on his face as he kisses me good morning.

I go into the house and get us some cereal and milk and glasses of orange juice. We sit on the back porch eating breakfast, and then I wash the dishes and put them away. When I get outside, Sebastian has taken down the tent and he's loading our stuff into the trunk.

"We're doing this, right?" he asks me.

"We're doing it," I say.

Then we hop into the car and take off.

        ⑥ ⑥ ⑥ ⑥

"What are we going to tell them?" Sebastian says once we're on the road. "Like, are we going to say we're not returning home unless they accept that we're together, and maybe it's awkward but they'll have to deal?"

"Something like that. And let's hope they accept it quickly, because I have to be at work at six tomorrow morning."

Sebastian grins sideways at me. "The towel hero is needed."

"That can be your next picture book," I say, laughing. "A superhero called Towel Woman."

"Purple-haired, of course," he adds.

It's a short drive to Lincoln Township, and we find parking right away. We walk along a cobblestoned path through the town green. There's a cell signal in this town, which is the primary reason we're here.

"Ready?" Sebastian asks. He's sitting next to me on a bench, holding my hand. He offers to take a walk while I make my call, but I say I need all the support I can get.

I scroll through my contacts, trying to figure out if I should call Dad or Mom or even Anaïs. Then I see Byron's name, and I remember how he stood up for me yesterday. But it's not just that. I'm thinking back to how close we were when we were younger, before he grew up and I grew up and a million forces pulled us apart.

"Gin?" Byron asks after I dial his number. "Are you okay?"

"Yeah," I say. "I just—"

"Is it Virginia?" I hear Mom's voice say. "Mike, it's Virginia! She called Byron's phone."

Dad gets on. "Are you okay? Where are you?"

"Connecticut," I say. "We just drove into town."

"She's in Connecticut," Dad says to whoever is listening. Then, to me, he says, "How did you get there? Did you take the train?"

"I . . . uhhh." I pause. "I took the car."

"You got the car out of the garage?" Dad says, his voice rising. "Without telling me? Those are some major highways. We haven't practiced—"

"Sebastian drove," I say quickly.

"She's saying that Sebastian drove," I hear Dad say in the background.

All of a sudden there's a squeal. Two squeals. I recognize those voices. But what are they doing in my house?

"Is that Shannon and Alyssa?" I ask into the phone.

Sebastian raises his eyebrows at me. I shake my head like, *I have no idea*. But before I can ask Dad what's up with Shannon's and Alyssa's voices being there, my sister gets on the phone.

273

"Hey," she says.

"Is that Shannon and Alyssa?" I ask again.

"Yeah," she says. "Hang on . . . I'm walking into your bedroom . . . I'm closing the door. I want to talk to you in private."

"What are Shannon and Alyssa doing there?" I ask. I'm utterly confused. It's in the realm of possibility that Alyssa could come to my apartment on a random Sunday morning, but Shannon is hiking the Pacific Crest Trail. Just a few days ago I mailed her a letter to someplace called Truckee, California.

Anaïs explains that my parents didn't actually have a play to go to this weekend. That was all a cover. The real reason we weren't supposed to go to Connecticut is because Shannon was flying into New York City last night. That's why they said yesterday that the tickets were coming. The tickets were Shannon. It turns out she'd had enough of the Pacific Crest Trail, so her parents called my parents from a pit stop and arranged for Shannon to stay with us for the rest of the summer while they finish the hike. They brought Shannon to the airport in Reno, Nevada, and she flew in last night and took a car service to our apartment, and Mom planned the whole thing as a surprise for me.

Anaïs is a little less clear on what Alyssa is doing at our place. Something about how when Shannon arrived last night and discovered I'd run away, she texted Alyssa, who convinced her uncle to drive her into the city this morning to help find me.

The whole time she's talking, I'm shaking my head in disbelief. I can't imagine my parents and my siblings and Shannon and Alyssa all in the same apartment, trying to manage a crisis.

I actually love that image, like maybe it's the start of something new and much more real.

"I'm sorry I didn't have your back yesterday," Anaïs says. "I feel awful about that. You're completely right about how you love who you love."

"I am?"

"Of course you are." Anaïs pauses. "Mom and Dad know that, too. That's why Mom didn't bust you last night. I think it wasn't as much that they were mad about your boyfriend as they're worried about how it all could affect Byron."

"Anything new on that?"

"It's the weekend, so things are slow, but it looks like nothing has changed with the plea bargain deal. The district attorney told Mark Levy that he doesn't believe you were coercing the Mills family."

"Hang on," I say. "What did you say about Mom not busting me last night?"

Sebastian raises his eyebrows again. Again I shrug. I definitely didn't expect my call going in this direction.

"Mom knew that you and Sebastian were at the house," Anaïs says. "I have no idea how she knew. She didn't tell Dad, which was probably for the best."

"I thought you said secrets aren't good."

"Dad would have flipped. He would have driven up in the middle of the night."

"But the car wasn't there . . ."

"Yeah. Well. I think you're going to get in trouble about that one."

"Better that than about Sebastian," I offer.

I hear a knock in the background and Shannon's voice saying, "Can we talk to her?"

"I better hand you over," Anaïs says. "More later, okay?"

A second later, Alyssa shouts, "You're on speaker!"

"Hey!" I say to both of them. "What's going on, Shan? You left the PCT?"

"The thing about the PCT," Shannon says, "is that on paper it looks good, right?"

"Not exactly," I say.

"No way," Alyssa says.

"Okay, well, to *some* people it looks good," Shannon says, "all the hiking and mountains and scenery. And it *is* amazing. But imagine being with your parents twenty-four hours a day, seven days a week. I started wanting to get eaten by a bear."

"So you came home," I say.

"Well, I came to your home," Shannon says. "But you're too busy running away and smooching it up with some cute boy."

"I'm here, though!" Alyssa says. "And I can't believe you didn't tell me who Sebastian is, that he's *her* brother."

"I'm sorry," I say. "It's—"

"I'm just giving you a hard time," Alyssa says. "I totally get it. It was too scandalous. But maybe we should try to, you know, talk about things more."

"Definitely," I say.

As Shannon jokes about how they're going to try on my

makeup and dig through my drawers, I notice she's not stuttering. She rarely stutters with me, but she does with most other people. The fact that she's not stuttering around Alyssa means she's comfortable, which makes me excited for fall because now I'll have two good friends who like each other, too.

"Hey, girls," Mom's voice says. "Can I say hi?"

"Of course," Shannon says. "W-w-want us to leave?"

Mom always makes Shannon stutter. It's been that way since the first time they met.

"No, that's fine. I'll just take it off speakerphone if that's okay with you." There's a pause and then Mom says, "Are you okay, honey?"

Color me shocked. Mom never conducts family business in front of outside people.

"How did you know where I was last night?" I ask.

"Remember Divya? From the golf club?"

"I think so," I say. "The one with the daughter who wants blue hair?"

"Exactly. She lives nearby, so I had her drive by the house last night. She saw a light on in the bathroom."

Enter another shock: Mom not only involved a friend, but a *golf club* friend, in a family crisis?

We talk for a few more minutes. Mom tells me that she's proud I've cultivated such amazing friends who come through for me when I need them. She also tells me that Dad wants to make sure Sebastian drives the car back to the city, something about a rule from the driver's ed course. She briefly mentions that Dad is upset I took the car, but we'll figure that all out when I get home. And then Mom delivers one final, earth-shattering shock.

"Can you please tell Sebastian to call his parents? I talked to his mom last night. She's quite worried."

"You talked to Sebastian's mom?" I ask, hunching forward in disbelief.

Sebastian whips his head toward me. I listen, stunned, as Mom explains how, when I didn't come home last night, she guessed I was with Sebastian, so she checked if Byron still had Annie's number in his phone, which he did. Then she majorly sucked it up and called Annie and explained who she was and asked to speak with their mom.

I'm practically falling off the bench by this point, not to mention that Sebastian is gaping at me with a shocked expression on his face.

"It's not like we're going to become friends," Mom says. "But we both care deeply about our kids and want to make sure they're safe. Once the legal stuff is over, Byron is going to send Annie an apology letter. He's already started it. He knows he has a lot of repair work to do, both with himself and with the people he's hurt."

"Did you . . . or did Sebastian's mom . . . say anything about us?" I ask.

"We did." Mom pauses. "We both talked about staying out of it. It's not our business."

Maybe I'm reading between the lines, but I'm totally translating that as they're going to let Sebastian and me be together.

I give Sebastian space to call his parents. He didn't ask for it, but he looked nervous when he got his phone out, so I told him I was walking to a café across the town green to get us bagels. He asked if they were going to be the best bagels in Connecticut. I kissed him and called him a snob.

When I return to the bench ten minutes later, Sebastian's face is pointed toward the sun and his sea-glass eyes are clear and blue.

"Well . . . they're not going to kill me," he says.

"Not being killed," I say, sitting next to him, "is a good start."

"My mom actually liked talking to your mom. She said it was refreshing and even healing to remember that Byron's parents are people, too."

"Wow," I say.

"I know."

"Did she say anything about us?" I ask.

"About the same as what your mom said. She also told me that she and my dad are looking into places for Annie to get help. What happened with Byron triggered a lot for my sister. My mom said they want to make sure Annie deals with the trauma of what happened so it doesn't haunt her for her entire life."

"Like an in-patient place?" I ask. Some of Mom's patients have checked into facilities in Westchester County, and she's even driven up to visit them.

"They didn't say," he says. "All they said is they're considering bringing Annie back to Saskatchewan for the rest of the summer. They want to help her remember what she likes, what makes her happy. I don't know. I'm just glad they're getting her help. This whole thing has been really hard. For all of us."

Sebastian lets out a slow breath, and his shoulders sag.

I touch his arm. "So what now?"

"Now we sit and eat the best bagels in Connecticut."

"No bagels." I hand him a bag and a pile of napkins. "Blueberry muffins."

Sebastian and I rip off chunks of our muffins and begin eating. Something about this road trip has left us both famished.

"So what now?" he says when we're done eating.

"I guess let's just be here."

Sebastian brushes a crumb from the edge of my lips. "I like that. We are here."

"We are here," I say.

I rest my head on his shoulder and squeeze his hand. Yes, this is messy and complicated. But it's happening. Our life is happening. And we are here.

# ACKNOWLEDGMENTS

Thanks to my agent, Jodi Reamer, for saying an emphatic *yes* when I told her I wanted to write this novel, and then working her ninja powers to make it happen. Thanks to Cindy Loh and the entire Bloomsbury crew for your every bit of awesomeness. This book would not be what it is without: Diane Aronson, Erica Barmash, Hali Baumstein, Beth Eller, Cristina Gilbert, Courtney Griffin, Melissa Kavonic, Jeanette Levy, Donna Mark, Lizzy Mason, Brittany Mitchell, and Emily Ritter.

Thanks to Judge Kevin McGrath, my guide to arrest proceedings, criminal court, and the Pen. Thanks to my early readers, Dr. Vijayeta Sinh, for lending a psychologist's eye to my characters' struggles, and to Barbara Stretchberry for her expertise on all things teen.

Thank you to my friends and family for being here for me through highs and lows. Thank you to my readers who have written me the most powerful and honest letters about their connection with Virginia; I'm delighted to share more of her.

And a special thanks to Jonas, Miles, and Leif Rideout for showing me what true love looks like.